What the c

D0497529

About Payton's Passion:

"…wonderful insight into the lives of a lot of married people and what time, stress and children can do to it. Andy is a fighter who's not ready to give up on his marriage and does whatever it takes to get it back. Payton doesn't want to lose her husband but isn't quite sure how to get back what they once had. Anyone who has been through this will identify with the characters, and those who haven't will get clued into what could happen. All around this is a fun read with plenty of laughter mixed in." – *Angel Brewer, The Romance Studio*

About Authors In Ecstasy:

"The tension between Candy and Charlie is electrifying. … AUTHORS IN ECSTASY is truly that -- two authors discovering what real love is for the first time. Ms. Andre's debut novel with Ellora's Cave is a real winner. Don't miss it!" – *Denise Powers, Sensual Romance Reviews*

Discover for yourself why readers can't get enough of the multiple award-winning publisher Ellora's Cave. Whether you prefer e-books or paperbacks, be sure to visit EC on the web at www.ellorascave.com for an erotic reading experience that will leave you breathless.

PASSION AND ECSTASY
An Ellora's Cave publication, 2003

Ellora's Cave Publishing, Inc.
PO Box 787
Hudson, OH 44236-0787

ISBN # 1843607417

Payton's Passion:
ISBN MS Reader (LIT) ISBN # 1-84360-666-6
Authors In Ecstasy:
ISBN MS Reader (LIT) ISBN # 1-84360-651-8
Other available formats (no ISBNs are assigned):
Adobe (PDF), Rocketbook (RB), Mobipocket (PRC) &
HTML

PASSION AND ECSTASY edited by Raelene Gorlinsky.
Cover art by Darrell King.

PASSION AND ECSTASY

Payton's Passion

by Ruby Storm

Authors In Ecstasy

by Bella Andre

PAYTON'S PASSION

Ruby Storm

Chapter 1: The Early Years

Payton Jamison sashayed into the dull and austere college classroom. Her presence created an instant contrast to the beige setting of square desks and plain brick walls. The red knit shirt she wore stretched tightly across her huge breasts, teasing the nipples that nearly bored holes through the shiny fabric. Endlessly long tanned legs stretched from beneath a short skirt that hugged her upper thighs.

Andy Duncan, who sat at the back of the classroom, quickly poked his roommate in the shoulder to gain the man's attention and nodded in the direction of the open door. "Tony! Fuck! Take a look at what's coming in."

Tony swiveled on his seat to discover what his friend wanted him to see. Instantly, his clean-shaven jaw dropped open. "Holy shit," he whispered, not even giving a second glance at the brunette who walked beside the blonde bombshell.

The object of their tongue-hanging-out perusal glided to a desk at the front of the class. Andy had a great shot of her tight round ass as she twisted to sit in the chair, which gave him an instant hard-on before the two perfectly matched round globes disappeared from view.

Tony glanced at Andy with an appreciative smile that stretched wide across his lean face. "Hey, I got a hard-on just looking at her!" he whispered, then chuckled with eyebrows raised and lips shaped in a feigned pout.

Andy sniggered along with his buddy, but scooted forward in his seat to hide the bulge at the front of his pants. Unbelievably, he'd had an immediate sexual reaction to the blonde when she strolled through the doorway. And if his friend discovered his arousal, there would be no getting around having to listen to Tony's pointed jibes the rest of the week.

Hell! he silently corrected himself, *the rest of my life!*

His green eyes narrowed as he methodically examined the blonde. She had casually crossed one long leg over the other as she sat sideways in the chair and giggled with her friend who sat across from her. His gaze devoured the blonde's exposed upper thigh, which was as tanned as her lower legs.

Andy swallowed to clear his head. He would bet anyone that she didn't have a clue what she was doing to the guys in the room. She didn't seem to sit haughtily at the front of the room, hoping she was the objection of attention. Andy had seen other girls do that transparent act—it always turned him off.

He rested his chin on a closed fist and continued to study her. It wasn't anything he could quite put his finger on, but if the innocent way she crossed her arms before her chest as if to hide her breasts was any clue, she would probably die of embarrassment if she knew how many erections in the room probably stood at attention right now.

"Who in the hell do you think she is?" Tony kept his eyes on the blonde's voluptuous chest when he whispered across the aisle to Andy again. "I haven't seen her around campus, have you?"

The two men had attended four years at the University of Minnesota and were now starting their graduate classes. They had been in residence for the last two weeks, getting themselves ready for yet another year of college, and attended every pre-semester party. Not once had they come across a find like the one who sat at the front of the class. They sure as hell would have remembered if they had.

"I don't know who she is, but I'm damned well going to find out."

"Fuck you! You can get any girl you want—let me have a chance at her."

Andy opened his Psychology textbook when the instructor entered the room. "Fuck you, Tony," he muttered a firm response. "She's mine…"

* * * * *

After the class, Andy quickly dumped Tony and caught up to her in the hallway. He maneuvered himself directly behind the slim rolling hips as she strolled with her friend to the double glass doors leading outside.

Andy rounded her, laid a hand on the metal door lever, and stared straight into a gorgeous, if not surprised, deep blue gaze.

"Hi."

A tiny smile tugged at the corners of her mouth when Andy held the door open. She exited the building with her giggling friend in tow.

He quickly caught up with them again, switched his backpack to the other shoulder so it wouldn't bounce against her arm, and adjusted his pace to hers.

"I haven't see you on campus. Did you transfer in?"

Before she could respond, her brunette friend piped up. "Hi, we're both new to Minnesota. We completed our first four years at Luther College in Iowa."

Andy clenched his teeth at her interference. *Go away! I wasn't talking to you!* The blonde widened her smile when she glanced sidelong at him, and his heart beat a little quicker.

He ignored her friend. "I'm Andy Duncan—" He left the sentence hanging, hoping she would respond. She did.

"Hi, Andy Duncan. I'm Payton." She wasn't about to give him her last name—not yet.

He decided to plunge right in before her pest of a friend contributed anything else. "You know, I could give you a few tips about the U. This is my fifth year here. What do you say we duck into a coffee shop? My treat."

The brunette opened her mouth again, but before she could say anything, Andy decided to set the situation straight. "I don't think your friend would mind if I stole you away for a little conversation." He actually crossed his fingers that were hidden inside his jean pocket.

The other girl apparently took the hint.

"Well...you go, Payton. I'll see you back at the dorm." She hiked her backpack a little more firmly on her shoulders and waved goodbye before she headed across the street and down the sidewalk.

Payton watched her go. It wasn't hard to miss the flash of trepidation in her eyes when she turned back to face him. "You know, thank you for the invitation, but—"

"I promise I'm not a serial killer. I just couldn't help but notice you back there in class. Come on. What will it hurt to have a cup of java with me—there will be tons of people around."

The straight line of her white upper teeth nibbled indecisively at her bottom lip.

"Please? I'll make a deal with you. You give me a half an hour. If by then I haven't convinced you that I'm one helluva great guy, I'll crawl away and never bother you again."

His stomach did a little flip when her smile widened at his comment.

"All right. You've got thirty minutes."

* * * * *

Payton sat back and wiped the tears from her cheeks. Only twenty minutes had passed since they entered the coffee shop with its strange Bohemian interior, but she was totally at ease with the carefree man who sat across from her. Andy had kept a constant stream of conversation going since ordering them both steaming mugs of cappuccino, and coaxed one laugh after another from her.

She watched him settle back against the red fake leather backrest of their booth and take a sip from his cup, and ignored the jump of her heart when he flashed another one of his sexy smiles in her direction.

"So, Miss Payton Jamison." He raised his arm and glanced at his wristwatch. "Do I need to spend another ten minutes totally captivating you or do I have you convinced that I'm safe to be with?"

She sipped from her own cup above bent elbows. She would not tell him, but nothing could convince her to leave now. Andy's exuberant personality had completely captivated her. "How about I give you another thirty minutes to assure that I've made the right decision?"

He expelled his breath, not realizing until that very moment he was holding it while waiting for her response. "Okay, how about you tell me a little about yourself. Tell me how the stars lined up perfectly—and how the registrar's office set up the same class—allowing us to cross paths this morning."

She giggled again. *How do I tell him about me? That I'm from a farming community? That up to this point, no boy has ever really taken an interest in me?* She still felt uncomfortable in her new look.

Payton had met Angie at Luther College when they were assigned the same dorm room. It was Angie who couldn't wait to get her away from Iowa and give her a complete makeover—a look that would send her parents into an apoplectic fit if they saw her now.

Gone were the thick lenses, the straight blonde hair, and the baggy sweatshirts that hid her feminine shape. In their place were the results of a trip to Lenscrafters for contacts, an afternoon at a beauty shop where her hair was permed and tinted, and a fanatically giggling day at the Mall of America. Her sweatshirts and baggy jeans were packed away in the back of her closet, replaced by short skirts, tight tops, and the latest fashions. Angie insisted that if she had it, she needed to flaunt it—and it was something she was still a little uncomfortable with.

She glanced at the smudge of lipstick on the edge of her cup. She had never even worn makeup in her life, but now spent each morning applying it, even though the woman at the makeup counter had continually dribbled on about how she wished she possessed the naked beauty of her customer's plain Iowan features. Payton possessed dark, thick lashes around her blue eyes and a natural country-girl healthiness that shined beneath the thin layer of foundation and blush. Years of working beside her brothers at the farm kept her tall body toned. There wasn't an ounce of fat to be found anywhere. She eyed Andy above the cup.

"Well, I'm from a small farming community. My parents own a dairy farm. I guess I was lucky enough to have good grades and received an academic scholarship or they would never have been able to send me to a four-year institution. I received a Bachelors degree in Business at Luther College. My friend, Angie—that would be the girl you so obliviously dismissed a while back," she watched his face take on a slightly rosy hue with her comment, "talked me into coming here to complete a Master's degree in Administration. I applied for some scholarships and worked hard at odd jobs to make some extra money. So, here I am. That's about it in a nutshell."

He watched her closely, mesmerized by the blue eyes, full lips, and the sight of the red material stretched across her breasts. A quick flash of what she would look like naked pricked at his brain. Andy found it hard to imagine that the stunning person across from him was as 'simple' as being wrapped up in a tiny nutshell. He wanted to know everything about her, including what it felt like to have her lying beneath him.

Chapter 2: The Wish

Andy kicked off his boxers and used his toe to flick the underwear on top of the pile of clothes lying on the bathroom floor. As he stepped into the hot spray of the shower, his thoughts were filled with Payton.

They had ended up having lunch before returning to their afternoon classes. He was lucky enough to pull the Numerical Analysis course with her, but had to part ways when he headed for Finite Mathematical Groups.

Screw the numbers... He had found it difficult to concentrate on the professor's droning mathematical equations in that last class. Finally the hour ended and he managed to hook back up with Payton and her friend, Angie. A quick invitation to a frat party on Friday ended up with Payton answering quietly that she would go but only, she insisted, if Angie was included.

He consented immediately — anything to spend the evening with her. Payton had invaded his thoughts every minute of the day and if Angie had to initially be a part of his time with her, then so be it.

He tipped his head back and enjoyed the feel of the steamy water running down his body. Grabbing a bar of soap, he built up a mound of suds between his large hands, dropped the bar back into the soap holder, and vigorously scrubbed his chest. An instant image of Payton sharing the heated shower space with him appeared in his head.

Andy's hands stilled while he imagined the feel of her large breasts beneath his fingers as he soaped her chest. A split second later found him staring at the shampoo bottle and wondering how he would manage until morning to see her again.

"Man, do you have it bad," he muttered as he closed his eyes to picture her again.

He was acutely aware of his sudden erection. Even though she had walked into his life only twelve hours earlier, Payton did something to his insides that no other woman ever had. Andy had his share of sexual experiences throughout his college years, but no one person had ever affected him so completely.

His soapy hand brushed across his hardening penis as he washed himself. The combination of visions of Payton and thoughts of what he wanted to do to her body brought his fingers back to his erection. His heart beat a little quicker, but he jerked his hand upward and reached for the shampoo. He quickly washed his dark, wavy head and tried to ignore the release he needed.

"Fuck—I haven't jerked off in years…that shit is for teenagers…"

He forced the image of jutting nipples and a round ass out of his brain, but it wasn't long before a picture of the two of them showering together reappeared. Andy leaned against the shower wall and squeezed his eyes tightly. His jaw clenched with indecision.

You're not a kid thinking about his first time…

It wasn't long before his hand traveled back to his crotch. Tentatively, he grasped his throbbing penis, lost the final battle with his conscience, and began to stroke his hard length.

He envisioned Payton standing beside him, her blonde hair plastered against her skull, her full slightly smiling lips half open, and then imagined the press of her heavy breasts against his chest. She reached out to take his cock into her slender palm.

Andy stroked harder. His head fell back. It was now Payton's hand that brought him nearly to the peak. He pumped against his palm, felt the stirrings of heat pierce through his firm belly, and groaned loudly when semen joined the swirling water around the drain.

He stroked until he was emptied, knowing with certainty that he couldn't have slept a wink tonight if he hadn't jacked off. With a shake of his head, he grabbed the soap once more and rewashed his crotch.

"You better get her in bed quick or Tony's going to wonder why you spend so much time in the shower..."

* * * * *

The two women lay across from each other on twin dorm beds in their pajamas. It was Thursday and their stomachs were full of pizza that Andy had insisted on buying tonight.

Payton stared at the ceiling, thinking about the coming weekend. She was acutely aware that Andy had simply put up with the presence of her friend over the last three nights.

Tomorrow might be different. When they spoke at the beginning of class or during the private lunches he managed to maneuver her into, he intimated that he wanted to be alone with her and not have Angie tag along.

"I think I created a reverse monster of sorts."

Payton turned her head on the pillow to stare at her friend. "Why do you say that? Who's the monster?"

"You are."

"What?" Payton sat up and fluffed the pillow behind her back, then leaned into the downy softness. "Why do you say that?"

"Because I took the little 'farm girl' out of you, helped you to spend some of your hard-earned cash, and turned the ugly duckling into a swan. Now, I think I'm going to lose you to the handsome rooster who's been chasing you all week."

Payton blushed at the observation. She had just been wondering the same thing, but wasn't going to admit it out loud. "Don't be silly. I'd never let a man come between us."

A snort erupted from Angie's throat as she scooted up, crossed her legs, and peered at her friend closely. "He wants to fuck you, you know."

"Angie!"

"Oh, come on. It's about time you get used to that word. I use it all the time."

"Don't I know that," Payton returned with a roll of her eyes.

"Christ, Payt, he's been panting after you all week." Angie's look became thoughtful as she crossed her arms. "I'm going to bow out of the party tomorrow night."

"The heck you are. I need you beside me. I'm swimming in uncharted waters here. I've never had someone interested in me before."

"That's because you've never looked the way you have before. Don't you see how the guys watch your every move? And, Andy—well I sure as hell can see what you do to him. Haven't you ever noticed his hard-on when he's around you?"

Payton leapt from the bed, grabbed a basket of clean clothes, and started folding them. "Contrary to how you handle yourself in public, I'm not in the habit of looking at guys crotches."

Angie tucked the blankets around her knees and stared at her friend. The corners of her mouth curved up in a smile. "Well, you should—and you should take a closer look at what you're doing to Andy. Man, I wish I had a guy that wanted me as bad."

Payton remained silent and continued to stack folded shirts on the chair.

"What are you afraid of, Payt?"

She shrugged her shoulders. Payton put together her thoughts before she turned to face her roommate. "This is all so new to me. I've never had a 'boyfriend'. Angie, I never even was asked to prom or, for that matter, any dance while in high school. I was always the little Jamison girl who studied hard—the little 'ugly duckling' as you so aptly put it. My parents never gave me a chance to date. Once in college, I worked hard and then went home to them every weekend."

Angie left her perch on the bed and moved to help her friend with the basket of clean clothes. "Don't I know it. They always made sure you were too busy with projects at home to have any fun. That used to bug the hell out of me. You're here, though—miles away. They don't run your life anymore."

She grabbed Payton's shoulders, turned her around, and forced her to look in the mirror. "You see that pretty girl looking back at you? You've always been there, hiding inside." A quirky smile appeared on Angie's face. "You just needed me to spruce up the 'old' you a little, and voila—the beauty queen appeared. And, the prince is just waiting to get his hands on you."

Payton trembled slightly and remained serious. "I think he'll try and kiss me tomorrow night."

Laughter bubbled in Angie's throat and escaped a moment later. "So? Let him! Quit being such a virgin. Christ, you're twenty-three years old! A goddamned dinosaur! Your parents ought to be horsewhipped for keeping you hidden out there in the country. You're not on the farm anymore, Payton. You're an adult that can make decisions for yourself. You've got a body that won't quit; you're smart and beautiful. Enjoy it. If he wants to go to bed with you, what the hell? He's a great specimen. May as well lose your cherry to him than someone who shovels cow shit on a daily basis."

"You're impossible!" Payton's cheeks deepened to an even rosier hue.

"But I'm right. I don't know if it was your mom and dad who pounded it into your head that you had to be a virgin when you got married or what. That's not the way of it, kiddo. It's not the dark ages anymore. Have some fun—and have it with Andy."

Payton picked up a pile of clothes and placed the folded items into her drawer. "I have to admit that the thought of him kissing me gives me tingles, but to go to bed with him? I think not, dear friend. I've got too much work ahead of me the next few years to become that deeply involved. I can't jump into bed with someone I just met."

"Tingles?" Angie's jaw dropped with an incredulous shake of her head. "The man makes my panties wet and all you can do is tingle?"

Angie placed a fist on her hip, and she laughed again at her roommate. "As much as I want to see Andy and Tony's place, you're going alone tomorrow. If you don't come back to the dorm, I'll know you've spent the night."

"I'm not sleeping with a stranger."

"Yeah, we'll see about that. Even if you do stop him from feeling you up and putting his dick in you, I still want to hear all the juicy details."

Chapter 3: The Date

True to her words, Angie disappeared the following evening before Andy stopped by to pick up Payton. Now she sat on his living room couch at the party with his arm slung casually across her shoulders.

Payton had to admit that she enjoyed his attention immensely. He was funny and watched over her, assuring that everyone in the room was aware she was his date by the constant handholding and his nearness. She found herself looking forward to the end of the night, innocently hoping he would kiss her when he dropped her off. It was beyond her realm that he would want to jump in bed with her so quickly — they had just met a mere week earlier.

Payton's brain was a little fuzzy — no doubt caused by the three screwdrivers she'd downed already. She wasn't used to drinking all that much, but discovered she liked the warm wooly feeling that threaded its way through her limbs. Lifting the plastic glass to her lips, Payton downed the last few remaining sips of her drink. Feeling totally at ease, she glanced up at Andy's chiseled face and smiled.

"Want to get me a refill?" she hiccuped.

His gaze settled on the empty glass in her hand. "Are you sure?" He peered into her eyes. "You look like you've probably had enough."

Finding courage, she leaned closer to him. "Oh, come on. I'm a big girl." She was, wasn't she? For the first time, she was actually enjoying the 'extra curriculars' that college had to offer. "You've already had two to my every one. Are you going to call it a night? I'm really having fun." She waited patiently for him to do her bidding.

Andy felt the unintended slight pressure of one large breast against his arm. Instantly, his stomach muscles tightened. It was going to be tough keeping his hands off of her.

Earlier, as he drove to her dorm, all he could think of was somehow manipulating her into having sex with him. After spending time, however, talking with her through a simple meal of hamburgers and fries, he realized there was a lot more depth to Payton than the beautiful exterior. She spoke to him about her family and growing up on a farm; about working hard in school and her dreams and goals for the future.

Once back at his house—the one that his parents financed—and the party that was in full swing, every guy in the room continually eyed her up and she didn't even notice. There wasn't an ounce of phoniness in Payton, and he wanted to explore that. As he sat on the couch with her slim body protectively held in his curved arm, Andy had come to the decision that he didn't want to take the chance of losing her by fulfilling his earlier fantasy. He was determined that the evening wouldn't end as a one-night stand.

"I really would like another drink." She stood, albeit a little wobbly, grabbed his hand, and pulled him up from the couch. "Let's find the bar."

Giving in, Andy rose and led her to the kitchen. He let her walk through the swinging door first, enjoying the smell of her perfume as she drifted by him, and then nearly walked up her heels when she stopped on a dime. They both stared at another couple wrapped in the deep throes of a passionate embrace. A young man had a girl backed up to the counter while he kneaded her breasts and kissed an exposed shoulder. The girl's hand reached down to caress the bulging crotch of his pants with encouragement. It wasn't long before the lovers realized they weren't alone.

Payton simply stared at them as the embrace broke apart. She also heard the smile in Andy's voice when he spoke behind her.

"Excuse us. Didn't mean to interrupt anything." He wiggled his empty glass in the air. "Just needed a refill."

The woman took her drunken boyfriend by the hand and strolled past them. "No problem. We were just thinking about heading upstairs anyway." She winked at a wide-eyed Payton before the two disappeared through the doorway.

Andy cleared his throat and walked around a silent Payton, then took the empty glass from her hand. "Okay. One screwdriver coming up."

It wasn't long before he had both drinks poured and ready to go. "Here, taste this and see if it's okay. I made it a little light so you're not sick in the morning." He held the glass to her lips. Payton took a sip as she met his gaze over the rim.

Andy watched her slender throat quiver slightly as she swallowed. When she didn't make an attempt to take the glass from him, he reached down, took her hand and wrapped her fingers around it, never taking his eyes from hers.

"Could I kiss you, Payton?"

Her tongue instantly darted out to wet her lips. "I…I think I'd like that."

Andy set her glass on the flat surface beside him, moved to stand before Payton where she leaned against the counter, and placed a hand on either side of her.

She blinked and wet her lips again.

He lowered his mouth and brushed his lips against her moist ones. The slight intake of her breath encouraged him to deepen the kiss, but he kept it soft. She tasted sweet.

He ended the kiss and hugged her gently. "I've wanted to do that since the moment we met," he whispered against the soft mantle of her hair.

She lifted her arms and clasped them around his neck. "Then, do it again."

He complied, this time a little more sure that she enjoyed it as much as he did. Andy ran his tongue across the seam of her mouth, slanted his head, and pulled her closer.

Payton came willingly, but didn't open her mouth as he thought she would. *Funny…you'd think that at the age of twenty-three, she wouldn't mind a French kiss.*

He didn't wait for her to come to that decision. Andy gently forced his tongue between her lips, and he was inside her mouth. Andy groaned with pure enjoyment. After searching for her tongue and not getting much response, he ended the kiss and leaned back. Payton glanced up from beneath heavy lids.

"Kiss me back. Kiss me with your tongue."

She nodded and pulled his mouth back to hers. She met his tongue tentatively, and then discovered the joy of kissing this way. Andy swirled his tongue against hers and they were lost in the intense sexual feel of the intimate embrace.

He couldn't help himself when he slowly dragged his hand around her slim waist and clasped a succulent breast. Payton gasped against his mouth, withdrew her tongue, and opened her eyes wide to stare at him.

"Is this okay?" He didn't pull his hand away. "God, you have beautiful breasts."

Her nipples hardened instantly. It was the first time anyone had ever felt her breasts. The heat of his caress was overwhelming. Her answer was to simply start kissing him again. *What could it hurt to let him touch me? I'm a grown woman…*

Waves of heat radiated from his light strokes across her nipple. Her intense pleasure doubled when his lower body pressed her more firmly against the counter and her other breast was grasped. The outline of his erection burned against her stomach, but didn't frighten her. She met his kiss with even more enthusiasm.

Andy was in heaven. Having her huge breasts in his hands was unexplainable—as were the emotions that ran through his brain. Exploring Payton's body was utterly unlike any other encounter he'd ever had. As much as he wanted to drag her up the stairs for some hot sex, he knew he wouldn't do it. Andy didn't want their relationship to start that way.

A thought pricked at his conscience while he kissed her. *Relationship?* He'd never used that word before, because he'd never had a relationship. He'd enjoyed some fantastic sex with willing girls who meant nothing to him. But, Payton?

His hands dropped from her chest and wound their way around her waist again, and then dropped to her ass.

He pulled her against him and ground against her. He wanted to fuck the hell out of her.

"Whoa!" Andy dropped his hands and took a quick step back. Payton would have toppled forward if he hadn't caught her by the arm to steady her.

"Andy?" Confusion shot from her heated blue gaze.

He breathed in deeply and ran his hand through his thick hair as he continued to steady her with one hand on her upper arm.

"Andy? What's wrong? Did I do something I shouldn't have?"

He dropped his chin for a moment before he answered her. Finally catching his breath, he met her questioning gaze.

"Oh, no. You did everything right. I...Payton, this is going to get out of hand if we don't stop."

She couldn't forget the unexplained heat she felt building in her body. Through the course of the embrace, her curiosity had changed to slight fear at first, and then to an emotion that she had never felt before. She wanted it to continue.

Payton reached up and caressed his chin. "I've never felt that way before."

"Me either. That's why we need to take our drinks back in the other room and join the party." Andy needed some time to cool off and examine these new feelings — feelings of wanting her naked in his arms, yet needing something else. He was confused about the instant emotion of wanting to protect her always, to do this right and to not push her into something that might make her disappear from his life.

The drinks that she had already consumed made her brave. Payton didn't feel like herself. At the moment, the young girl from the Iowa farm had disappeared. In her place was a woman who had experienced her first sexual tension.

She placed her arms around his neck and smiled up. "Kiss me again." She rose on tiptoes and brushed her parted lips against his, searching for the jolt of heat to run through her belly again.

Andy firmly removed her arms from his neck and set her away from him. "I think it would be best if we just left this where it was."

Her swollen lips turned downward in a frown.

"Payton, don't look that way. I don't know what it is, but be assured I want to keep touching you. In fact, I would love to take you upstairs and spend the night with you, but it's not going to happen."

She reached behind her, grabbed her drink, and took some hefty sips to cool her sudden embarrassment. He was right. What on earth had gotten into her? She handed him her half empty glass without looking directly at him. "Would you freshen this up?"

Payton couldn't meet his eyes. Now that her heart had slowed and she wasn't so caught up in the physical excitement of his touch, reason returned.

She watched him from the corner of her eye as he added ice, vodka, and juice to her glass before he silently grasped her elbow and guided her back to the living room.

Chapter 4: The Awakening

Two hours later, Payton slowly swiveled her head to ask Andy for another drink and faintly wondered why everything in the room blurred somewhat. The evening had flown by as she downed one drink after another, bereft because Andy had not touched her again.

She had to go to the bathroom again but couldn't, for life of her, remember where it was. She heaved herself up from the couch, waited for the room to quit spinning, and looked around.

Andy glanced up with a crooked smile and watery eyes. "Where ya goin'?"

Payton held onto the arm of a chair to steady herself and forced a smile to her lips, even though she felt like weeping. "Gotta find the restroom again." Her gaze bounced around the room again. "You know, I can't remember where it is."

Andy pushed himself up from the soft cushion. "Come on." For the first time since the episode in the kitchen, he took her hand and weaved a course through the many bodies occupying the living room. When they reached the hallway, he discovered a long line of giggling women. He sighed heavily and glanced over his shoulder.

"There's another toilet upstairs. Let's go."

She followed him back across the living room and up the stairs. Andy took her hand again and pulled her down the hallway. One more turn brought them to an empty hallway. He stopped before a painted door, bent at the waist, and swept an unsteady arm outward. "Here you go, Mi Lady. I'll wait for you."

Payton brushed past him and closed the door a second later.

Andy leaned against the wall and closed his eyes with a heartfelt sigh. He'd purposely avoided touching her since the incident in the kitchen, something that despite the cavalier attitude of the last few hours, was getting more difficult to manage. Normally he would have had his date between the sheets by now. With Payton? No.

He suddenly found himself thinking about the future. Andy sighed deeply and crossed his arms. He'd never given much thought to being with one woman exclusively. Payton was different. She'd crept unexpectedly into his life and blindsided him. He wasn't about to mess it up by tossing her on her back.

It wasn't long before he heard the toilet flush. The lock clicked, and she appeared shortly to stand before him. He straightened — and wondered why she remained silent and only stared up at him through wide, blue eyes. She wavered slightly and, he could have sworn, blinked back tears.

"Are you angry with me?" she asked.

"No. Why would you think that?"

She drew in a breath. A breath, he couldn't help but notice, that tightened the material across her mounded chest. He quickly brought his gaze back to meet hers.

"You've hardly said a word to me. I felt like your date when we got here. Now, it's like you want to get rid of me. That's fine," she shrugged. "I'm ready to leave anytime you want to bring me home."

He watched her struggle to hide a hiccup. He hadn't meant to hurt her feelings. Andy couldn't stop himself when he reached out a single hand, laid it on her slender shoulder, and then gave it a reassuring squeeze. "Sorry, Payton. I didn't mean to ignore you. It's just..." he looked at the ceiling and tried to figure out what he wanted to say. "It's just that I don't quite trust myself around you — especially after what happened in the kitchen."

She blinked again, but failed to stop the single tear that escaped down a smooth cheek. "Was it so bad kissing me? I haven't kissed many boys." *I've never kissed any boys...*

Christ — she thinks I didn't like it... "That's not it at all. Payton," he grasped for the right words of explanation again. "I don't want this to be our only date. I want to continue to see you."

"But, why wouldn't you want to kiss me again if that's true?" She adjusted her stance with eyes closed, lost her equilibrium, and swayed forward. Her breasts innocently brushed his chest. Andy quickly captured her in his arms to stop her fall, which nearly sent them both tumbling to the carpeted floor. His chest immediately burned where her nipples touched him through his thin cotton shirt. His semi-erection grew even harder.

"Payton, you're pretty drunk. Maybe we should get you back to your dorm room."

Her arms snaked firmly around his waist. "Andy, please. I want to be like the girl in the kitchen. I want to kiss you." Payton's chin came up. She stared at him and unconsciously licked her lips. The simple action drove him crazy.

His erection was now rock hard. He'd never held a woman in his arms and experienced a reaction like the one that now heated his blood.

Before he could utter another word, Payton drew his head down and kissed his mouth. A small mewling growl emitted from somewhere deep in her throat as she worked her tongue between his lips.

Andy was lost. The many drinks he'd consumed to forget the feel of her in his arms now spurred him to pull her closer. His lips slanted across her full ones as he forced his tongue deep in the warm depths of her open mouth.

It took only two steps to have her pressed against a closed door on the opposite wall of the hallway. A strong hand urged her thigh to wrap itself around his muscular leg. It was the first time he had molded her feminine mound squarely against his erection. She fit perfectly. He reached up and kneaded a swollen breast.

Payton clutched his shoulders, an age-old instinct instructing her to grind against him as his fingers gave her pleasure like she'd never known.

Andy knew he had to be inside of her. The thought of plunging into her hot pussy had his penis throbbing.

Payton seemed oblivious that they were in the hallway where anyone could see them. She moaned against Andy' lips again.

Andy's hand left her breast and quickly spun the brass knob on the door behind her.

He kicked the door shut with the heel of his shoe and walked her backwards to the double bed against the wall. A quick spin to change positions with her in order to take the brunt of the fall caused them both to lose their balance. Payton was like dead weight on top of his body as they fell backwards across his bed. Her flailing arm nearly knocked the dimly lit lamp on the bed stand to the floor.

Andy's hands immediately grasped her firm ass and held her in place until the room quit spinning. Payton lay motionless on him, so he flipped her onto her back. He was mesmerized by the blue eyes that fluttered open and the lazy grin that appeared on her face.

"Whew — was it the kiss or have you been spinning me around?" She lay with her arms spread out at her sides, her blonde hair spread across the pillow.

He smiled along with her slurred remark.

"Kiss me again," she mumbled.

He dropped his mouth to do just that, and then he mumbled against her lips. "We weren't supposed to be here, but I love the feel of you lying beside me."

"It's alright, Andy." She playfully nibbled at his lips. "I want to be here."

Trembling hands slowly unbuttoned her shirt and spread it open to reveal an unadorned white bra that covered what he hoped to be the nicest set of breasts he had ever seen. It didn't take him long to wiggle his hands behind her back and unhook the double clasps to find out what he suspected was truth. He tossed her shirt and bra to the floor.

He lay on his side and squeezed one soft mound, and then the other. Payton's contented sigh whispered past his ear. Raising up on a bent elbow, he dipped his head and rolled a pink nipple inside his mouth with his tongue.

"God, Payton. You've got great breasts." He sucked harder on the now erect nipple in his mouth and massaged its twin.

Payton's head spun as she tried to keep up with his hands and mouth. No one had ever made her feel like this before. Andy scorched her skin wherever he touched.

Is it wrong? Her mother continually warned her about what boys would try to do to her. It was easy to keep her promises when she remained the ugly farm girl. Angie had turned her into a different person, however—one that boys and men whistled at—one that found a man's attention wasn't as bad as she was led to believe. She was finally going to find out about what her friend constantly told her was a great experience. If Andy stopped now, she would simply die. Payton needed to know what being with a man was like.

The bed she lay on creaked. Gentle hands rubbed the naked skin of her midriff. She forced her eyes open, focused on Andy kneeling beside her, and then watched as if in a dream when he leaned forward to kiss the area beneath his gentle hands.

Payton sighed. "Mmmm...that feels good."

She bucked slightly when a hand fondled the area between her legs, and she automatically spread her jean-clad thighs. A hot dart of something indefinable sparked its way from her belly to the hand that massaged her crotch.

Suddenly, Andy's mouth whispered against her lips. "Do you want me to finger you?" The pressure of his hand between her legs heightened as he asked. Angie had told her about this. At the time, Payton didn't think she could ever let anyone do that to her. Now, she yearned to experience it. Her hand flailed in the air momentarily before dropping to cover his large one to urge him on. Her eyes snapped open to stop the sudden spinning of the bed. Andy's smile met her own.

He rose to his knees, used both hands to unfasten the snap of her jeans and tugged the open waist down. She lifted her hips slightly to help him along, and felt the material glide down past her shapely calves. Her silk briefs followed. The cool air in the room caused goose bumps to appear on her legs and arms.

Andy leaned back and took in every inch of her length with his hot gaze. Payton sprawled naked across his bed was a sight to behold. Her thick blonde tresses cascaded over the pillow and, even though her breasts were huge, they were firm enough to point upwards. His glittering eyes followed the path from the large mounds to her slightly parted legs. A light blonde tuft of hair hid the slit he craved to see.

He was in dangerous territory. His initial plan was evaporating as fast as her clothes had. It pricked steadily at his conscience. Fucking Payton would be an experience, but fucking her when she was drunk would be taking advantage of something he wasn't quite sure she would have submitted to in another circumstance. His throbbing erection disagreed, but he finally won the battle.

"I think we better get you dressed and back to your room. If we keep this up, I won't guarantee what will happen." *Christ — Tony's going to laugh his ass off about this one.*

"You don't want me here anymore?" Her voice sounded like a hurt little girl as she rolled to her side to face him.

"It's not that, Payton. I want to be inside of you —"

Her heart jumped at his words.

"But I don't think tonight is the night. We've both had too much to drink." For some odd reason, he wanted the first time to be perfect.

Payton reached out a hand. It was Andy's turn to buck slightly when she dropped her palm squarely on the bulge in his pants.

"Payton," he hissed out as she fondled his hidden erection. Andy grabbed her hand and half-heartedly tried to force it away. "You're not making this easy for me."

"I don't want it to be easy. I want…I want you to do to me what you said before. I want you to…finger me. I want to see what it feels like."

"Jesus," he breathed out into the dimly lit room.

Payton grab his hand and dragged it to the apex of her spread legs—and waited for the hot flood of feelings to start again. "Kiss me, Andy. I want to keep going. I want to see what it's like."

He didn't move his hand away from the heat between her legs. Rising to his elbow again, Andy stared down at her. His mouth dropped to kiss her again when he inserted a finger into her hot pussy. She jumped beneath his touch.

"You're drunk, Payton." Suddenly, something hit him square in the gut—something she had just said. As impossible as it seemed, he had to ask the question. "Is this the first time anyone has ever done this to you?"

She stared at him, and then swallowed. Payton nodded her head.

He pulled his hand away from between her legs as if burned and jumped to his feet. A second later, he grabbed her shirt and pants from where they lay on the floor. "Get dressed."

"I'm twenty-three years old, and I don't want to be a virgin anymore. I want you to be my first." The vodka gave her the courage to make the request.

"You're drunk."

"Yes I am."

Her crooked smile melted his heart.

Payton rose to her wobbly knees and reached out to grab his arm. She yanked on it until he was forced to look at her again. "I want you to do things to me. I want my first time to be with you, and I want it to be now."

He remained silent. Payton sidled closer. One of Andy's shirttails hung lose from his belted waist. She wiggled her hand beneath the cotton material and caressed the firm skin of his belly. His stomach muscles contracted under her searching fingertips.

"Make love to me, Andy." Her hand fluttered from beneath the shirt and rested over his erection. "Please, show me what it's like." She increased the pressure of her hand against him.

Andy lost the battle she waged.

He kneeled before her on the bed's surface, removed his shirt, and pulled her into his arms. As he kissed her, Andy used his right hand to unbuckle his belt, snap open the button fly, and work the zipper down. He took her hand and guided it inside his boxers.

They both gasped lightly against one another's mouth when she grasped his penis in her hand.

"Have you ever touched like this?"

"No," she mumbled.

He pushed her backwards and kissed her breasts as he removed his jeans and underwear. Rolling to his back, he took her hand and brought it back to his penis. He cupped his own over her fingers and showed her how to stroke, a slow sensuous movement that nearly drove him wild.

Payton was amazed at how the satiny length felt in her hands. Her head lifted and she stared down at the slightly purplish head. Suddenly, she was frightened. Angie told her that sex would hurt the first time. She didn't have much time to dwell on it, though.

Andy dragged her hand away with a large intake of breath. "You've got to stop or this will be over before you know it." Having her fingers around his penis had him tottering on the edge of coming.

He gently forced her onto her back again and suckled her breasts as his hand dropped to the curls between her legs. Payton instantly forgot her fears when he ran his fingers across her moist slit.

"God, Payton…spread your legs a little more."

She willingly dropped her knees wider. He dipped his middle finger inside her pussy.

"Christ, you're tight." He withdrew his wet finger and rolled it across her clitoris. "I've never fucked a virgin before." She felt the pressure of his cock against her hip. The combination caused her to arch against his hand.

He pumped his finger in and out of her wet pussy as he moved his mouth to hers. "Have you ever come before?" Andy swirled his tongue around her earlobe.

"I…don't know what's going to happen," she whispered breathlessly and wiggled beneath his hand.

He smiled into the cloak of her sweet smelling hair and inserted another finger. "Just go with it, baby."

She moved her hips, clenching her pussy around his fingers.

"That's it. Does it feel good?" His fingers slid out. He circled her clit momentarily, then inserted one finger with more force than earlier.

"Oh, God…" She searched for more of the heat that invaded her belly, knowing that there must be something else about to happen. "Please don't stop."

He chuckled. "I don't plan to." His cock throbbed. He wanted to stop with this play and simply come inside of her. Another part of him, however, wanted her to experience her first orgasm without any pain.

He worked her clitoris with his thumb as he continued to fuck her with two fingers now and suckled the hard dart of her nipple.

Payton writhed beneath his hand, pumping against it, still searching for some elusive feeling to end her torture. She spread her legs wider and arched against his palm. Suddenly, hot wet waves shot out from where his thick fingers played inside her and followed a molten path upwards to her breasts. She groaned loudly with the intense shock waves that caused her to clench her vaginal muscles.

"Andy!"

He inserted a third finger, thoroughly enjoying the pulsing waves she experienced simply because of what he was doing to her. Payton was in the middle of her first orgasm. Her knees came up, and she squeezed her thighs around his hand and bucked wildly.

The pulsing around his fingers slowed and finally disappeared. Payton's knees weakly dropped open. Andy withdrew from her wet heat and slid his hand upwards to capture the fullness of a breast.

Her eyes fluttered open. Deep satisfaction settled in her gaze. A pink tongue moistened her full, parted lips. "I've...I've never felt anything like that in my life. I didn't know a man could do that with his fingers."

A smile creased his face. "Oh, you haven't even experienced all of what my fingers can do to you."

Her brow dipped in an instant frown. "But...you didn't get to feel anything, did you? I can feel wetness on my thigh. Did you get to do it, too? It was so wonderful!"

His penis leaked pre-ejaculate. He'd done everything in his power not to come when she bucked beneath his hand. "No, I didn't come, but I'm gonna have to if I ever want to sleep again. Payton, you're something." Andy dipped his head and kissed her. "I don't think I'll be able to wait once I'm inside of you, though."

He rolled to his back, grabbed her hand and wrapped her fingers around his cock. "You're going to have to use your hand and get me off. It won't be any fun for either of us if we do it when I'm in the state I am at the moment."

He gasped when she held him tightly and immediately began to run her closed fingers up and down the length of him. "There's no way...fuck," his eyes snapped shut, "that I can hold it for long... I don't want to come immediately when..."

Waves of ejaculate squirted out across her closed fist and onto his belly. Andy held her hand tightly and groaned as he emptied himself. He shivered when she sucked on his nipple, and then smiled when she giggled as his breathing slowed.

"What?"

"That was something new for me. What do we do next?"

He burst out laughing, grabbed a towel that lay on the floor beside the bed and cleaned himself off. By now, he felt pretty sober, but he wasn't too sure about Payton. He eyed her. "Are you still drunk?"

"The bed's not spinning like it was, but I'm still feeling pretty fuzzy." She leaned forward and kissed him, absolutely surprised at herself that it didn't bother her in the least to be naked in front of him. "I have to admit that I was pretty out of it earlier, but I'm a big girl, Andy. And, I want to do the rest of it."

As much as he wanted to keep going, reason took hold of him. Payton was a virgin, and when they finally made love, he wanted her to be sober and know completely what they were doing. He took her hand in his.

"I want to do the rest of it, too. But, it's not going to happen tonight."

"But—"

"But nothing. Listen to me, Payton. This was different for me tonight. I can't believe I'm about to say this. I'm going to bring you back to your dorm. I want you to think about this when you haven't had anything to drink." He tucked a wayward strand of hair behind her ear and ignored the confusion in her eyes. "We started something here tonight, and I want it to continue. I don't want you to wake up tomorrow thinking I took something that wasn't mine to take. You walked into that classroom at the beginning of the week and got under my skin like no one else ever has."

She remained silent as she dropped her gaze to the bed's surface, wondering if she should be embarrassed now to find herself in this situation. His next words, however, calmed her fears.

"Let's get dressed before someone comes in. I never even thought about locking the door. I don't want people to think we came up here, knocked off a piece, and did it just for the hell of it. You're special, Payton, and don't deserve that. Let's wait a little until you know that you're absolutely sure."

That was when she fell head over heels in love with him. He wasn't willing to compromise her reputation, even at the expense of depriving himself of something she suspected most men his age would never have walked away from.

As much as she wanted to experience for herself something that Angie had told her about countless times, he was right. The first time that they actually made love would be something she remembered forever.

* * * * *

A full week passed by. In that time, Payton spent every possible moment with Andy that she could. They found themselves kissing in hallway alcoves between classes. His touch drove her insane. All she could think of was the hot emotion that he drew from her body the night he used his fingers to make her orgasm for the first time.

Payton climbed into bed at night, her body hot and aching with the need to make love with him. Angie continually teased her about her inability to concentrate on any subject at hand. Her friend had begged for the juicy details of their first date, but Payton remained closemouthed.

No one had ever consumed her every waking thought like Andy did. She had even forgotten to call her parents the following Sunday night—something she had done every week since leaving home the summer past.

Now, Payton readied herself for her second Friday night date with him. They were going with Tony and his date for pizza at an on-campus eatery. There had been talk about hitting a movie afterwards.

Fine. That's just fine. But there's no way I'm having even one drink. There were two reasons for that decision. She had been sick the entire weekend after drinking so many screwdrivers the last time. The thought of feeling that way again turned her stomach as she applied her lipstick.

Payton planned to stay completely sober. Tonight, she was going to finally lose her virginity. She'd had enough of Andy's intimate touches through her clothes. She would force the issue if need be, but didn't think Andy was in the frame of mind to wait any longer either. His constantly hot gazes and hard erections pressed against her when they kissed were proof.

She leaned back, crossed her arms, and studied her reflection in the mirror. "I can't believe you're planning this out the way you are. A week ago, you had never even been kissed."

A slight twinge of guilt ran through her brain when she thought of her parents and all their warnings. Having sex was something her mother toted to be a horrible experience for a woman—a duty to be performed by a good Catholic wife for procreation.

She shook her head, but couldn't help the smile that suddenly appeared in the mirror. Angie was right. Times were different. Payton's parents were good people, but her friend commented once that they kept Payton hidden and ugly on the farm just because they were so old fashioned.

Payton finally saw the truth in her friend's words. Thank goodness she'd come up with the idea to come to Minnesota.

She stared at her reflection again. "You'd never have met Andy if it wasn't for Angie's urging and guidance."

Her smile widened as she rose from the chair and grabbed a sweater.

Chapter 5: The First Time

The evening dragged out for both of them. Tony's date turned out to be a snobbish hometown girl from Minneapolis who whined continually about how the beer wasn't cold enough or how she would have much rather had a steak at Delmonico's than a greasy pizza. By the end of the meal, Payton could see that Andy had had enough.

As they rose to leave, he grabbed her arm and pulled her back against his chest. Tony and his date walked through the mass of students to the cash register as he whispered into her ear. "After we pay the tab, pretend that you have a stomachache and want to go home. There's no way I'm listening to Jennifer bitch through the entire movie."

Andy had just given Payton her excuse to be alone with him. She nodded with a smile.

They paid for their meal. As they left through the doors painted with the colors of the Italian flag, Payton drew in a deep breath.

"Jennifer, it was really nice meeting you, but I think I'm going to have to bow out of the movie. That pizza isn't sitting too well. I think I'll just have Andy bring me straight home."

Andy tightened his arm protectively. "We'll just say goodnight and I'll get her home. You two have a fun night." He ignored Tony's look of disapproval and urged Payton toward his car.

They waited until the car doors were closed and Tony and Jennifer were out of earshot before they burst out laughing.

Payton wiped at her eyes. "Did you see the look on Tony's face? He doesn't believe for a second that I'm not feeling well."

"Fuck him," Andy laughed. "Why should all of us suffer with Jennifer's attitude?" He started the car and pulled into traffic. "Mark my words, he'll figure out a way to dump her at some point, so don't feel sorry for him. What do you want to do?"

Payton scooted across the bench seat of his Chevy and laid her head on his shoulder. "Let's go back to your place and be alone. I'm not in the mood for any more crowds."

Andy clicked on the blinker and just made the exit ramp to get him out to the freeway. "Sounds good to me."

He wondered if tonight was going to be the night.

* * * * *

Payton stood beside Andy as he unlocked the door, her heart pounding in her chest, trying to figure out a way to broach the subject that had been on her mind the entire week.

He flicked the light on when they entered the living room, tossed his keys on the coffee table, and clicked the door lock. As Payton made to walk by him to the television, he gently grasped her arm, pulled her close, and kissed her deeply.

When the kiss ended, he smiled down. "I've been waiting all night to do that. Jennifer bitched, Tony joked, and all I could think about was kissing you."

She tightened her arms around his neck. "Me, too. I'm so glad you came up with the get-away-quick scheme. I don't know how much more I could have taken of her incessant whining."

Payton settled herself on the couch. Andy joined her a second later with the TV clicker in his hand. They channel surfed until coming to an agreement to watch an old John Wayne movie.

"You know, you're the first girl I've ever known that would willingly watch the Duke with me."

Payton shrugged with nonchalance. "What's the big deal? I love westerns. My dad and I watched them all the time when I lived at home."

"I don't know, I just think it's kind of cool that—"

She elbowed him ribs, and then smiled when he grunted. "Shut up and watch the movie."

* * * * *

An hour later, they still sat compatibly, he with his arm around her and Payton with her head nestled on her shoulder.

Andy rubbed his hand gently across the smooth skin of her upper arm. He glanced sideways, finding it hard to believe she was as engrossed in the movie as she portrayed. He leaned slightly forward and brushed his lips across the skin just beneath her ear, loving how she smelled.

Payton's head dropped to the back of the sofa to allow him all the access he wanted. The Duke was instantly forgotten. She turned her face and met the warm lips that were mere inches from her face.

They kissed silently, letting the liquid heat build as he opened his mouth and found her waiting tongue. Payton groaned when he gently forced her onto her back and stretched out beside her. His hand found her breast a second later. He wasn't sure until this very moment if she would want a repeat of their first date.

She simply kissed him with more passion than a moment earlier in answer to his thoughts.

Andy opened her blouse one button at a time to reveal her breasts wrapped in a low-cut lacy black bra with a clasp at the front. The surprise in his eyes was replaced by a smoldering look as he ran one finger lightly down the edge of one lacy cup, into her cleavage, then back up the opposite side.

"This is a change from last week. You look great in it."

"I bought it especially with you in mind. I hoped you would like it."

"I'd like it off you even better." His fingers made quick work of the clasp. Her breasts spilled out of the confined space. Andy buried his head against her chest, then kissed a nipple, teasing it into a tight dart.

His lips traced a path to the other breast as his hand massaged the taut skin of her midriff. His fingers trailed lower until his hand rested between her legs.

Payton's hand drifted to his chest, then down past his stomach to his hardening erection.

He raised his head and stared down into her smoldering eyes.

"Let's go upstairs, Andy. I'm perfectly sober, and totally ready to be with you. Please don't say no."

"God, Payton, you don't know how much I want to make love to you. Are you sure?"

"I thought about it all week. I want nothing more than to feel you inside of me."

He stood, helped her to her feet, then lifted her into his arms and headed for the steps.

* * * * *

Andy let her body slide down the length of him when he reached his room. He was rock hard and ready to make her his own.

Hooking his thumbs beneath lacy straps, he slid both her bra and shirt off her silky shoulders with one fluid motion. Payton stood quietly as he grasped both her breasts and squeezed them together. He loved the soft feeling of the two mounds in his hand.

"God, you make me hot, Payton. Why in hell did it take you so long to come into my life?"

As he massaged her, Payton's hand dropped to her waist. She slid the jersey material of her leggings over her hips to reveal a matching black thong. The thin lacy material lay just above the line of blonde pubic hair. She wiggled the pants down to her ankles and kicked them aside.

Andy whistled softly. "Wow, I don't know if I even want you to take that off." He walked around her to see what she looked like from the back. A thin strip of material disappeared between two beautiful ass cheeks. His hands urged her back against him, and then he threaded his arms around her tiny waist.

Kissing the side of her neck, he kneaded her breasts before sliding his palms down to her flat stomach. One long finger drifted along the band of black lace that lay against her belly, tempting her, promising her what was to come. Payton's head fell back against his broad chest as her hands covered his. The slow sensuous feel of her ass brushing against his erection caused his heart to thunder in his chest.

His large hand disappeared inside the lace. He pressed the flat of his palm against her pubic hair and flicked a finger against her clitoris, relishing the heat and the moistness he found inside the black thong.

Payton arched, her body silently begging for more.

As much as he hated to let her go, Andy moved to stand before her.

Flaming passion leapt from the blue depths of her eyes.

He knelt and gently drew the thin straps of the waistband over her narrow hips, past her knees, and down to her ankles. Payton stepped from the small circle of lace at her feet.

Gentle hands grasped her buttocks and urged her pubic mound forward. Andy rubbed his cheek against the downy softness of curling hair.

Payton clutched his shoulders to keep her knees from buckling, breathing deeply to maintain her composure. His fingers slid down the inside of her ass cheeks to play at the opening of her pussy, maintaining the pressure of his hands on her ass to keep her body close to his face.

"You're wet for me already. I'm glad you're as turned on as I am."

"Andy, please…" She didn't know how much more of this slow seduction she could stand. Being in his clutches was better than anything she had imagined the entire week before.

Andy stood and stripped off his t-shirt. His jeans lay on the floor a moment later along with his boxers.

She stared at his penis, which was erect and already glistening with pre-ejaculate. Payton moved in a dreamlike state to the bed when he took her hand and urged her along.

Andy stretched beside her on the flat surface. They faced each other as he ran a hand across the gentle curve of her hip, then kissed her softly. He tipped his head, kissed her once more, and curled his fingers around a breast. "I don't want to hurt you, but I think I will. I don't know if it will be as wonderful for you as it is me."

She touched his smooth cheek. "It has to happen. Then it'll be over with. I want this, Andy."

He already had it planned. He was going to turn her inside out with pleasure and, just as she came, he would enter her. Maybe then, it wouldn't be too painful.

Andy began a tortuous path with his lips from Payton's mouth, down across her breasts, and to her stomach. His hand ran a smooth course from her knee to an inside thigh, lightly brushed past the heat between her legs, and then trailed down her other leg.

Silently, he crawled between her legs, opened her knees wide, and looked at her for the first time. Payton curled her fingers into the pillow and watched his every move.

He slid a finger down her glistening slit, then back to her clit. Nothing had ever excited him as much as the moment when he dropped his mouth and captured her clit between his lips. Payton bucked on the bed, but his grip was firm on her hips as he rolled his tongue around the swollen bud.

Payton's gasping pants met his ears. The sound urged him on. He stretched out between her legs, opened her pussy lips wider with his thumbs and licked her from bottom to top, stopping to nibble her clit once more before he stuck his tongue inside of her.

"Andy..." Payton squirmed.

Knowing that she was close, he pulled his mouth away, rose to his knees and bent to suckle her clit again while simultaneously sticking a finger into her pussy.

Payton reared up and met each stroke of his tongue. Her head rolled wildly on the pillow. Small groans emitted one after the other from her throat.

Another finger joined the one that moved in and out of her pussy. His mouth lapped at her sweetness. Andy knew the exact moment when she exploded. A scream accompanied the throbbing waves of her vagina.

Never hesitating, Andy quickly plunged inside of her. He felt the momentary pressure of skin against the head of his penis before he broke through to capture the last pulsing waves of her orgasm around his cock.

Payton groaned loudly and instantly stopped her movements against him. Andy lay motionless, waiting for her body to let him know if he needed to stop. He kissed her lips, not caring if she let him continue or not. Buried inside of Payton was a sensual experience in itself. Somehow, he would pull out if that was what she wanted.

"It's all right, Andy," she whispered into his ear.

He began to stroke gently, waiting for her to join him. Her hips finally moved against his and found the rhythm he waited for.

Payton squeezed her eyes tightly and waited for the last remnants of pain to subside. Surprisingly, it did. In its place, the warmth of his embrace erased any fear that it would ever return. She began to meet his increasingly stronger thrusts.

It was beautiful. It was better than she could have ever imagined.

When he withdrew from her body, Payton thought he was finished, disheartened that their lovemaking was over — until he repositioned himself on his knees between her spread legs, guided his cock back into her, and then moistened his fingers with his tongue. He touched her clit and rolled it to the rhythm of his strokes. Payton felt the spikes of heat begin to build again.

"I want you to come again. I'm going to rub your clit until you do." He worked her body until she met each stroke, clutching with her vagina at his penis to draw him deeper inside of her.

Andy watched her eyes darken again with passion and increased the tempo.

Payton nearly fainted when the waves washed over her again. Andy grabbed her hips and emptied himself inside of her.

Chapter 6: Twelve Years Later

Andy's body jerked. His eyes snapped open as he looked about the living room. A television sportscaster announced the final football score. Apparently he'd missed the Vikings getting walloped again by the Green Bay Packers.

He sat up, leaned his elbows on his knees, and ran his large hands through the thick head of tousled hair.

"What the hell?" he muttered. It was then that he noticed his hard-on.

He had dreamed again about the time when he first met his wife, the first time he ever screwed her; correction — the first time he'd ever made love to her. That was twelve years ago.

He dropped back to the soft cushion of the expensive leather couch and slung an arm over his brow. He could hear the laughing voices of his two sons playing some kind of cop and robber game in the front yard, completely oblivious that their father had almost had a wet dream — all because of the sex life he used to have with their mother, who at the moment was shopping for a pair of shoes for their daughter, Sara.

Andy's dream had him thinking now about their life after that first encounter. Three months after that first week of graduate school, he and Payton stood before a Justice of the Peace, planning for the baby that was on the way. He had been so intent on finally showing Payton the pleasures of sex, that it never occurred to him she wasn't on the Pill.

Payton's parents insisted they marry immediately, but even so, Andy had never felt trapped. He was the happiest guy in the world to have such a beautiful, smart wife and never regretted a day of their forced marriage or the three children they shared. He loved her deeply.

Those first few early years were hard. Thank goodness, his parents had enough money to help put both of them through the last years of college. Payton's parents had bowed out after their initial demand that they marry. He could still see her father's pissed off features at the wedding reception when he told Payton she was cut off from any money for school. *Dumb bastard – he doesn't know what he's missing now.*

Her mother then informed Payton that she had made her bed, now she would have to lie in it and suffer the consequences. His new wife's brothers stood by, looking like they were ready to punch his lights out. *God damned Puritans.* They never saw too much of her family after that.

"Like Tyler was something that made us suffer," he muttered out loud again. If anything, the little baby boy born that next summer completed the joy both he and Payton shared.

He worked two jobs to support them, and went to night school, never complaining. His own parents were good enough to watch Tyler while both he and Payton completed course after course with honors. Andy now remembered how he wished, at the time, his father would have been even more generous with his checkbook. Those four years were tough, but their trials had only fortified a solid foundation of love. And, to top it off, the night they both graduated, Payton's gift to him was the announcement that another baby was on the way.

As soon as Scotty was born, Payton found a job with an international computer software company and climbed her way up the ladder quicker than anyone he knew. She was a great supervisor, made tons of money for her company, and worked her way right out of their bed — or did so after Sara was born three years ago.

The hours she was asked to work took something away from the marriage. *That's why I dreamed again about the fun we used to have between the sheets.* Payton always seemed tired and managed only quick fucks on the weekend. She hurried through the sexual encounters like she hurried through cleaning the house, preparing meals, and through the door when she left for work.

It drove him crazy. Her disinterest didn't cause him to love her any less, but it continually pricked at Andy that he had one of the sexiest wives around and their sex life sucked. The men he worked with told him how lucky he was. Payton was more beautiful now than when they married, and she never complained when he did things with the guys, only smiled and told him to have a good time. She'd give him a peck on the cheek and send him golfing.

Andy worked hard to try and carve out time for his wife to enjoy her life. He hired a housecleaning service, but it didn't make any difference. Payton, in her anal retentive way, cleaned the night before they showed up. He stopped more often after work to pick up carryout so she wouldn't rush in to cook, or most times started dinner for them all because he arrived home first. Well, then, she would rush to the basement and throw clothes in the washer or hit her computer for a little extra project to complete, therefore taking the pressure off her shoulders the next day at work.

He sighed heavily into the lonely room. He had to find a way to get back the good old days when they enjoyed one another to the fullest extent.

* * * * *

Andy thrust one final time into his wife's body, waited until he emptied himself, and then rolled to the side a split second later. The mattress dipped in response to his splayed body as a satisfied sigh escaped into the total darkness of the bedroom.

At the same time, Payton gritted her teeth at the sound. Once again, he had left her hanging by her toenails, frustrated because he had come quickly before she had a chance to find her own satisfaction. These days, it took forever to get her mind off of work and family and give him the attention he was due. Because of it, she was just warming up when he released himself inside of her and called it a night.

She sat up and, before her searching fingers found the switch on the bedside lamp, Andy's big hand cupped her breast.

"Wow, babe—" he declared as his roughened palm danced over the soft mound, "I can't believe that after all these years, your pussy is still as tight as it is. You'd never know that you've had three kids."

The sudden glare of light caused both of them to squint when the lamp flashed on. Payton rose from the bed, crossed to where her shabby bathrobe lay in a heap on a chair, and shrugged the garment around her naked shoulders just as her husband's low whistle of appreciation met her ears.

"Hey, Payton—" he rumbled from the bed.

She hid the irritability in her blue gaze and glanced over her shoulder.

Andy watched her with a gleam in his eye.

"You've got one great ass." He reached down and pulled at his flaccid penis. "How about you come back here and rub it on me. I'm sure I could get it up for another fuck."

Her shoulders instantly fell with a silent sigh. *That's what he always calls it – fucking. Couldn't he at least once use the words 'making love'?*

A wry smile curved her lips to cover up the sting of the word he used, and she shook her long, blonde hair. "You're out of luck, big guy."

"Oh, come on, babe," he whined.

"Nope," she returned, "I've gotta get up for work tomorrow."

"Hell! So do I."

Payton tightened the cotton sash around her waist as an exasperated sigh crossed her lips. "Yeah, but you don't have to put the final touches on a budget proposal. I've worked like crazy on it for two weeks and it's still not done. Andy, I work for a huge corporation that doesn't care if you get laid for a second time tonight." She sighed again. "Thank God it's Friday tomorrow – I've had a hellish week at work, and I'm exhausted. All I want to do is make it through one more grueling day, then I can sleep in on Saturday."

Andy gave her that little boy look he was so good at. "Sure I can't change your mind?"

She shook her head. "I'll be right back."

Payton opened the door, and he watched her sumptuous figure disappear into the hallway. His easy smile turned instantly into a frown when the doorway was empty. He flipped onto his flat stomach and smacked his pillow with a closed fist.

"Shit," he mumbled to the empty room, "when are we going to get this right again?" A second later, he flipped back to stare at the ceiling, wondering if he should entirely blame himself. Once again, Payton hadn't experienced the pleasure of an orgasm—no matter the small moans that emitted from her slender throat or the hip motions meant to try and fool him. But, no matter that she didn't come once again, Andy could not hide the pleasure he found inside her body.

He had tried since the beginning of this week to have everything done for her so she wouldn't be so damned tired. He knew she appreciated every ounce of effort, but still didn't seem too enthused to have a little romp before Saturday night. *We're like an old couple with our Saturday night fucks. When the hell did that happen?* Tonight he'd whispered breathless, dirty words into her ear in an attempt to increase the passion of the typical bedroom episodes. It was something that used to turn her on. Now? Nothing. Zero. Zip.

Andy battled his own frustration at being unable to draw his wife into a gratifying sexual encounter. Somehow, he had to discover a way to fix this one important missing part of their marriage—the part where two people found complete enjoyment in one another's bodies.

"Christ," he muttered aloud again, "I don't know what the hell else I can do to prove how much I love her...to show her how much she turns me on." A quick picture of her lying naked beneath him flashed in his brain. Andy got hard again with just the thought. She had a way of doing that to him at the oddest moments of the day. He couldn't even watch her vacuum without becoming aroused.

He ran a hand through his thick dark hair, squeezed his eyes shut, and willed away his erection. *Baby — I can only hold out so long when you're under me.*

Andy understood that Payton wasn't frigid and never had been. She was simply too consumed with family and work to see what she was doing to not only herself, but to their sexual relationship.

He remembered the many times he quelled his own needs, trying to get her to respond to his gentle ministrations, his adoring hands, and his wild kisses. When he asked if she liked something in particular — like sucking on her breasts, or if he worked her clitoris to assure she would come when he was inside her, she would simply shake her beautiful blonde head on the pillow and tell him to hurry up.

A couple of times over the last year, he persuaded her to watch porn with him, but eventually her cheeks would flame with embarrassment and she would ask him to shut the television off before the kids woke up.

Andy sat up, punched his pillow one more frustrated time, and settled back into the softness. Over the last couple of years, they had lost the special sexual communication they'd always had between them. Now he was at a loss as to what to do to make things better for his wife.

Chapter 7: Payton's Problem

Payton poked her head through the baby's doorway and was assured that Sara slept soundly. A few more steps brought her to the boys' bedroom. They too, were sound asleep. Glancing at the floor, she tiptoed past the twin beds, spent five minutes picking up the toys strewn across the carpet, then turned and pressed soft kisses on each of her sons' forehead. A moment later, she exited the room and retraced her way past the master bedroom suite. Andy lay motionless in the rumpled bed.

Hmmp – so much for another round. Good, I'm too damn tired anyway...and, besides, there's a quicker way... She continued down the wide hallway.

Payton closed the bathroom door behind her, turned the lock as she switched on the light, then spun the dimmer knob until the room was bathed in a soft glow. She moved to stand before the rectangular mirror above the vanity. Her gaze studied the reflection in the mirror. Indecision sparked momentarily in the blue eyes that stared back at her before her bathrobe was slowly opened to reveal heavy breasts with huge dark pink nipples, a flat stomach, and gently curving hips.

As her hands fondled the breasts reflected in the smoky glass across from her, Payton's mind wandered. She loved Andy with a passion. He was a great father, a husband who supported her in everything she did, and a wonderful provider.

His one fault, though, led to these sporadic nightly forays in the bathroom. For some reason, he wasn't the best of lovers anymore; he never gave her time to catch up with him. Just when she felt she was ready to meet him, he came and the session was over. Consequently, she had to take care of her own orgasm or spend another hour in his arms. If Andy came once, then resumed another session of sex, he could go on forever. These days, she just didn't have the energy.

The times she actually came when his erect, long cock was in her were few and far between. He simply never waited for her anymore. He would be done, and she would be ready to go.

Payton's bright gaze followed her hand in the mirror as it left her breast and traveled along the smooth tautness of her abdomen. Her fingers brushed across the golden curls of her pubic hair. Her stomach muscles immediately clenched and her mouth dropped open in response. She knew if she inserted a finger into her pussy, still wet from Andy's semen, it would only be a matter of seconds before she would be grinding against her hand.

My mother would die if she knew I masturbated on a regular basis. She tossed away the thought. In this room, behind the locked door, she could be whatever she wanted to be and find her own pleasure.

She ran her right palm lightly again over the curly pubic hair, whisked a finger quickly across the moist folds of her body, and teased an erect nipple with the fingers of her free hand. The action was enough to make her sag against the tiled wall behind her.

Payton was tuned now to the simple erotic pleasure of kneading her hands up and down the front expanse of her well-shaped body. She observed her breasts swing gently in the mirror as she bent forward to stroke the skin of her firm inner thighs, always hesitating at the opening of her pussy. She teased herself mercilessly by refusing to dip her finger into the moist darkness. Her clitoris throbbed with the burning need to come.

She turned completely away from the mirror, looked back over her shoulder, and lifted the heavy mane of blonde hair, letting the silky strands fall sensuously across her shoulders. Payton reached behind her and massaged the round spheres of her tight ass that Andy loved so much. She closed her eyes and pretended the sensuous strokes were her husband's hands that now caused her to drip with excitement. Her body screamed to have something inside it.

Unable to wait any longer, Payton flipped back around to face the mirror and shoved a finger of her right hand into the slippery heat of her vagina. The index finger of her left hand became Andy's in her mind, and she flicked her clitoris until a low moan escaped from between her lips. Another deep groan echoed off the tiles. She became weak-kneed and came immediately in hot waves that ran from her fingertips up through her belly.

Payton collapsed to the carpet-covered floor, leaving her finger inside her body in order to feel the last hot throbbing vibration of her climax. She clenched and unclenched her pussy lips around its slender length until at last her heart slowed and she was able to breath normally again.

Her head lolled against the wall and a sigh escaped from her lips. *If only Andy could make me feel this way...I would have the perfect marriage again.*

Payton pondered her situation. She found it hard to believe that any woman would have to masturbate on a regular basis to get off—especially when a hunk of a man like Andy lay waiting in her bed.

She flushed slightly with guilt. *Is it really Andy who isn't a good lover, or is it me? It's so hard to switch gears at the end of the day.* Payton rubbed her forehead, trying to find the courage to admit the real problem.

It was she who had to spend a few minutes in the bathroom after he came in her. Andy always gave her a chance, but in reality, for some odd reason, she couldn't get past the thought of endless files in her desk or mapping out rides for the kids to various school events. It wasn't until she entered the serenity of the dimly lit bathroom and concentrated on her body, that she was able to relax.

Something had to be done to fix this—and it would be up to her. It amazed Payton that Andy could enter a room and just his appearance would set her heart on fire. The women she worked with nearly swooned like Southern belles when he visited her at work. Most times, he was simply surprising her with a luncheon invitation, or had found the time during the day to drop off a rose for no reason whatsoever.

His dark swarthy looks, muscular chest, and arms that bulged beneath his shirt drove them all wild. Those silly women always asked what it was like to be screwed by him. She's sit silently at her desk, refusing to answer, amazed at their bluntness. Many times she could hear them in their cubicles giggling that he made their panties moist, that just the sight of him made them horny as hell. They all thought she was the luckiest woman in the world...

And I would be if I was simply better in bed or could at least find a way to get synchronized with him.

Payton pushed herself up from the floor, wrapped her robe around her slim body, clicked off the bathroom light, and returned to the master bedroom. She slid beneath the covers and relished the immediate warmth of her husband's body. He lay on his side and faced the wall. Tentatively, she wrapped her arm around his muscular chest and breathed in the scent of his skin. Andy automatically grasped her small hand in his large one and tucked it close, then sighed contentedly in his sleep.

Andy, I promise you that I'll try to make things better for us...

Chapter 8: The Guilt

The following Thursday evening, Payton trudged up the stairs to flop into bed. The horrendous week was nearing an end. Somehow, she'd managed to revise another budget proposal over the course of three days when the first one was rejected.

"That rotten bastard," she mumbled to the stairwell. "'Sure!' he says, 'Our Payton didn't realize...blah, blah, blah.' What *our Payton* really didn't realize is that she doesn't have a life anymore." She was so tired from the fourteen-hour days that she was numb. "If that asshole hadn't accepted this last proposal, I think I would've punched him in the face."

She opened the bedroom door and spied Andy, who was sound asleep amidst the rumpled sheets and blankets. Her gaze took in the dirty pair of socks strewn across the dresser and his slacks in a pile on the floor.

Payton was just about to wake him up and give him hell, but instead flopped into a chair and stared at him. His thick, dark hair was tousled against the pillow. Her gaze followed his broad, naked shoulders, and then down the smooth line of his back to where a hint of his buttocks peeked above the edge of the sheet.

She leaned back, ran the fingers of both hands through her blonde tresses, and sighed heavily. In another life, she would strip naked, jump in bed beside him, and probably play with his penis until his erection woke him up. Now? No way would she chance waking him. All she wanted to do was sleep the blessed sleep of the dead.

Payton couldn't discount how sweet Andy was the entire week. Her gaze dropped back to the wrinkled slacks on the floor. So? What if he didn't hang them up? Every night this past week, he'd cooked the meals for the kids, cleaned up the dishes, and even washed clothes and never complained once. Payton knew he did those things to make her life easier. Her husband understood the stress she was under.

And what do I do? Nothing – absolutely nothing. Not even a thank you kiss.

Payton battled with herself. She should climb in beside him and give him some great sex. A tiny smile appeared on her lips. *Wouldn't that surprise the hell out of him?*

Her mouth opened in a gaping yawn. "But, not tonight."

She heaved herself from the chair and crossed to the master bathroom. It wasn't long before she came back through the doorway with one of Andy's t-shirts on and climbed into the bed.

As she pulled the bedspread over her shoulders, Andy raised his head from the pillow. He'd never even heard her come in.

He rolled to his opposite side, drew her close, and spooned around her. "Hi, Baby. Are you just getting in?" He nuzzled the thick length of her hair.

"Yeah. I finished the proposal. Now all I have to do is stay awake for eight hours tomorrow and it's the weekend."

"Good for you. I know how tough the week has been for you. You called that you would be late. Did you even eat supper?"

"Brenda and I had takeout. It didn't pay to come home until we had everything ready for the presentation tomorrow."

A wind-up clock ticked on the bureau.

"Andy?"

"Yeah?"

"Thanks for helping around the house this week."

His hand moved up to grasp her breast. He kissed her neck. "No problem." He breathed deeply. "Your hair smells great." His hand left her breast and ran across the curve of her hip.

Payton tensed when he rested his palm against her covered crotch.

"I missed you this week." His voice sounded slightly tentative in the darkened room.

Andy rose on his elbow and nibbled at her exposed neck. His finger slipped inside the elastic at the top of her leg and caressed her pussy.

Payton didn't move. "I'm really tired, Andy."

"Come on, Payton. I've hardly seen you all week." His finger found her warm, moist hole. A split second later, he withdrew it and rubbed her clit.

Payton grabbed his forearm and yanked his hand out of her underwear. "Not tonight."

In a flash, he dragged her on top of him and fit her pubic mound against his erection. Andy squeezed her ass gently. "I want to fuck you, Payton. I've been thinking about it all week."

She used her arms against his broad chest to push herself off his body and grabbed the bedspread again. "I'm not in the mood. I'm tired, dammit."

Andy opened his mouth to throw a comment back at her, but snapped it shut before anything came out. He wouldn't endear himself by bitching about not getting laid.

A heavy sigh left his lips. He rolled over and punched the pillow before he buried his head in it.

* * * * *

Music blasted into Payton's consciousness. She lifted her head from the pillow, squinted at the clock, then reached out an arm to bat at the offending noise. Her fingers finally connected with the snooze bar and suddenly the horrible woman who screeched at the top of her lungs went away. Payton rolled slowly to her back and fought the idea of having to get up for work. She was dead tired.

She lay in the bed, trying to come up with yet another reason why she could dump work for the day, knowing no matter how she argued with herself, that like a good girl, she would get up and start some breakfast for her and Andy before the kids hit the floor running.

Payton slung her arm over her eyes and wiggled back into the soft pillow. *Just five more minutes. That's all I want.*

Fifteen minutes later, Andy came into the room wrapped in a towel and eyed his snoozing wife. "Hey, Payt—you better get up or you're gonna to be swearing.

She pulled the blanket over her head, rolled into a ball, and mumbled something unintelligible from beneath the covers.

"Come on, babe. One more day. You can sleep in tomorrow." He strolled past the bed, swatted at the general area of her butt, and was rewarded with a responding grunt. Andy dropped his towel on the floor and dug through his drawer to find a clean pair of boxers. "Pa-a-a-y-t-o-o-o-n, I know you're in there," he warbled in a falsetto voice over his shoulder.

"Oh, shit," she sighed tiredly.

Andy smiled to himself when he heard the huge sigh that followed her curse and stuck his long legs into his underwear. "'Oh shit' what?"

"Oh, shit, I hate to think of getting up." The voice still came from somewhere beneath the covers.

"Come on, get up." He slapped her butt again as he walked by on his way to the closet. "I'll tell you what. You get up without any more prompting, and I promise I'll take the kids to the park in the morning. You can lie in bed and watch Saturday morning cartoons." He disappeared into the walk-in closet.

She heard his muffled voice a moment later. "Maybe you'll get enough rest to remember that it's fun to have sex."

Payton bolted upright and eyed the closet opening. She was certain he hadn't meant for her to hear his remark, but it still angered her. She waited with her lips drawn in a tight line.

Finally, he appeared. Her husband walked back through the closet doorway with a white shirt in his hands. His perfectly pressed slacks hung open from his slim waist. Andy stopped short and stared at her. "So what the hell do you look so pissed about?" He threaded his arms into the shirt and waited for her answer.

"Is sex the only thing you think about anymore?"

The normally gentle look in his eyes disappeared instantly. "So now I can't even think about it?" Andy sat on a chair and jerked a sock over a waiting foot.

"That's not what I said."

"You might as well have."

"If you're referring to last night, I was tired."

"You're always too goddamned tired, that's your problem," he spouted back. "You're not the only one in this family that works their goddamned ass off."

Andy's rare anger surprised her. He was the one who always kept a level head when they argued. Now his nostrils flared when he stood to yank his pants open and stuff his shirttails past the waistband. "It's okay if I open my pants in front of you, isn't it? I'd hate to go to work with my shirttails hanging out." He hesitated a moment. "I'd also hate to offend your virginal sensibilities and have you think I was making a pass at you."

"Where do you get off acting like such an ass this morning?"

"Where do you get off—" His hands stilled as he stared at her. "Wait a minute, I stand corrected. You never get off. That's why I'm acting like an ass, Payton. I'm sick of how you don't want me anymore. I'm sick of wanting to hold you in my arms to feel the sexy woman I married. I'm sick of going to bed and wanting you so goddamned bad that it hurts." He yanked his briefcase off the desk before he pierced her with another glare. He'd finally gotten out what he wanted to say to her, but the sight of Payton sitting forlornly in the middle of the bed softened his tone. "I just want it to be like it used to be between us. Just once, I'd like to know that I drove you over the edge of reason like I used to. No more fake moans. That's what I want."

An immediate flush of red spread across her cheeks and extended down into the neck of the t-shirt she slept in as his observation hit her square in the stomach. The ruse was up. She hadn't fooled him at all.

Andy's shoulders rose and fell with a sigh. He grabbed a suit jacket from the back of a chair and headed for the door. "I'll start breakfast. You better get in the shower."

He disappeared into the hallway and missed Payton's reaction to his dismissal. She flopped back onto the pillow and stared wide-eyed at the ceiling. A second later she pulled the sheet up to her chin and squeezed her eyes shut to stop the tears.

Chapter 9: The Fix

Andy reached for the carton of eggs, yanked out a bowl from the cabinet, and cracked six eggs into its center. A second later, he whisked them into one swirling yellow mass, then poured them into the heated frying pan. His actions were automatic as his brain raced in circles. It was a good thing, because all he could think about was Payton's reaction when his flippant comment about her faking it met her ears. She was flushed with obvious guilt when he left the bedroom.

Christ almighty, she's a grown woman with three kids. She used to be turned on by me. What the hell does she want? He jabbed at the eggs with a wooden spoon, stirring them until they began to congeal into lumps.

His broad shoulders fell again with the deep sigh that left his lips. Andy dropped the dirty wooden spoon on the counter, his thoughts still on his inflexible wife, and pulled three more bowls from the cabinet. A box of Fruit Loops followed. He dumped everything on the table in the breakfast nook so things would be ready when the kids woke up.

With another heartfelt sigh, Andy sank onto the bench, rested his chin on a closed fist, and stared out the window. *I've got to do something about this. Enough is enough. She's driving me insane.*

He dropped one elbow to the surface of the table and watched two squirrels dash up and down the oak tree in the back yard. One chased the other. It didn't take Andy long to realize that it was a male in pursuit, and the female wanted nothing to do with him.

"Good luck, buddy, but if it's anything like mine, you won't be getting any fucking in today — or tonight."

"Daddy, what's uckin?"

Andy spun to see his three-year-old daughter standing in the kitchen doorway. Her ragged pink blanket dangled on the floor as she looked up at him with big blue eyes that mirrored Payton's.

His own eyes slammed shut for a second as he admonished himself. "Nothing, baby. Come here and see the squirrels."

Sara scampered across the kitchen floor. Andy hoisted her into his lap a second later. She leaned forward and rested her forehead against the pane of glass. Mr. Squirrel was still in hot pursuit of his frigid wife. Her chubby finger pointed out as she looked up with serious intent at her father. "Squirrels uckin?"

"No, Sara, squirrels are *funning*. They're having *fun* and playing in the yard." His eyes rolled heavenward in hopes that she would catch on. Payton would have his balls if she thought he was teaching their daughter to curse.

Suddenly, the smell of burnt eggs reached his nostrils.

"Shit!"

He carefully dumped Sara onto the chair and hurried to the stove. Smoke billowed from the pan. Andy grabbed the handle and slid the pan under running water to cool it down. "Fucking eggs…"

Sara tucked her ragged blanket beneath her chin and watched her father scrape the burnt contents of the pan into the sink, then switch on the garbage disposal.

A moment later he turned with a furrowed brow and tight lips, leaned against the counter and counted silently to ten. Another angry sigh left his mouth.

"Shit, daddy!"

His eyes flew open. "No, Sara."

His daughter clapped her hands. "Eggs ucking shit, daddy!"

"Sara, you can't say that. Here—" he hurried back to the table and poured Fruit Loops into a bowl. "Eat your breakfast. Mommy will be here soon."

She looked at him with wide eyes and a smile as she picked up a spoon with her chubby fingers and waited for him to finish pouring milk into the bowl.

"Frue Oops!"

"That's it, baby. Let's get your mind on something else. Good Fruit Loops—look at all the colors."

Once he had her mind going in another direction, Andy's spun back to the problem with his wife. He had to figure something out or he was destined to burn eggs the rest of his life.

* * * * *

Later that morning, Andy sat and stared at his computer screen. Nothing made sense inside the flickering monitor. He hated himself for blowing up at his wife when all he really wanted to do was fix their problems. And that was it in a nutshell. It was their problem, not just Payton's. He shouldn't have placed the blame entirely on her beautiful blonde head. Andy was just as guilty for letting this...lag...in their sex life happen.

Determination suddenly squared his jaw. He left his chair and crossed to the open door of his office. Closing it, he returned to his chair and clicked the Netscape icon. Placing the curser in the Google search box, he typed in the word *sex*, then quickly backspaced to erase it. He leaned back in the chair and stared at the screen.

"Think, Andy."

He leaned forward again and typed in *problems, sex, spas, seminars, Minnesota.* He waited until his choices appeared. The first three pages were Internet sex sites. His eyes examined each line. His dark eyebrows lifted as he read. "Holy shit." He was surprised at the lurid choices that were presented. "I don't want to buy it, I want to do it with my wife for chrissakes."

He continued to click through the pages, searching for what he wanted to find, trying not to get discouraged.

Ten minutes later, he found a site that looked half-assed promising.

"Sex and Love, Inc. promises to make your deepest fantasies come true…

He clicked on the URL and watched the page load.

Sex and Love, Inc:

Capture that lost feeling; recreate the sex you've only dreamed about; become the love slave you've always wanted to be…prepare yourself to lose all inhibitions. Serving the surrounding states of Michigan, Wisconsin, and Minnesota.

Andy clicked on link after link and read about a small business outside the city of Detroit. Sex and Love, Inc. was a spa/seminar of sorts that catered to couples who were having sexual problems. It could be considered a learning experience if a patron wanted, or simply a hedonistic weekend getaway where no children were allowed.

He read on, getting more excited by the minute. This was the kind of place he was searching for. Hot tubs, spacious, luxurious rooms—a place created for the art of seduction; a place where he could find the old Payton and bring her back.

Andy grabbed a pen and scribbled down the toll-free number. He closed out the site, grabbed his cell phone from his briefcase, and dialed the number with a smile splitting his face.

* * * * *

Payton swore again, pushed herself away from the computer, and grabbed her coffee cup. A quick glance at the clock told her it was only two o'clock.

For the past two hours at work, she had managed to slowly mess up every document she worked on. Her presentation had gone well this morning and was accepted unanimously. Now she was in the implementation stage, but numbers meshed into one large jumble as thoughts of her morning argument with Andy still rang in her head.

He knew. Andy wasn't fooled by her fake moans. Her cheeks stained a dark shade of red. All this time, she apparently hurt him with pretending that she enjoyed every sexual encounter they'd had. It would have been much smarter to simply be honest with him.

She bolted from her chair and headed for the staff lounge to refill her cup. As she entered the austere room, she breathed a sigh of relief. It was empty.

Payton poured herself a cup of coffee, sank onto one of the hard chairs around the ugly brown table, and stared at the corkboard filled with stupid memos.

What the hell am I going to do? She leaned forward and rested her forehead against her hand as she blew lightly into the hot liquid, and then took a sip.

This morning, she entered the kitchen and he could hardly even talk to her. He seemed preoccupied during his usual morning tasks and didn't quite meet her eyes when she spoke to him.

"Not that you had anything interesting to talk about," she mumbled into the cup. "You're going to lose him, Payton, if you don't do something."

The door opened behind her. Payton glanced around to see her coworker, Brenda, enter the lunchroom.

"Hi, Payton."

"Hi, Bren." Payton said no more—and only sipped at her coffee.

Brenda poured herself a cup while keeping an eye on Payton's slumped shoulders. She placed the pot back on the burner and seated herself in a chair across the table. "How's the implementation policy going?"

"It's not."

"Payton, if it's any consolation, everyone thinks Mr. Henderson is an ass to expect you to get on it so quickly, but you've got to present something in a few hours. Need a little help?"

The blonde woman simply sipped at her coffee with a faraway look in her blue eyes.

"Payton? Did you hear me?"

"What?"

Brenda placed her cup on the table. "All right. What the hell is going on with you?"

"What do you mean?" Payton looked confused.

"You don't think you've been acting strange all morning?"

Payton shrugged.

"Shit. You've been swearing under your breath since you got here, you seem nervous as a cat, and just the fact that you haven't got the policy together — like yesterday — is proof enough. You're always on top of things at work."

I should be on top of something else... Payton almost gasped out loud at her silent retort.

"Anything I can do to help?" Brenda leaned across the table and clasped her friend's hand. "Are you having some sort of personal problem? I don't mean to pry, but we've worked together for six years. I've never seen you like this."

How could Payton tell her that she was in danger of losing her husband — the one that everyone thought she was so lucky to have? *To hell with the numbers and the policies.* She wanted to say to hell with work, call Andy, and meet him in some hotel room before she went home. She wanted to tell him that she was sorry for the years of always trying to be the upright and hard-working woman her parents expected her to be.

Why should I care what they think anyway? They've done nothing but look down their self-righteous noses at me since I got pregnant with Tyler.

She sat stunned. Is that what she had been doing? Working like a maniac to find some acceptance from parents who never just simply loved or forgave her when she'd made a mistake?

It's Andy who never left my side. It was Andy that worked two jobs to assure I had time to study and reach for my goals — not them.

She wanted to go home.

"Payton? You sure you're all right?"

Her mind raced. There was no way she could get out of work today, yet the meeting would be useless because she had nothing to give them. The implementation plans were a bunch of computer printouts from the week — nothing solid and nothing that would endear her to her supervisor.

"I just want to go home. I can't keep my mind on what I'm doing — I can't get anything together." She sat back and looked at Brenda with a dawning look of discovery in her eyes. "And you know what? The strangest thing is that I don't give a shit. I could walk out of here right now and never come back."

"You're scaring me, Payton. You? The office goddess who never does a thing wrong? You've got to pull yourself together and get that plan down. This organization is depending on you."

"Screw them."

"Payton! I don't know what's gotten into you!"

I know what's going to get into me...

"But I'll help you out. I've had lots of experience with budgeting and the type of policies that Ol' Man Henderson likes to see. Come on. Let's get something together. You can go home at the end of the meeting, then come back on Monday and say, thank you, Brenda, for saving my ass."

Payton shook her head as if hearing Brenda for the first time. "You'd do that for me?"

"You'd be there for me if I needed it. Come on. We can pull something together even if we have to dazzle them with a little bullshit. Whatever is bugging you will have to wait until 6:00." She stood and waited expectantly for Payton to join her.

Chapter 10: The Solution

Payton eased her Blazer into the garage and pressed the button on the automatic closer. It didn't take long for the sun to be blocked out as the square door lowered to the cement.

She slid out of the vehicle and hesitated a second to gather her wits about her. Over the course of the ride home, she had practiced her apology to Andy over and over. Payton planned to be honest and open with her husband for the first time in a long time.

Opening the adjoining door, she entered into the kitchen. The house was completely silent.

"Hmmm, that's odd." She dropped her briefcase and purse on the counter and walked into the living room. The TV was off and the blessed silence was almost eerie.

"Andy? Are you here?" she called up the staircase. "Where are the kids?"

Receiving no response, she turned to walk back to the kitchen. Nothing was pulled out of the freezer for supper. Payton popped the fridge open and inspected the contents. There wasn't much but staples like milk, cheese, and some fruit.

Shoot — I'll have to get something going. Oh, to hell with it. I'll call him on his cell and order a pizza if he didn't pick something up.

As she turned for the phone, a shuffling noise to her right caught her attention. Payton swiveled to see Andy in the hallway entrance. He leaned against the jamb with his arms crossed before his broad chest and one ankle propped against the other.

She took in his long muscular length. He simply stood there and stared at her. His expression was unreadable. Her heart sank.

"Hi, where are the kids?" It was difficult to keep her voice level. Suddenly, she was frightened beyond belief, and she wasn't sure why.

"At my mom's."

Her slender eyebrows dipped in a frown. "Your mom's? What are they doing there?"

"I sent them off for the weekend."

Payton's blue eyes widened as she chewed on her bottom lip. "Why did you send them there?"

Andy swallowed silently and continued to watch her closely. *Don't turn me away now, Payton.* "Why don't you sit down for a minute? I've got something I want to discuss with you."

She recognized the seriousness in his gaze. Payton swallowed back the instant fear that pierced her heart. She had waited too long. Andy had had enough of her virginal responses over the last few years of their marriage.

She crossed stiffly to the breakfast nook and seated herself with an air of calmness even though her hands shook.

Andy seated himself on a stool across from her. His stare unnerved her.

Payton ran a hand through her hair and glanced up at him. *Figure something out! You can't let him leave you. Andy – I love you so much! I'm sorry...*

Her husband cleared his throat, then leaned back against the counter and crossed his arms again. "Payton, I sent the kids to my parents because I wanted to be alone with you. We really need to discuss something, and I didn't want them around."

"Andy—"

He lifted his palm in the air to interrupt her. "Let me talk, Payton." His gaze softened slightly. "First off, no matter what, I want you to know how much I love you."

He's saying goodbye... Instant tears burned behind her eyelids. She tipped her head to hide them.

"I think you're the greatest wife in the world. Do you know that even after all the years we've been together, all you have to do is walk into a room, and I get excited as hell?"

She opened her mouth to speak.

"Let me talk, Payton. We've got a great thing going here—except for our sex life."

Her chin dropped, and she stared at the floor while her fingers played nervously with the edge of a green placemat.

"When I make love to you, it kills me afterwards that you're not getting out of it what I am. I'm sorry for being so rude this morning. I could've been a little nicer about how I blurted out the fact that I know you've been faking it with me. For some reason, it was if I'd finally run into a wall—my male ego couldn't handle the fact that I can't make you feel the way you used to when we're having sex."

"Andy, I—"

His large palm raised in the air again. "I want to try to fix that this weekend. I want you to have as much pleasure out of my body that I have out of yours."

Payton's head snapped up. "*What?*"

"That's why I sent the kids to my parents. I don't expect every time to be...earth shattering...but I want to have sex with you and go away knowing that you're thinking about the next time; that one fantastic sexual encounter will lead to another that's even better. Give me this weekend. Let me show you how much fun we can have with one another. And, if you discover that it's too much for you, I'll understand. But you've got to at least give me the chance."

"What are you talking about exactly?"

"I have a bag packed for you. I made reservations at a —" she noted the slight hesitation, "a resort...of sorts."

"Where?"

"Detroit.

"Detroit? That's quite a ways from here. I have a busy week at work coming up." She wanted to take back the words as soon as she said them. Work was the reason they were having this discussion now.

"You're not going to work next week," he stated firmly.

Payton straightened in the chair and forgot her self-reprimand of a moment earlier. "Yes, I am. I can't just call in Monday morning and tell them that I won't be in."

"I called your supervisor already."

"What?"

"Don't be pissed, but I told your office that your father wasn't feeling well and that you needed to go home to help your mother for a few days. I asked them not to say anything to you so you wouldn't be upset while driving home."

Her mouth dropped open. "Why would you tell them a lie like that? Everyone knows I don't see my parents very often. You had no right to do that."

"I had every right. To hell with what they think anyway. That's the only explanation I could think of. Your boss had no problem with it whatsoever. He said you've been working like a dog and it was time to take a few days off. I took next week off, too. We're going away for the weekend. If we don't feel like coming home on Sunday, then we'll just get in the car and go somewhere; anywhere, Payton. It doesn't matter. I just want to be alone with you."

Her anger left as suddenly as it had built. How could she be upset with him? He had manipulated her next few days simply because he wanted to be with her. Andy hadn't done that in a long time.

Payton rose from the chair, took three steps, and stood before him. She reached out a hand and cupped his cheek. The textured feel of his slightly whiskered cheek was wonderful beneath her fingers. He stared into her eyes and hope jumped into his dark gaze. She also saw a look of tender love and acceptance, even if she would have disagreed with him.

* * * * *

Five hours later, Andy eased Payton's white Blazer into a brightly lit parking spot. When she wasn't sleeping in the front seat beside him, she was begging him to let her in on where they were going. Andy remained firm. It was a surprise. Besides, he wanted to assure she was far enough from home before possibly blowing up at him and demanding they turn back. Even then she would admit they were too far from Minneapolis to turn back.

He simply hoped like hell when she realized what he had planned that she wouldn't freeze up on him. Andy put the vehicle in Park and pulled the keys from the ignition.

Payton's fingers gripped her purse strap as she glanced warily at the unassuming but very large building before her. Her gaze followed the cement walk to the front area, then along the wide porch that ran the length of the cream-colored structure. English ivy draped its way lazily up the supporting poles and across the roof.

Andy glanced across at her to gauge her reaction. "Looks like a nice place, huh?"

She could clearly see at first glimpse that the setting was purposely fashioned to put guests at ease, but breathed in deeply to control the erratic beat of her heart when she noted a dimly lit sign with etched letters that read *Sex and Love.*

"What is this place?" she muttered into the darkness of the vehicle.

"Just a place for us to spend the weekend finding each other again."

Payton pried her fingers from the leather strap, dug inside her purse, and silently pulled out her lipstick. A moment later, her compact followed. She flipped open the visor and immediately light flooded the area where she sat.

Watching her dab on the lipstick first, Andy couldn't help but notice the flash of disquiet when her eyes darted in his direction as she applied the berry color to her bottom lip.

Payton's eyes returned to the mirror when she ran a soft powered pad over her nose and cheeks.

Andy waited quietly for her response.

She drew in a deep breath and turned in the seat to stare evenly at him. "So, what is Sex and Love supposed to mean? What did you get us into?"

"Absolutely nothing. This is a spa of sorts that caters to couples who seem to be having some sexual problems."

"Jesus Christ, Andy…"

He reached out and gently laid his hand on her arm. "Just give it a chance; give me a chance. This isn't a place that has you doing anything kinky. It just reminds couples to remember what they once had. The woman I spoke to explained that there are many different options, and we can pick and choose as we please—or we can simply spend the time alone—together."

Payton rubbed her temple. "You've talked to someone about us?"

"No—I just answered a few questions. Come on, Payton. Let's go inside and check in." He waited patiently for her to make her decision. He'd gotten her this far and wasn't about to chance ruining the weekend by letting her know she was starting to piss him off. He'd worked hard to arrange this getaway.

Payton dropped the makeup into her purse and popped the car door open. Andy quickly stepped from the vehicle. It took him only a moment to grab their bags from the back seat, lock the door, and slide the keys into his jacket pocket. Walking around the front of the Blazer, he clasped her hand and headed for the softly lit porch.

Chapter 11: Sex & Love, Inc.

Payton was not prepared for the intimacy of the foyer interior when she walked through the double oaken doors. Instead of the usual bright lights of a hotel lobby, the check-in area was bathed in muted red lights. Soft guitar music filtered from hidden speakers somewhere within the room, lavender-scented candles sputtered from the top of every table, and a huge tabby cat slumbered on the back of an expansive leather couch.

"This doesn't look like any hotel I've ever seen," she whispered. "I don't even see a check-in area."

A movement to her right garnered her attention as Andy closed the big door behind them. A woman with exotic dark features and draped in silk came forward, a gentle smile curving her ruby-red lips. She held out her hand and took Payton's palm in hers.

"Welcome. You must be Payton and Andy."

Andy recognized the husky voice from the phone.

"How…how did you know that," Payton stuttered.

"Your husband described you on the phone. You're as beautiful as he said. I'm so glad you decided to spend the weekend."

An instant flush spread across Payton's cheeks when she remembered why he had made the reservations. Before she could think of something to say, however, the woman escorted them forward toward the steps leading to the upper level.

"Come. We'll get you settled into your room. As soon as you're comfortable, I'll be up to have a little chat. My name is Velvet, and I'll be your host for the weekend."

Payton swallowed back her embarrassment, sent her husband a look that could kill, and followed the woman up the sweeping staircase. Her round blue eyes widened even further as she eyed the pictures on the wall that lined the steps. Naked painted couples lay sprawled in various sexual positions, their limbs entwined together, in the different sized frames.

Surprise hit her a second later when she realized she wasn't offended by the portraits of love like she usually would be, but rather more curious at the total expression of love and pleasure in the faces as they stared into each others eyes.

Her gaze met Andy's. He winked, and she could have smacked him right then and there. Instead, she hid the tiny smile that threatened to appear when she turned her back to him. He was like a little kid in a candy store.

"They're beautiful portraits, aren't they?" Velvet stated when they came to a stop before another massive oak door. "That will be you and your lover after you have finished our course. Payton, I want you to know that you didn't make a mistake coming here. I know you're probably a little apprehensive, but we'll talk shortly, and I can put your fears at ease." She opened the door and motioned her guests forward. "Just settle in. There's a carafe of wine and a bottle of the vodka you requested on the counter. Pour yourself a drink and relax. See you soon."

Velvet nodded her head, turned, and retraced her steps down the wide staircase with a gentle swishing of her gauzy robe as it flowed around barely discernable slim ankles.

Slightly more at ease, Payton walked a little less hesitantly into the room. Her slim brows arched high when she took in the plush surroundings of expensive furniture. Again, lavender scented candles flickered throughout the room.

"Holy...shit..." she breathed out softly. Her jaw dropped in shock. If Payton had thought the pictures hanging along the staircase were enlightening as to the workings of sex, the ones she stared at now were audacious. Her purse dropped from numb fingers to the floor with a muffled thud. Andy took a few steps and set the two overnight bags beside it. A low whistle from his lips escaped into the room.

They were both drawn to the far wall behind the king-sized bed. An expansive six-by-six-foot picture took up most of the area above the ornate headboard. They leaned forward in unison, hardly believing what they saw.

A woman's fiery red lips were wrapped around the shaft of an erect penis. That's all that was in the frame — just the close-up of feminine smiling lips and a glistening penis. The painting was so real that Payton reached out, expecting her fingers to come away wet with the man's semen and the woman's spit. Her stomach constricted as instant moisture leaked into her panties.

Shaking her head, she dragged her gaze from the portrait to find her husband staring at the other hedonistic representations decorating the walls of the room. One of the framed portraits was a vagina spread wide as two men's tongues lapped at the sweetness it offered.

Another was of a voluptuous woman. She lounged against a carpet of grass with her head thrown back in ecstasy as her lover leaned close to the apex of her legs. The man suckled his own fingers. Payton knew with certainty where the masculine digits had just been. Her heart thudded. She closed her eyes a second to regain her equilibrium.

The rush of adrenaline caused from the picture of the sex act before her caused her body to tremble. As much as she felt like running from this room to escape, another more primal need urged her to stay. Suddenly, her work, the kids, and even the past problems she and Andy experienced seemed to melt away.

She moved quickly to the crystal carafe, poured a splash of berry-colored wine into the goblet, and tossed it down with one swallow.

"Whew," the sound of her breath was invasive in the quiet of the room. Her voice lowered to a near whisper when she squeezed her eyes shut. "What the hell kind of place is this?"

Her husband moved to stand beside her. He took the glass from her fingers, splashed some more wine into it, and repeated her actions. It was gone in a second. "After I called to make reservations, I went back on the Internet and accessed a few chat rooms to ask some questions. There wasn't a person that had a bad thing to say. More than one couple said spending a weekend here saved their marriage."

Payton's faced paled at his words. She sank to a velvet-covered chair and stared up at him with wide eyes. "Is that where you think we were headed?" she whispered out. "Have I been that awful that you thought of leaving me?" Her hands trembled in her lap.

He set the glass on the counter before he stared down. "I don't know, Payton. I didn't think we would split because it was my idea. I wondered, though, if you found life with me too boring to try working at it anymore. That's why I searched for this place. I thought you might want to leave me."

"That thought never crossed my mind. Do you know, this is the first time that I've stopped long enough to actually think about what my life's been like." She stood and wrapped her arms around his neck. "I'm sorry. I'm sorry that I made you and the kids take a backseat to my job."

He squeezed her waist and kissed the tip of her nose. "No apologies. We're here now and, hopefully, this weekend will fix everything." His gaze settled on the bags in the middle of the floor as he pulled her close. *If everything goes the way I planned, I could've left those bags home. Payton, dear, I plan to keep you naked as a jaybird...*

Chapter 12: Let the Games Begin

A knock from the hallway echoed through their suite. Payton sat up from the chaise she reclined on, sipping at the last of her third goblet of wine and watched Andy stroll to the door. A slight shake of her head helped to clear away the slightly fuzzy feeling that engulfed her brain.

Payton was no dummy. Andy was transparent as hell with his drivel about completing some remodeling on the house as he continually kept her glass filled. *That shit...*she smiled inwardly. *He's trying to get me drunk.*

Velvet stood in the corridor with another carafe of wine. "I see you're both relaxing. That's good. It's why you came here." She floated across the thick carpet, poured herself a small bit of the amber-colored liquid, then draped herself across an overstuffed sofa. The woman's fluid motions were feminine and sensual. Payton hugged her oversized sweatshirt to her body and sat primly on a chair—and waited.

"I see that the two of you are relaxing. That's good. Now, first I'd like to discuss why the two of you are here. The reasons simply help me to tailor the weekend to your needs." Velvet's statement drifted across to the couple.

Payton shrugged her slender shoulders, glanced at her husband, and remained silent. Her nervous blue gaze darted about the room.

Andy had no such qualms. "I guess my reasons are that we need a little more excitement in bed."

Payton wanted to crawl under the chaise, but stayed where she was.

"We used to have a great sex life. I guess work, kids, whatever, has just got in the way." He took his wife's clammy hand in his and gave it a squeeze. "I want a weekend filled with pure, unadulterated sex with my wife."

His hand was the only thing that kept her on the chaise rather than on her knees to try and find a hiding spot.

Velvet smiled at her. "My dear, Payton. You look like you're going to bolt. You can look at me." Her guest tentatively brought her chin up. "While you are here, we need be truthful with each other, say exactly what we feel, and state exactly what we want. You two will leave on Sunday afternoon with a rare truthfulness to your marriage that not all couples have discovered. This is going to be a weekend of pure sex for both of you. It's not going to be nasty or dirty. It's going to be exactly as it should between a man and woman who love each other deeply."

Velvet rose from the divan and crossed to a cabinet. She clicked open the brass lock and let the heavy doors swing wide. "In this cabinet are various 'tools' that are at your disposal. There is every sex toy imaginable. Each comes with its own set of directions." Her fingers ran across the outside jackets of stacked DVDs. "Visual aids are on this side and over here—" she pointed to the opposite side of the middle shelf, "are manuals." She turned with a wide smile on her face. "Not that you need a manual after being married for so many years. But, always keep your mind open to possibilities that you haven't thought about."

Payton's breath caught in her throat when she turned her head to catch Andy staring at her. Her breasts instantly tingled with his hot look that nearly devoured her whole. A moment later, she blushed again when she realized Velvet was witness to her husband's ogling.

"You must not be embarrassed to have your husband show how much he wants you, Payton. That's why you two are here — to rediscover and find anew the sexual experiences that you've only imagined. You're a beautiful woman."

Andy chuckled. "That she is. I plan to spend the weekend letting her know that."

"Andy!" Payton hissed, but a smile curved her full lips. How could she help but feel sexy and loved? Andy's desire and love for her blazed in his eyes. The idea of how much work awaited her when she returned to her office receded further.

Velvet waved her hand indifferently. "On the bed stand is a phone list and menus. Feel free to order anything you like. That includes food, snacks, drinks, and masseuse services. It's included in the weekend price. You'll also find an agenda of different seminars that will be held tomorrow. Feel free to join in a group or reserve a time for just the two of you. If you'd like to try one of our Fantasy Rooms, call and ask for a time. I've never had customers who weren't thrilled by creating their own fantasy and having it come true."

She closed the cabinet doors and turned to face them one last time. "If there is something that we haven't thought of, something you feel you need while experimenting with sex, you simply pick up the phone and ask for it. I guarantee that it will be delivered to your room. You can eat meals with our other patrons, or have meals delivered here. It's up to you if you'd rather stay closeted to enjoy one another or join in on some group sex. Any questions before I leave?"

Payton sat stunned.

Andy wondered if Velvet had spotted his hard-on yet.

"Well, you two have the first part done. You subconsciously were looking for an answer. The proof is in the initiative it took to make the phone call to me."

Velvet brought her red-tipped fingers to her lips and blew them both a kiss. "Simply because it's midnight does not mean that you can't begin your new discoveries. The weekend is young. Happy orgasm." Payton's face paled at her host's choice of words. "Don't be shocked. You two are going to find yourselves energized."

With one last smile, she exited the room and closed the door quietly.

* * * * *

The door latch clicked. Payton didn't know what to think. Andy did. He already had the cabinet open again.

She eyed his backside as he rifled through the inner contents. "Pretty subtle, Andy."

He poked his head around the edge of one door with a grin that stretched across his face. "Come here, Payt. You gotta see some of the shit in here!"

She heaved herself up from the chair, refusing to admit out loud that her interest was piqued. "So much for romance," she mumbled.

"Wow, this stuff is wild!" His muffled voice reached her ears from somewhere inside the cabinet. A second later, he pulled out a board game, held it out for her to see, and grinned even wider. "*Foreplay!* Can you believe there's a game called *Foreplay?* Christ, K-Mart would make a killing at Christmas if they were smart enough to put in an adult sex aisle. Let's play!"

"You're like a little kid in a toy shop."

"You got it, babe. And it's right behind those oak cabinet doors." Andy hustled across the room to a round table, shook off the cardboard cover, and pulled out a set of directions.

"Aren't we supposed to read a manual or something, then follow an agenda?"

He shot her a quick, cursory glance before bringing his gaze back to the paper in his hand. "Go ahead and see what it says in the book by the bed stand. I'm going to run through these directions." He glanced up again, this time his eyes glittered with hot anticipation and promise. "There's no way I'm letting you out of this room until we've played this game."

Her heart did a little flip. *I wonder how many months he's been sending me that look and I've been too busy to notice it.*

Payton perched on the edge of the bed and flipped open a manual called, "A Weekend of Sex: Sex & Love, Inc." The room became silent as both she and her husband read.

Payton was engrossed in a list of experiences the Spa offered. She was on the third page when suddenly, a pair of hands grabbed her shoulders, and she was gently shoved backwards to the bed's surface.

Andy stared down from where he lay on top of her. "So, what does the manual say? Do we fill out a questionnaire or just commence to screw like rabbits?"

She gazed up at her husband, taking in the handsome line of his square jaw and the lock of wavy hair that rested across his forehead. His erection pressed against her. A sexy smile rested on his lips, and hot anticipation rested in his gaze.

Payton's tongue moistened her lips. "You know, Andy, I think I'm starting to warm up to this idea. I'm sorry it took so long."

She ran her fingers through his thick hair, pulled his mouth to hers, and kissed him softly. "The book says we can start however we want to. It just listed some examples."

"Like what?"

She giggled at his eagerness. "Like your damned board game."

Andy levered himself from the bed, grabbed her hand, and pulled her to her feet. "Honey, I promise you this is going to be better than any Monopoly game you've ever played." He gave her a peck on the nose before he turned for the game.

"Where are we going to play?"

"Right in the middle of the bed." Andy set up the board and placed a pile of pink cards on her side and blue ones on his.

"Don't peek at the questions. I'm going to mix us both a drink." He was back in a flash with two huge crystal glasses filled with vodka and orange juice.

Payton took a sip. "Screwdrivers? I haven't had one of these in years."

He joined her on the bed. "I know. Remember the first time we dated? That's how I want you—like putty in my hands."

She simply shook her head and eyed him over the rim of her drink—and hid a smile.

"Okay, the directions say that we're supposed to have a drink first—I imagine to get us in the mood. We're supposed to tell one another why we first fell in love and why we're here. Do you want me to go first?"

"Would I be able to stop you?"

He smiled. "That's what I like about you, Payt. You're a cute smartass. Okay, let's see." He leaned against the footboard, crossed his arms, and heaved a sigh. His eyes swept the length of her.

The quiet inspection heated her blood.

"I'll never forget the first time I saw you. I don't think you had a clue how beautiful you were. You swept into Psych class and gave me an instant hard-on."

"What!" she burst out.

"Yup. Never told you that, did I? You sat down at the front of the class with your tight red top and all I could think about was getting my hands on your breasts."

Her mouth dropped open in surprise. "I can't believe that you remember what I was wearing. I can't even remember that."

"Man, Payton, I don't think I'd ever seen a woman as sexy as you. Tony wanted you, but I told him to back off. I told him you were mine."

"Tony? He doesn't want me anymore, does he?

"He damn well better not. If he or any other guy would have tried something with you back then, I think I would've knocked them flat on their asses."

"My knight in shining armor."

He grinned at her observation. "It's almost embarrassing how badly I wanted you. At first, having sex with you was the only thing on my mind until that following Friday when I finally got you in my bedroom. After having listened to you at dinner, how eloquently you spoke about family, your goals in life, and the future, I realized there was a lot more to Payton Jamison than just a beautiful body. I was starting to feel guilty with my earlier, lurid thoughts of what I had planned for the evening. You already had become an important part of my life."

Payton blinked back the few tears that threatened to appear. Andy's last words were spoken from the heart.

"I still find it hard to believe that at twenty-four, I had this beautiful, totally drunk blonde in my bed, begging me to have sex, and instead I brought you home — although, I couldn't help myself — I had to play around a little. But, as the session on the bed wore on, I suddenly didn't want to take advantage of you, because by that time, I had decided then and there that I was going to spend the rest of my life with you."

A stunned Payton sat quietly for a moment before she spoke. "Are you saying you fell in love me the first week?"

"Love — or lust — a combination of both." Andy shrugged his broad shoulders. "I just knew I didn't want to scare you away." He took a swig of his drink.

Payton leaned forward and rested her elbows on her bent knees. A breathless question soon followed. "And why do you still love me now?"

His green eyes narrowed in thought. "Because I have a deep respect for you. You're a great mom. Even with the work schedule you've insisted on keeping, those kids always know you love them. You constantly rearrange your schedule so you don't miss a single Little League or soccer game. You're also smart, you're a hard worker, and you're even prettier than when we first married. You make my life complete."

"But, what about the reason we're here?" She suddenly felt small and undeserving of his compliments. "What about how I've neglected you?"

Andy's chuckle rattled across the space between them. "You haven't really *neglected* me, Payton. You just got caught up in our dreams and goals. I have to admit there were many nights when I wanted to scream at you for not responding to me in bed. That's my male ego problem. But, how could I point a finger at you when really what you were doing was working your ass off and trying to juggle everything in our lives? I loved you when we got married, and I love you now. Even more. I wanted this weekend because we just haven't given enough time to you and me. I plan to remedy that over the next few days. Okay—your turn."

Payton took a sip of courage, and then ran a slender finger around the rim of her glass. Finally, she looked up. "You're a tough act to follow. Okay, let's see. I fell in love with you despite your boyish charm that first three months. I saw beneath that flamboyant exterior of yours. You were always funny and had me in stitches, but you actually possessed more maturity than most of the boys— men—that we attended grad school with. You had goals; you worked hard at your studies, despite all the parties."

She cleared her throat and took another sip. Payton nibbled her bottom lip. Andy wondered how many times he had seen her do that endearing little action over the years. She glanced back up and met his gaze squarely.

"Your love for me was expressed by the way you stood by my side when I discovered I was pregnant. You supported me when my parents treated me like a piece of shit because I'd suddenly become an embarrassment in their eyes. I know how hard it must have been to continue school, work two jobs, and give up the college party life because we were young parents with tons of responsibility. You never walked away from me—even over the last few years when I haven't acted like a wife should—a wife with a totally handsome, sexy husband who makes me feel special by all the extraordinary little things he does to make my life easier."

Payton's eyes glistened with happy, hidden tears. "I love you, Andy. I always will. I'm so glad you concocted this weekend to be alone with me so I can prove it to you."

"Come here. We're not supposed to kiss yet—the directions say so—but fuck the rules."

They leaned across the board and pressed their lips against one another. Payton was warmed by his touch.

Andy leaned back, took another sip of his drink before he set the glass on the bed stand, then rubbed his large hands together, his earlier seriousness suddenly gone. "All right, let the game commence."

Payton burst out laughing at his obvious anticipation of the sex game. "All right, let's play. No cheating. I just want you to know that I'm going to show no mercy."

His dark brows literally bounced over his green eyes. "I was hoping you'd say that." He picked up the dice and tossed them onto the board with a flick of his wrist. The total of the roll was five. "Now you roll. Whoever has the higher number picks the first card. Oh, when we get through these first piles, then we use a second set of cards. That's when the real fun begins."

Payton rolled her eyes, grabbed the dice, and tossed them back onto the flat surface. "Boxcars! I'm first." She selected a pink card from her pile and read out loud. "Have your partner tell you, of the following three, what you like most to be done to you." She hesitated and blushed slightly.

"Come on, what does it say?" Andy urged her on.

"Okay, A: lick my nipples."

"Oooo, I love this game already."

"Oh, shut up. B: rub my breasts or C:" she giggled, "tit-fuck."

"Definitely tit-fuck," he responded.

"You've never done that."

"But, I'm going to before the night is over. Definitely tit-fuck is my answer. Do you agree?"

Payton giggled louder. "Once again, do I have a choice?"

Andy grabbed a card from the blue pile. "My turn. Oooh," his lips smacked together. "I got a bonus card! You have to strip from the waist up before I can ask the question."

"Give me that card, you liar!" Payton made a grab for it, but Andy pulled his hand away.

"Strip, baby."

"I don't know why I have to be the first," she mumbled as she pulled her t-shirt over her head. Payton unclasped the hook between her breasts. A moment later, her chest was bare for his viewing. Dark pink nipples puckered instantly when he whistled. "Now, ask your question, you cheater."

"It's kinda hard to think when all the blood is rushing to my other head."

"Would you stop already?"

"Okay. Which position will your partner say she loves most? A: Missionary style, B: Doggy style, or C: on a chair." He glanced up, breathlessly waiting for her answer.

Payton pretended to ponder deeply. She pursed her lips and glanced around the room. "Hmmm. I don't know. I guess we'll have to try all three later on. Then I can give you my final answer."

"You're a shit, Payton. I'm getting hornier than hell. Let's screw this game."

"No way! You're the one who wanted to play. Besides, I can't wait to get to the second pile."

This was the other Payton whom Andy had missed so much; the one from years ago who never told him no to anything he suggested. It was going to be a great weekend.

Chapter 13: Discovery

They played on, laughing, giggling, and drinking their way through the first set of cards. By the time Andy reached for the next set, both were completely naked, slightly drunk, and ogling one another's body across the bed.

"Okay, my turn to go first." Andy grabbed the blue card from the top of his pile and licked his lips. He studied his card as a wide grin split his face. "Looks like there's no more questions. Now, we have some scenarios to play out. Shit—we should've used this pile first." His gaze scanned the card. "Wow! We definitely should've started here." He glanced up, his eyes dark with desire. "Have your partner spread her legs. Run a finger gently down the outside length of her vulva."

Payton breathed deeply to clear her head. Her drinks and his constant ogling fueled her courage. She leaned against the headboard, never taking her eyes from her husband's glittering ones. Slowly, she bent her knees upwards, spread her legs—and waited.

Andy moved the board and cards to the edge of the bed and crawled forward, stopping an arm's length from her splayed knees. He reached out tentatively with a finger. When her touched her, Payton jumped slightly, and then chewed nervously on her bottom lip.

She was hot to his touch. Andy ran his finger down the outside of her labia, stopped just before he reached her anus, then traveled back up the other side. Payton's chest inflated with the next deep breath she took.

"God, you've got a beautiful pussy. Want to say to hell with the game?"

Her blonde head shook slowly from side to side. As much as she wanted to be done with the play, the intimacy forced upon them by a simple few slips of paper promised to be too much fun.

"Okay," he muttered as he sat back and reached for a pink card. "Here you go." He held it out so she could read it. Payton scanned the writing.

She sat up. "Lie on your back."

"What else does it say?"

A secret grin was instantly displayed on her lips when she snatched it from his grip. "Don't worry, I won't cheat. Lie on your back."

Andy settled himself on the bed. Payton moved between his legs and pushed his thighs apart. His erection was rock hard. Slowly, she massaged the insides of both thighs, each time brushing closer to his pubic area. Soon, she lightly swept her hand across his pubic hair, careful not to touch his penis. Andy groaned.

She continued the massage until she ended it with a quick, gentle roll of his testicles in her hand, and then sat back.

"What the hell? You're not going to stop now, are you?" Andy was immensely turned on.

She shrugged. "Just following directions. I wasn't supposed to touch your penis."

Andy grabbed her used card where it lay on the bed. He quickly read it. His wife hadn't lied. "Fuckin' game."

Payton giggled at the look of remorse on his face. "It's going to last forever if you don't pick another card. I can't wait to see what's next."

He sat up, selected another blue card, studied it, and then tossed it to the floor, never taking his eyes from her heavy-lidded gaze. "Oh, you're gonna get it now. Lie on your back."

She did.

He stood and gently dragged her body closer so she lay across the bed with her hips near the edge. Her blue gaze smoldered.

Placing a hand on each of her calves, he positioned her feet on the edge of the mattress, which raised her knees slightly.

"Spread your legs wider, Payt. I want to see you."

Her knees dropped open for his viewing. He reached out with trembling hands and kneaded the inside of both her thighs.

To hell with the card telling me to simply French kiss her for two minutes. She'll never know — and I never promised not to cheat...

Her pink, down covered lips now glistened before him. Andy ran a finger the length of her slit again, and couldn't help himself when he inserted a finger into her pussy. He was done with the stupid game.

Payton arched on the bed and curled her hands around a pillow. "Oh, God, Andy." She wasn't thinking about the game any longer either.

He kneeled down, grasped her hips, and raised her buttocks slightly. Licking his lips, he moved his mouth to the inside of her left thigh and ran his tongue upwards until he had created a moist path across her flat stomach.

He kept her torture going until he ended up on her opposite leg. He could smell the feminine muskiness that came from her body and wondered if his erection was going to burst.

Andy tipped his head up slightly to meet Payton's gaze. "I'm going to make you come in my mouth, then I'm going to make you come with my fingers."

Her head lolled to the side.

"Play with your breasts while I'm doing it."

She did as commanded, a lazy smile on her lips and heat sparking from her eyes as she looked up, squeezed her breasts together, then played with her nipples.

Andy looked at the downy tuft of her pubic hair. He used his fingers to spread her wide and expose her clitoris even more. His tongue lapped at her bud.

Payton gasped and ground against his lips.

Andy circled her clit with his tongue, loving how slick she was and how sweet she tasted. It was a dream come true to come down on his wife like this—it had been far too many months.

His mouth circled her clit again. He flicked at it with his tongue, and then began to suck hard.

Payton groaned as she grabbed his head. She forced his mouth tighter against her body and bucked until hot shards ripped through her body. He could feel the waves of her orgasm when he stuck his tongue inside her pussy. Andy sucked and ground his mouth against her until she collapsed with her arms spread wide across the bed.

"Andy," she panted, "that was…indescribable."

"I'm not done with you yet, baby."

He slipped two fingers into her pussy and began to finger fuck her. He used his other hand to stimulate her clit, loving the sight of her body writhing on the bed. Andy worked her until Payton ground against him. Leaving his fingers in her, he bent and sucked hungrily at her clit once more and inserted a third finger. It didn't take long for him to feel another orgasm wracking her body. Finally she wasn't faking her orgasms any longer.

Payton screamed, grabbed his hand, and helped him with the pumping motion. "Oh, God, I'm coming again!"

He smiled greedily with her pleasure — and his own.

Andy rolled her limp body to her stomach, pushed her slightly forward onto the bed, then positioned her knees forward until her ass and pussy were raised for easy access. She was putty in his hands — exactly what he had promised her earlier. Taking his cock in his palm, he guided himself into her. Payton slammed against him instantly, rocking up and down his length.

Andy went wild with lust — she drove him crazy with her round little ass and velvet soft pussy lips. He grasped her hips and drove himself time after time into her until he came hard. He groaned as he buried himself as far as he could, and then collapsed on the bed next to his panting wife.

They lay spent, breathing hard, and totally satisfied with the sex they shared. It was like nothing either of them had ever encountered for more than a few years. When Andy's strength returned, he dragged Payton across his chest and kissed her deeply.

"I love you, woman. I knew we could get this back."

Payton tightened her arms around him and laid her head on his chest. She could hear his still-pounding heart.

"I always want it to be like this with us. I'm sorry I let everything get in the way."

Andy flipped her onto her back and stared down into the face he loved. He brushed the damp blonde strands from her cheek, moistened his lips with his tongue, and kissed her waiting mouth. "So am I. Payton, I didn't love you any less because of it. I've never been sorry one day that we've been together. I just always felt awful that I couldn't make you as happy as I used to. You've always made me happy. Don't ever think that you haven't. I wouldn't give up you and the kids for anything."

Payton smiled softly. She could never ask for more as far as her gorgeous husband was concerned. "Can I tell you something?"

"Sure."

"What we did? I used to consider that fucking." She blushed slightly, but charged on. "That's how I had come to think of it. I would get so upset when you called it that. But you know what? I've come to realize that's what it is. Pure, unadulterated fucking—but it's also making love. It's making love because it's one person doing anything for their partner to give them pleasure; allowing anything to be done to their bodies because both parties find extreme joy and satisfaction in the act."

She pulled his mouth to hers and kissed him lovingly. "I want to continue to experiment. I want to continue to have orgasms every time we make love. Not only this weekend, but forever. I always want to be thinking of the next time."

His lips dropped to her mouth. "That's a deal that I'm going to hold you to."

Chapter 14: Wet 'n' Wild

Payton awoke, but didn't open her eyes. She lay on the bed beneath a down comforter, thinking how cozy and comfortable she felt.

Someone must have covered me…

She was definitely aware of how sore her vagina was from Andy's fierce fucking, but a smile split her face nonetheless.

The evening was like no other, and despite the soreness, all she wanted to do was get fucked again. Andy had awakened the sexual need that she'd forgotten about for so long. Her eyes fluttered open to see his head on the pillow beside her.

He smiled. "Hi, sleepyhead."

"I fell asleep, didn't I? Sorry. What time is it?"

"There are no clocks this weekend, Payton. Want to sit in the hot tub? I found some strawberries and champagne in the fridge after you fell asleep."

She stretched like a lazy cat. "God, that sounds relaxing. You're going to turn me into not only a sex addict, but an alcoholic to boot."

He chuckled when he kicked the blanket from his body and swung his long legs over the side of the bed. "The sex part is fine. An alcoholic? That's a problem you'll never have, hon."

She watched his tall, lean body disappear through the bathroom door. When he exited, she took her turn, stopping long enough to find her toothbrush to get the taste of stale screwdrivers off her tongue before she joined him in the other room.

Payton caught a glimpse of her naked body in the vanity mirror. She hesitated as her gaze inspected her full breasts, slim hips, and shapely slender thighs.

You'll never have to stand in a mirror and satisfy yourself again. She had rediscovered the joy her husband's body brought her. Payton would never forget that again. A smile creased her face as she hurried to join him.

* * * * *

Andy and Payton lounged in the Jacuzzi situated in a romantic corner of the room. Hot bubbling water forced billows of steam up and around their naked bodies. She had never felt so relaxed and so completely satisfied in her entire life. She lifted a slender eyebrow in the direction of her husband and a giggle burst from her throat.

"What?" Andy grinned back as he lounged against the opposite marble side.

"Look at us! What the hell was I thinking the last couple of years." She shook her wet head in wonder. "This is absolutely fantastic."

"You were overwhelmed. I'm never going to let it happen to you again." He left his molded seat and effortlessly moved through the bubbling water to be closer to her. Andy grasped her hand and pressed a warm kiss against the center of her palm. "Agreeing to come here without too many questions shows how much you really still love me."

He slid his lips around one slim finger and sucked gently. Payton watched his mouth. An immediate rush of excitement laced its way through her belly.

"You doing that to me is turning me on."

"Good, I'm just getting you ready."

Her eyes darkened with desire. "Ready for what?"

"You've suddenly turned into my little nympho, haven't you?"

"I want to feel the same way I did earlier. I can't wait to see what you've planned next. Tell me."

"Uh-uh, Payton."

She poked his powerful chest with a finger. "Come on. Give me a little hint."

He shook his head again and droplets of water sprayed lightly around him. "You can't get me to buckle under."

A sly smile flitted across her lips when he refused to answer even the tiniest of questions. She reached beneath the bubbles, found a firm hairy thigh, and then ran her hand along its length. A second later, she cupped his balls and rolled them gently in her hand,

Andy's breath caught in his throat when she wiggled the fingers of her other hand before his face, and then dropped them beneath the water's surface to encase his cock with her palm at the same time. Even though his penis was limp, she was amazed at how big it was. "Well, I think I could coax you into at least one little hint."

He grasped her hand beneath the water and ran it up and down the length of his cock that quickly hardened under her tender ministrations. His eyes darkened with passion. "There's something to say about bringing out the inner wanton hidden behind big breasts and a wet pussy."

Payton locked gazes with him. Courage and complete freedom to ask what she wanted filled her. "Would you fuck me now?"

He silently stood, and the warm water streamed off his muscular build. Andy shook the water from his hair; the simple motion reminded Payton of a wild animal. He grabbed her hand and pulled her up and against his full erection.

She was breathless and excited that she had discovered the audacity to make the first move after so long.

Andy kissed her deeply and ran his hands down the length of her back to massage her firm ass. "Do you want to come with me over there," he nodded in the direction of the bed, "or do you want to fuck right here?"

She leaned back in his embrace and gazed up into his handsome face. "It would be a little difficult here, wouldn't it?" She rubbed her breasts across the smooth chest before her. "I really want to feel the smooth skin of your cock inside me. Should we go to the bed now?"

One large hand left her ass and found its way down past her belly to between her legs. A split second later, he buried his middle finger into her pussy. Payton gasped and her knees nearly buckled beneath her.

Andy held her upright with his free arm and worked her clitoris. "You're dripping already."

Payton's mouth only sagged open, and her lids dropped close.

"I'm going to fuck you right here," he whispered into her ear before she could utter anything. He flipped her around and bent her forward. "Lay your body over the edge. I want to see what I'm fucking."

Payton shivered when the cold edge of the tile came in contact with her breasts and stomach. She felt as if she was in a novel. She was the captured heroine, and Andy was the wild pirate who would never take no for an answer.

He spread her legs further apart and ran his fingers down her crack and slipped his thumb into her vagina. "God, you've got a hot pussy!"

Her head rolled slowly against the tile. "Please, Andy. I want you inside of me..." Payton was startled at how fast her body reacted to the promised sexual pleasure. He was examining her pussy and it excited the hell out of her. Now, she wanted him to fill her.

He ignored her plea. Andy's other hand that rested on her ass, slid slowly down to her crotch. His other thumb joined the one inside of her. "You have a great ass, Payton. And, this-" he applied a little more pressure with his thumbs. "You're lips are a pinkish color and you don't have too much pubic hair. I like that." He continued to thumb fuck Payton as he stretched her open wider and stared into the cavity that gave so much pleasure.

She rocked against his hands.

"Andy...please!"

The tip of his cock nudged at her opening a moment later. He inserted it only an inch and then backed out again, only to return a second later with the same motion. Payton tried to back onto his erection, but he only pulled back further.

"Settle down, Payton. Try not to move."

Her head lolled on the ceramic tile again. "I don't know if I can. Christ, I want you in me."

"Try. Just let me fuck you a little at a time and think about how it's going to feel when I finally ram inside of you." He continued to tease the opening of her pussy for endless minutes, then held his cock and ran it up and down her ass crack. He worked his other hand around her hip and flicked at her clitoris as, once again, he barely inserted the tip of his dick.

Payton's hands were clenched and she moaned against the ceramic tile. "Please, Andy, you have to fuck me now. I can't wait!"

He slid into her slowly, and she accepted his entire length. A growl rumbled in his broad chest, and then escaped through his lips, but he remained motionless as he gripped her hips firmly and held her tightly against him. His teasing drove her mad—him lying inside her and not moving was unbearable.

Payton wiggled and tried to get him to find the rhythm.

"That's it, Payton. You've got the idea now. I'll let you take the lead. You pound all you want."

Payton raised herself up onto her hands and slid down the length of him as her husband supported her body by lifting her hips. She remained impaled on him with only the palms of her hands touching the tile. "Oh, God, you've got a big cock…"

She enjoyed the feel of his cock inside her and remained motionless, knowing she teased him now with her simple words. Her feet found the marble seat beneath the water, and she was able to leverage herself into an even better position. She rocked against him slowly, drawing herself up and down his long length. Payton increased her tempo, savoring every inch of his throbbing erection.

Soon, Andy grunted, and then followed her lead. His every thrust became harder as her ass slapped against his thighs.

Payton exploded with an orgasm that appeared from nowhere, but still Andy rammed into her. He never stopped the motion even when he maneuvered her body back down to the tiles. He slammed, and she groaned with pleasure until the heat built again. Andy quickly changed his position by supporting his body with a bent knee beside her shoulder on the tile — and rammed harder.

The cold tile scraped her breasts. Payton realized she was going to be bruised, but she could do nothing but urge him on. "Fuck me, fuck me harder. Oh, god, fuck me...fuck...ohhh!" Another orgasm slammed through her as hard as the thrusts from the man behind her.

Andy threw his head back and groaned as he emptied his semen. One last thrust completed his own orgasm.

Payton lay sprawled on her stomach; the lower half of her body sagged into the bubbling water. "Jesus Christ," she whispered when she found her voice.

Andy dropped onto the underwater bench, pulled Payton across his lap, and shoved his tongue into her open mouth. His heart pounded alongside her breasts. She moaned against his lips and danced her tongue against his. Payton met his ardor and reveled in the moment.

Time passed before their mouths finally parted. She reached a trembling hand upwards and caressed her husband's square jaw. A smile played about his lips as he stared down.

"What?" he asked with a raised eyebrow.

Payton smiled gently and tipped her head, never taking her gaze from his. "I'll remember that forever. It was fantastic."

"Do you realize why?"

She simply shook her head, blinked her round blue eyes, and waited for the answer.

"Because you initiated it. You were the one who started that last session. It's been a long time since that happened."

He rose with Payton in his arms, then set her on her feet and gave her ass a light slap as he eyed the untouched bowl of strawberries. "Now, let's get something to eat. I gotta keep your strength up."

Chapter 15: Play With Me

"I can't believe this place. I know it's the middle of the night and, still, here we are, munching on lobster tails as if it happens all the time."

Andy pushed his plate aside with a grin. "Money will buy you anything, Payt."

"I meant to ask you about that." She dabbed at her lips with a linen napkin. "What is this little 'seduction weekend' of yours costing us?"

"Don't you worry about that. I've got it all taken care of. All I'll say is that it's been worth every penny so far."

Her blood instantly heated in her veins. For the first time in a long time, she wasn't tired; she wasn't worrying about getting up for work or if the kids needed something. It was simply she and Andy having the time of their lives.

"What about tomorrow? Should we check in to one of the Fantasy rooms?"

He shrugged. "I couldn't care less. You're fulfilling every fantasy in my head. It's up to you, though. In fact," he cocked his head and stared at her exposed cleavage, "maybe we should check this place out. You want to call now or are you too tired?"

Payton stood, rounded the table, and plopped in his lap. They both wore white terry cloth robes found in one of the closets. She slipped a hand into the opening at his chest and rubbed his hard chest. "I'm not tired. But how about we check out the rooms tomorrow? For now, I want you to make love to me again. Any way, any position."

Andy stood with her in his arms and strolled to the bed. Sleep was also the last thing on his mind. He lay her gently on her back, and opened the sash of her robe. When her breasts were exposed, he kneaded them softly, enjoying how quickly her nipples hardened beneath his searching fingers.

"Want a massage?"

"Oooh, that sounds simply delightful."

He dropped his lips and brushed them against her open mouth. "I'll get the lotion. Roll over and get ready for the time of your life."

* * * * *

A sigh escaped Payton's lips when she felt the warm lotion on her back. Five minutes later, she was totally at ease. Her stomach did a quick flip, however, when Andy's hands spread her legs slightly and worked the firm muscles of her inner thighs.

"How does that feel?"

"Mmmmm…wonderful," Payton murmured into the pillow.

As soon as the words left her mouth, she felt a massaging hand on her buttocks. Warm liquid dripped across the round spheres of her firm ass and traced a soothing path down the slope of her hips. A second later, Andy's other hand joined its counterpart. The gentle ministrations continued.

"Why don't you flip over so you can see me? Just lie on your back."

Payton did as she was told, smiling up at him when she settled comfortably in the middle of the bed.

"Close your eyes, Payton," Andy whispered, "and let me take care of pleasing you."

Her lids dropped shut. Payton shivered when warm lotion drizzled onto her stomach. A moment later, Andy's large hands moved in circular motions across her flat belly—a light feathery touch that sent a hot stream of desire straight to her core.

He leaned forward near her ear. Warm breath whispered against her cheek before he spoke. "You have a beautiful body." His hand brushed across her pubic mound and was gone a second later.

Her pussy was instantly wet.

She clenched her teeth when Andy spread her legs open with the slight pressure of his gentle hands. His palm brushed over the curly pubic hair once more, and then slid the length of Payton's legs, massaging the shapely limbs to the ankles and back.

Payton moaned slightly and her body arched when his fingers danced their way across her inner thigh, only to skip past the glistening folds of her vagina to again rub her flat belly with a circular motion. Her eyes flew open to stare at him. Soft pants left her lips.

She now remembered the hot passion of instant gratification. All she had to do was ask…

Before she could utter anything, Andy slid his hands upwards, a slow, sensuous path across her velvet skin to the swell of her firm breasts. His thumbs flicked across Payton's erect nipples. His gaze narrowed with lust when he spoke.

"Payton—I'll lick your nipples if you want."

The touch of her husband's mouth against her was something she suddenly and desperately wanted. No longer was she the overworked wife; no longer was she the mother of three children. She was a woman who wanted physical fulfillment; she craved the feel of his warm lips against her.

"Kiss me," she whispered.

"How?"

Andy's wonderful hands still massaged her heaving breasts.

"No — don't just…kiss," she panted out. "Suck them — suck my nipples — please don't make me wait any longer."

Andy knelt beside her. His lips wrapped around a large dark pink areola, and the intense sucking nearly caused Payton to scream out loud. Her fingers threaded their way into the soft waves of his dark head.

"Do you like it, Payton?" Andy mumbled against her breast as he nipped at the soft mound, then rolled his tongue around the perimeter of an erect nipple.

"Yes — oh God, yes!"

"Tell me what else you want me to do."

Payton's fingers splayed across the bed. One slim hand followed the length of his muscular thigh until she found his hard penis. Andy immediately rose up on all fours to give her better access to his erection. She had no sooner wrapped her fingers around him that he pumped his hips in rhythm with her gentle strokes.

Tender hands traveled the slopes of her body. They moved across her breasts, down around her inner thighs, and back across her stomach. Payton squirmed with desire.

Andy bent and mumbled against her nipple. "Ask me to lick your pussy."

Payton bucked at the mere question. Her legs bent at the knees and she spread them wide, thinking that the motion would clue him as to what she wanted — what she craved.

Suddenly, the hands that drove her to distraction and the lips that suckled her breasts disappeared. Payton's eyes snapped open in confusion. Andy leaned over her with his sexy smile in place once more.

"What...why are you stopping?"

"Tell me what you want me to do," Andy requested softly.

Payton's gaze examined his handsome face. "I want you to lick me...down there. Now — don't make me wait."

Andy rolled between her legs.

The woman lying on the bed moaned.

He slowly and worshipfully gazed at the delicately furred pussy lips before him and spread them wider with his fingers. His tongue extended from his mouth and, in one fluid motion, licked Payton from below her labia to her throbbing clitoris.

A low moan escaped her throat as she arched her body to search for more of the same.

Andy began a slow assault with his tongue. In between the long licks through Payton's wet folds, he would hesitate, then suckle Payton's clitoris.

Payton rolled and arched her body against his hot mouth. A searing line of fire built in her blood. His tongue darted in and out of her vagina. She thought she might faint with the sheer ecstasy of his actions.

It was when he vigorously fucked her with two fingers while he continued to lap at her that the intense heat of orgasm begin to build. Payton didn't think—didn't stop to wonder at how her husband could coax this wonderful feeling from her body. She simply tightened the muscles of her own body and rocked herself against the sensuous mouth that lapped at her.

The building heat burst. Payton gasped for air and let the waves of the intense flames shake her body. She screamed again when the climax continued to rock her to near oblivion. Andy continued to lick her until she lay with her legs spread wide, still shivering with the aftershock of the massive orgasm.

"Oh, God…I can't believe it…I—" She lifted her head from the pillow to stare in wonder at him. "I…it was so wonderful."

Andy kneeled between her splayed legs, took his penis in his hand, and rubbed the head up and down the slit of Payton's pussy. She jumped at the contact.

"Do you like my cock?"

"Oh, yes."

"Would you like me to fuck you?"

Suddenly, it was all Payton craved—to have his huge throbbing erection inside her. She still tingled all over. This weekend was about being filled completely—about reaching a precipice she'd never reached before.

"Fuck me."

"Fuck you hard?"

"Fuck me! Do it now!"

Her body arched when he dropped on top of her and jammed his erection into her dripping pussy.

Payton gasped and dropped her knees wider to allow him even more access. He filled her so completely and so perfectly that Payton groaned with the ecstasy of the beautiful feeling. Her body stretched to its limit around his long cock. She knew he would do anything she asked. She was the mistress—she was the woman who could take his penis and devour it.

"Fuck me harder," Payton gasped next to his ear. "Please, fuck me harder!"

He plunged deeply into Payton's vagina and nearly lifted her from the bed's surface. She screamed with the instant orgasm that shook her to her very soul. Andy pumped on, sliding his cock in as far and as hard as he could. He slammed himself against her inner thighs. The waves of desire continued to shake her. Payton had never experienced anything like it in her life. She wanted to faint, and she wanted to fuck forever.

The encompassing orgasm lessened, but still Andy didn't come. He only continued to fuck her hard—he rode her without mercy. Payton continued to meet each deep thrust with one of her own until the heat started again.

"Oh! I'm...I'm going to come again!" She bit his shoulder and raked her nails across the broad expanse of his back. "Fuck me, Andy," she urged him on again, "fuck me harder!"

As impossible as it was, Andy increased his tempo and Payton wrapped her legs around his back until her toes curled with the hot waves of yet another orgasm. A moment later, he shuddered in her arms and buried himself with one final stroke inside her wet pussy.

Chapter 16: The Garden Spot

They slept until nearly noon. Both woke with hunger pinching their stomachs and agreed before there would be any more sexual play, they needed to eat.

It wasn't long before a tray was delivered to their room and they sat on the veranda overlooking the garden of their suite. Both were cloaked in the white robes again, their travel bag of clothes untouched.

The meal turned into sexual play as they fed each other and found ways to delicately touch the warm skin of the other. It was when they discussed the Fantasy Room options that Andy grabbed her arm to gain Payton's attention.

"What?" She looked around.

"Looks like someone else is enjoying the garden view." He nodded his head. She turned to see a couple across the way exit their room to enjoy the warm sunshine also. A mere thirty feet separated them.

Payton turned back to him with her full lips drawn in a slight pout. "I was wondering when we would run into someone else. They must have the rooms soundproofed around here. Haven't heard a scream or squeaking bed springs yet. Should we go back inside?" Andy wasn't listening to her. His attention was drawn to the other couple. "Andy?"

"Turn around, Payt, and take a look at what's going on. I think they're going to fuck right in front of us."

She swiveled on the garden chair. A second later, her jaw dropped open.

The woman was in the process of helping her lover remove the white robe she wore. The man who stood behind her was already naked with a rock-hard erection. The terry cloth material dropped to the deck she stood on. She lifted her chin, stared squarely at Andy and played with her breasts.

Payton followed the line of the other woman's gaze straight to her husband's. She sat forward and snapped her mouth shut. "They want us to watch, don't they?"

Andy adjusted his chair for better viewing. "Yup. I think you just nailed it on the head. What do you think? You want to go inside or sit here and enjoy the show?"

The man stepped closer, wrapped his arms around the woman, and ran his hands up her body. He brushed her fingers aside and squeezed her huge breasts. The woman continued to stare at both Payton and Andy now as she raised her arms and ran her fingers through her long length of dark hair.

Her lover's fingers trailed down over a taut stomach and rested on the dark strip of pubic hair between the woman's legs.

A streak of heat darted through Payton's groin. She had never seen anyone else perform a sexual act—except in the few porno flicks Andy had exposed her to. Her nipples instantly puckered into hard points.

"Payton. I think they're waiting for us to make up our minds. What's it going to be?"

She turned, glanced at her husband, and ran her tongue across her full bottom lip. Her shoulders raised in a shrug. "What the hell? If they don't mind, why should we?" She adjusted her chair and settled back.

"Are you jealous that I'm watching a naked woman?" Andy asked unexpectedly.

Payton glanced at her husband again before bringing her gaze back to the other veranda. The man stepped away from his partner and seared Payton with his gaze while he stroked his hard-on. An impish smile appeared on her lips. She nodded her head to the goings on across the way. "Are you jealous? I think I'm going to enjoy the little show. He's hoping I'm watching him."

"You're a smartass, Mrs. Duncan."

"You started it. Shut up and watch the show."

His chuckle was hard to miss when he settled back in his chair once more.

Their attention turned to the other couple. It was hard to miss the understated smile on the other woman's lips as she turned and kissed the man she was with. He played with her breasts as she stroked his cock.

Payton found it slightly difficult to breathe at a regular pace when the woman sank to her knees.

The woman massaged her hands across the man's stomach before grasping his cock in her curled fingers. She stroked him as her tongue darted out to lick the head of his penis.

Payton's vaginal muscles clenched. She hadn't given Andy a blowjob in years. It was something she never quite enjoyed, so he never asked her to do it. But watching another woman perform the act was titillating to say the least.

She watched the woman's lips work their way down the shaft of the man's penis to where her fingers grabbed him at the base. It wasn't long before her head bobbed up and down at a frantic pace. The man pumped her mouth as his head fell back. His complete joy was seen by the widening smile when he turned his head and nodded at the couple across from him.

Payton swallowed and refused to turn her head to glimpse Andy's reaction. *I'll have to give this some thought...*

The woman stood, leaned back against the wrought iron railing and spread her stance. She played with her breasts while searching out Andy's eyes.

Andy's cock throbbed between his legs.

Her man stepped forward, extended one finger and inserted it into her pussy. He finger fucked her until she began to wiggle with excitement.

Then she turned her back to him, placed her hands on the railing and bent slightly forward to allow him better access to her ass. He squirted liquid from a tube between her spread cheeks and inserted a finger into her anus.

Payton nearly slid off the chair. "Christ," she panted out. "Is he going to do what I think he is?"

"Fuck, I hope so," was Andy's only response. He was having a hard time controlling his own breathing.

The man bent the woman slightly more forward before he grasped his cock and guided it between her cheeks. Slowly, he slid into her rectum. The woman gasped, threw back her head, and rocked against him. They both went wild.

He slammed into her time after time. The woman's breasts swayed crazily to the motion as she met each thrust.

A quiet, strangled moan left Payton's lips when she realized the man was coming—evidenced by his short, jerky thrusts into his wife's ass and the look of complete joy on his face.

The woman answered Payton's gasp with one of her own as she also came.

"Fuck…" Andy breathed out from where he sat on the chair. "That was better than any porno flick I've ever watched." He turned his head to stare at his wife. "What about you?"

"I'm not even embarrassed to admit I'm hornier than hell."

"Then let's do it. Let's give them a show back. Look over there. It seems like they're waiting for us now. Come on, Payt. No one will ever know."

Payton glanced at the other couple. Both leaned against the railing waiting to see what would happen.

"Screw in front of someone?"

"We'll never see them again. I want to fuck you in front of them. I want them to see me doing it to you. I want them to see what a sexy, beautiful wife I have."

Payton pushed aside the prick of conscience that jabbed at her. *So what if they see? It was fantastic watching someone else have sex…*

"You'll never tell anyone that we did this, will you?"

"Get over here, Payton." He dragged his chair away from the table and closer to the edge of the veranda. A second later, he shrugged off his robe. His erection glistened in the sunshine.

Payton drew in a deep breath of courage and stood. She strolled to his side, surprised that it was easy to meet the gaze of the voyeuristic couple across from them.

She sighed deeply when Andy opened the front of her robe so the couple could see his wife's breast. He slid his hand around the mound and massaged it. He leaned forward and murmured against her lips. "You taste like wine and feel like satin."

Payton's tongue circled his top lip before she nibbled at his open mouth. "I can't get enough of you. I want to stay here forever. Are they watching?"

A chuckle rumbled in his throat when he sat and pulled her onto his lap. Andy ran his tongue down the side of her neck, across her breastbone, then down to the full breast resting in his hand. "I think the guy's got a hard-on again. Let's give him a full view." His hand traveled down to the sash tied at her waist. He untied the simple knot, spread the robe open to reveal the smooth skin of her belly, and shoved the material from her shoulders.

Payton gasped quietly when he yanked the robe from her body and tossed it on the tile. "I want them to see all of you." He worked his palm between her legs and inserted a finger into her pussy. "I could fuck this forever. Spread your legs more so they can see what I'm doing."

Payton's heart pounded against her ribs as she spread her legs for him, enjoying the instant desire that raced up her spine, knowing that the other couple must be feeling as she did just a short while earlier. The heat of the afternoon sun didn't compare to the flame Andy built inside her as his thumb circled her clit.

"Come for me," he whispered close to her ear. "Just lie back and come in my hand."

Payton dropped her head until it rested against his arm. She reached down, covered her hand over the back of his palm as he stroked her harder, and urged him along.

"Use two fingers," she breathed. "Fuck me with two fingers." The other couple was forgotten momentarily when Andy immediately complied. Payton rocked against his hand, spread her legs wider, and clasped her pussy lips around his long digits.

"Oh, God…Andy!"

She arched back as each wave wracked her body. Andy buried his fingers inside and let her throb around them. As they slowed, he withdrew his hand, lifted her body and guided her legs until she straddled his naked lap, facing him.

"Let them see you put my cock inside of you."

Payton immediately reached her fingers down and guided his cock inside her. She moaned against his lips when his hands circled her slender waist to work her body up and down his erection.

She slid across his familiar length time after time until the heat started again. Suddenly, Andy slammed her down on his penis and held her there as he ejaculated. Her body trembled around his shaft as yet another orgasm wracked through her lower body.

Payton fell forward and rested her head on his broad shoulder, panting along with the heavy breaths in her ear. Her husband's arms circled her protectively before grasping the sides of her head with his big hands. It was as if he peered into her very soul when his gaze met hers.

"That's what I wanted him to see, Payton—that I'm the one person who can make you totally happy. I wanted him to know that only I can make you come like that."

Lovingly, he kissed her open mouth. "I love being the only one who can completely control your emotions. I love you."

A soft smile touched her lips. Payton swiped at a tear. "I love you too," she whispered. "Only you." As she laid her head on his shoulder, she glanced across the veranda. Only she and Andy were left to enjoy the beautiful gardens.

Chapter 17: The Sultan's Concubine

Andy pushed the door open with the flat of his left hand. The fingers of his right hand clasped his wife's gently as he led her into a dimly lit room. Earlier, the two pored over the different selections of sexual fantasy rooms and had decided to go with the Sultan's Palace.

Payton stood on her tiptoes and peered over his shoulder. "Holy cow…" A shiver of anticipation ran up her spine as her gaze moved around the room.

Even with the lights turned down low, multi-colored satin pillows shimmered around the room. A thin raised bed of sorts was placed in the center of the floor. Against the wall was a flat cushioned panel with fur-lined handcuffs attached on chains near the top and two more shackles near the floor. A quick glance at Andy revealed his lascivious grin.

Velvet entered behind the couple with a covered tray in her hands. She set it on a nearby table and lifted the cover.

"You'll find quite an assortment here of cold foods to enjoy. If you would like anything else, just give the operator a call and I'll have it delivered."

Payton and Andy silently followed her further into the room when she motioned them forward. Their host melted into the lush surroundings with her flowing red robe and exotic persona. She turned with a smile touching her full scarlet lips.

"I think you made a good choice. Role-playing in a room like this is always exciting. *Sex & Love* simply supplies various experiences for fantasy, but that surely doesn't mean you can't come up with something on your own once you leave here or even while you are here."

She rose, crossed to a chest and opened the heavy lid. "In here, you'll find clothes and various other objects that will help you 'get in the mood' so to speak." She lifted two thin leather-bound books from the interior. "Each of these manuals denotes if they are for a man or a woman. Take a few minutes to look through them. Each outlines role-playing ideas. You can try them or create your own scenario." She placed the books back inside the chest. "I've never had a customer that wasn't pleased with any of our fantasy rooms. Stay as long as you want. When you decide that you are finished here, feel free to check out the list on the hallway table and experience some other special offers from *Sex & Love*."

Velvet was about to leave, but hesitated a moment longer. She turned, clasped her hands lightly, and smiled wider. "There is one thing I'd like to mention. We have staff counselors if you'd like to set up an appointment. The choice is yours. I thought I'd mention it out loud again because, up to now, you haven't requested any sessions."

"Is it a required that we do?" Andy returned.

"Oh, no. Some couples need the outside help and some don't. I just want the two of you to get everything you need out of this weekend. Communication is a big part of a happy relationship."

Andy rested an arm across Payton's shoulders. "I think we'll just take your tips regarding the room and enjoy the rest of the afternoon. Payton and I have been talking," he squeezed her shoulder gently, "among other things."

Velvet nodded, crossed the room with her robe rustling around her ankles, and closed the door behind her as she left.

Andy immediately pulled Payton into his arms. He pressed his lips softly against hers and was surprised when she slanted her head and opened her mouth hungrily. The tender embrace quickly turned hot as she molded herself against his body.

Andy grabbed her ass and pulled her even closer. "Hell," he mumbled against her mouth, "I should have brought you here a long time ago. You know, I didn't ask you if you wanted to see one of the offered professionals. What do you think?"

"I can't get enough of you," she murmured back. "I'm not even embarrassed anymore in front of Velvet. We don't need anyone to tell us if there is a problem, because there isn't. I just wanted her to get the hell out so we could be alone."

Andy burst out laughing, but sobered quickly when his wife wiggled her hand between them and massaged his burgeoning erection. "You keep that up—pardon the pun—and we'll never even get to the manuals."

Payton floated from his arms with a wicked smile on her lips and crossed to the chest. "Just priming the pump, honey."

He hurried to her side and playfully swatted her on the ass. "You've become a horrible tease."

Payton handed him the bound manual. "Are you complaining?"

"Hell, no. I'm just wondering if I'm going to be able to keep up with you from here on out."

Payton turned to pull costumes from the chest. "I'll just have to find some young stud then to take care of my needs," she teased, and then yelped when he swatted her across the butt a little harder than the first time.

She spun back around and placed one fist on her hip. "If that didn't turn me on so much, I'd smack you back. Can't wait to start, big guy?"

Andy's eyebrows danced. "That's half the anticipation."

His wife shoved an armful of silky material into his waiting hands and nodded her head at an ornate hinged panel. "Go behind that screen and get dressed."

"Are you really going to make us put on costumes?"

"You're damned right. Look at this." She held up a cotton gauze, see-through robe. "I want to see what your reaction is when I put this on!"

"Ooo, my harem girl. I'll be right back." He scooted behind the screen. "This better not be a joke, Payton. When I come out, you'd better have that outfit on."

She was already pulling her shirt over her head and heading for another corner of the room that was screened off.

A few minutes later, Andy stepped from behind the privacy panel. He wore a long flowing sheik's robe, complete with headgear. "I can't believe I'm doing this." He glanced around until he saw her clothes hanging over the top of her dressing area. "Payton, you almost done back there?"

A rustle of material preceded her as she floated into the room.

A rush of air whistled across Andy's teeth as he stared at his wife who had suddenly transformed herself into an Arabic concubine.

She was stunning to say the least.

A silver band wrapped around her head just above her eyebrows. Matching silver hoops bounced from her delicate earlobes as she raised her chin a notch to let him view the sweet length of her slender neck. Payton had pulled her long blonde tresses into a swirling mass at the top of her head. Springing curls draped their way around her neck, making him want to reach out to feel their softness.

That need, however, didn't match the desire he felt to gather her body into his arms to assure himself she was real. The filmy gauze floated along the sensuous curves of her breasts and thighs. Her pubic hair was barely discernable beneath the white threads, and Andy knew the joy he would find just beneath the curly mound.

Payton's nipples immediately hardened when his heated gaze raked her from head to toe. Slender hands reached up to caress the muted pink nipples draped by the material. She brushed her fingers down past her hips, around to the apex of her legs, and back up to rest gently on her trim hips. "Do you like what you see?"

He nodded.

"It opens in the front. In just one little flick of your finger, you could be inside my robe."

He took a step forward, but she raised a palm to halt his approach.

"Not yet, though. I love the feel of this material against my skin. I want to stay dressed for awhile."

"You have nothing underneath it. It's pretty clear to me that all I'd have to do is lift up the hem and you'd be mine before you knew it. I don't need to open anything. I've got a hard-on that hurts just looking at you."

A satisfied smile turned up the corners of Payton's mouth. That's exactly the reaction she had gone for, but she was going to make him wait. Like he said; the anticipation was half the game.

Payton sank to a pillow and patted the one across from her. "Here, sit so we can talk. I took a quick glimpse at the manual. We're supposed to communicate orally first."

"You want *oral communication*? I'll give you *oral communication*."

"That's not what I'm talking about and you know it. But...I'll remember you said that."

His jaw clenched, but he sat across from her as ordered.

"You look handsome in that robe, Andy. With your dark masculine physique, you could easily be sitting in an Arabian tent with a camel waiting for you outside."

"I feel a little silly."

"Don't—the sight of you turns me on. It helps my fantasy along."

"Which is...?"

"In due time," she answered cheekily. "My manual gave me a few ideas, but it also asked me a question." The smile left her face as she reflected inwardly for a moment. "I'm supposed to discuss with you the exact moment when I knew you and I would make a life together—when I was absolutely sure you would always be by my side."

"Did something come to mind?"

"Yes—it did."

"And…?"

Payton leaned back against a larger pillow and stared at him. A soft, mellow love rested in her blue gaze. "At the hospital—after Tyler was born."

Surprise widened her husband's eyes. "I thought you'd pick some great sexual experience—like maybe a time when we connected more so than any other."

Her head shook slightly. "I heard you in the hallway talking to my parents after he was born. You're words warmed me and gave me security like nothing else ever has."

"I can't remember what you're talking about." He tilted his head, then shook it with uncertainty furrowing his brow. "A conversation with your parents?"

"Yes. I don't think I was listening to the first part of the discussion. I did hear, however, your voice charged with emotion—that's what caught my attention."

As she spoke, an emotion of protectiveness warmed his blood. He was beginning to remember now exactly what she was talking about.

"What did they say to you that made you respond the way you did? You told them that they were making a huge mistake."

Andy squirmed. It was a conversation he had buried, planning to never let Payton know how her parents were ready to throw her away. If it weren't for him, they would have walked out of her life after the wedding. But, numerous calls when Payton wasn't around had guilted them into visiting occasionally or to at least call her on the phone to see how the pregnancy was progressing.

"Andy? Was the mistake that...they had decided they didn't want me in their life anymore?" A lump formed in her throat. Payton was amazed that after all the wonderful years she created with Andy, her family still had the power to break her heart. She hadn't seen her brothers since the day of her wedding. "My parents aren't the kind of grandparents I thought they would be. The kids don't even know them. What did you tell them?"

He studied her beautiful features. Did he really want all this brought up now? It might put a damper on their weekend—especially when they'd had so much fun thus far. But, wasn't communication the reason they were here? "All right. I told them they were fools to put such stock in one mistake. I asked them to think about all the years you worked hard alongside them—to think about your high academic honors and how you never caused them an ounce of trouble your entire life. Those things had to count for something. I also told them you were still their daughter, even though you were beginning your own family."

"And why did you tell them that?"

Andy sighed. "Because they said that you and Tyler were now my responsibility. Their duty was done and they felt they failed. It was easier for them in their square little world to just dismiss you and go about their days."

An instant tear trickled its way down Payton's cheek.

"Christ, Payton. Talking about this does nothing but upset you. Fuck them. You've got me, the kids, and my parents, who love you deeply. Why are we talking about this anyway?"

She dabbed at the tear with the gauzy hem of her robe, then took a deep breath. "Because of the manual and its question to me." She leaned forward, held out her arm, and waited for his fingers to touch hers. It always amazed her how his warm touch seemed to make things right when her world became rocky. "I didn't hear that entire conversation that night. What I did hear was you speaking with love and emotion in your voice. You stated how much you loved me and, no matter what, you would never leave my side—that Tyler wasn't a burden or a mistake—that he was your son. You said you'd die for both of us before letting anything hurt us again."

"I meant it. You're my life, Payton. Love isn't even a big enough word to explain how I feel about you."

Suddenly, the weight of her parents' refusal to be a part of her life anymore lifted from her shoulders. Andy was completely right. She hadn't done anything to deserve their complete dismissal. What she had now, most women would die for.

To hell with them. Andy was her life now.

Payton rose and pulled Andy up with her. "You know, Mr. Sheik, all of a sudden I'm rather horny. I think I need to do something about that." Her gaze flitted about the room, and then returned to his slightly whiskered face. "Want to hear my fantasy?"

"Want to hear mine?" His eyes bored through the gauzy material.

"Later. I'm first. Let's see," she pondered as she urged him across the room. "Normally, a sheik is in charge of his kingdom. But, I'm the smart, intimidating woman that has overtaken the empire that the overbearing sheik has created. It's all mine now—and you have become my slave." Her slender hands shoved him against the padded wall.

Chapter 18: The Sultan's Kingdom

Andy smiled. "If I overtake you right now, I suppose your guards will take me down and make me pay for it?" He enjoyed the scenario she created and would play along.

"Oh, yes. You would be beaten and thrown into the dungeon. But," her finger traced a pattern across his chest, "I've decided that you would be better as a love slave rather than sending you to the fields to work out your days in the hot sun."

"I didn't know deserts had fields."

She grinned at his smart-assed comment. "It's my fantasy. I can have anything I want—and I think I want you."

Before he knew it, she grabbed his wrist, dragged his arm upward, and linked a handcuff around it. "If you fight me, remember the guards will be here instantly. You might not get to experience what the queen has decided." She clicked the handcuff shut.

Andy's breaths became heavier. "Your wish is my command."

"Lift your other arm up so that it can be bound."

He did and was rewarded with another click of the opposite handcuff.

The material of his robe rested over his erection. Payton eyed the area and whisked her fingers across it. "I see that you are a fine specimen. Big, long, and hard. Hmmmm. Remember, if you come too soon, I'll have you returned to the fields, never to have a woman interested in you again." She sank to her knees. "Now spread your feet wide enough so I can secure your ankles."

Andy spread his stance. Payton quickly wrapped the ankle ties around him and made certain they were fastened. Her sheik was totally immobilized. Rising to her feet, she smiled up at him. Andy licked his lips. Being completely at her disposal caused his cock to throb. He wondered what she had planned.

Payton dragged a three-tier stool closer to the wall where Andy was chained, and then returned to the chest. Withdrawing a soft feather whip, she turned to face him. Her head tipped to the side as she studied his body clamped to the wall.

"You are not to say a word unless spoken to. Only then, can you utter anything. If you do, I might have to use my whip on you. You are just a man with no power now. Only I have the power."

Andy was never so excited in his life.

She strolled across to him, reached out and caressed his balls gently through the silken material. The intake of his breath echoed in the room, but he remained silent.

"Very good. You obey rather well. We'll see how long it lasts. Nod your head if you're comfortable." A quick nod assured her that her sheik was at ease with the position he was in.

Dragging the wide stepstool closer, Payton placed it before him. A quick kick of her satin slippers and she was barefoot. She stepped regally up the three tiers. Her chest was eye-level with Andy's face.

He watched her closely, his eyes dark with lust.

Reaching a hand ever so slowly into the front of her gown, Payton massaged her breast before pushing aside the material to expose it to his view.

"I love having my nipples sucked, and I've decided to see if you are worthy enough to continue on with my desires. If not, I'll find someone else to take your place."

She leaned slightly forward and whisked her nipple past his open mouth, and then quickly pulled back just out of his reach.

A low growl erupted from Andy's throat.

In response, Payton undid the clasps at the top of her shoulders. The gauzy bodice material drifted down to the sash tied around her waist. She fondled both exposed breasts that were mere inches from his mouth. "I don't know what I was thinking. How could I tell if you're good at sucking nipples when I only offered you one?" Raising her arms, she placed her hands against the padded wall above his head and brushed the tips of her breasts across his face.

Andy snatched out at a wayward nipple with his mouth, captured it between his lips, and sucked with force.

Hot streams of excitement raced through Payton's blood. The idea that he would do anything she asked fueled her on. Pulling back to break the suction, she offered her opposite breast. Andy immediately imprisoned the hard dart of her nipple and swirled his tongue around its perimeter.

Payton grasped her breast and forced it tighter against his mouth. Her breaths were tiny pants as she fought to maintain control. "You're very good. That's it. Suck it hard. Just think what it would be like if you were putting your finger in me at the same time."

Andy groaned behind his closed eyelids and sucked harder. The muscles of his forearms clenched as he tried to pull free. He wanted to fuck her so bad that he ached. The nipple was pulled from his mouth. He eyed the breasts that hung just out of his reach with longing.

Payton's blue eyes danced about the room again. She scrambled off the footstool, hauled it out of the way, found one that wasn't as tall, and dragged it back before him. As she stepped up on her new perch, her gaze swept the length of him. "I don't think I like the fact that you're still dressed. Wearing that outfit makes you still look like the king in charge—and you're not. You're nothing but my slave." She reached up and yanked the front open in one fluid motion. The muscles of his chest quivered when she ran her hands across his breasts. Quick fingers untied the sash at his waist. Andy's erection was hard and dripping pre-ejaculate. Payton was quick to stuff the ends of the robe between her husband's body and the wall to keep the material out of the way.

She reached down, pressed her palms against the inside of his spread knees, and traveled a sensuous path up his inner thighs, swirled her hands around his balls, and then took his cock in her hands. Andy arched forward and expelled the breath he held.

"You can answer me now. You like this, don't you."

"Christ, Payton, you're driving me crazy…"

"That's all. You can be quiet now."

His mouth snapped shut.

Continuing to slowly stroke his hard length, she looked up at him. Andy's stare bore into her. "You've been so good, that we might continue this…" she squeezed her fingers around his cock, applied slight pressure, and then pulled her hands away from him, "…or not."

She watched his eyelids drop when he inhaled deeply.

"Or we could try this."

His eyes snapped back open when she dropped to her knees. Now her chest was even with his groin. Payton grabbed the sides of her breasts, pressed them together, and leaned forward. Lessening her hold slightly, she encased Andy's cock in her cleavage, and began to fuck him with her breasts. Andy immediately pumped against her chest. "You've been so good. You deserve a special little treat. I remember you saying when my guards captured you that you wanted to…what did you call it? Oh, tit-fuck."

Andy's jaw clenched tightly as he continued to fuck her this way.

"You can only talk when you think you might come. We have to stop before that happens or I'll have to send you to the dungeon." Payton ground out the words, trying to maintain a semblance of calm. The feel of Andy's cock between her breasts had her heart pounding. She squeezed them tighter around him and let him pump. The tempo increased and she wondered how he managed not to come. A slick line of wetness moistened her cleavage.

"Payton—"

She jumped back and watched his face as he struggled to take control. Andy sucked in several deep breaths, and then clenched his teeth. Soon, he found the control he sought and swallowed as his head fell back against the padded wall. Beads of perspiration dampened his brow.

Payton rolled the footstool out of the way. Turning her back to him, she stepped to the middle of the room and swiveled to face him again. Slowly, she untied her sash and let the gown float to the floor. His heated gaze scanned her nude body.

She lifted her arms overhead and twirled slowly so he could study her body. "Answer yes or no if you want me to come back over there."

"Yes," he shot out.

Payton dropped to the floor on all fours and crawled slowly up to him. Andy never took his eyes from her. She rose up on her knees once she was next to him again and grasped his ankles immediately above the soft shackles that held his legs apart and stared straight at his penis.

"I'm thinking you've been so good that you deserve another special treat." Licking her lips, she kissed the tip of his penis. Andy swayed in his bindings. "You don't taste like a peasant." She swirled her tongue around the purple head. "In fact, you taste like a king. Maybe we could rule our kingdom together."

"Payton—"

"Oh, no, you weren't supposed to say anything." She knew she was driving him over the edge. "No more licking—I'll just have to bite now instead of using the whip." She nibbled on his penis. Andy bucked toward her mouth.

Deciding not to torture him further, she opened her lips, placed the tip of his cock in her mouth, and swirled her tongue down the length of him.

Andy gasped.

Payton reached up a hand, encircled his thickness with her fingers, and began to suck in earnest. She stroked him faster and faster as her head bobbed up and down.

Andy groaned one time after another and did his best to keep his penis buried in her mouth. When his rhythm became erratic, she removed her mouth and stroked him harder until cum squirted onto her chest. She continued to stroke with her hand until his breath lost the hissing sound of satisfaction.

Andy sagged in the handcuffs and took a deep cleansing breath. His head rolled until he looked down at her with blazing eyes as his tongue wet his lips.

"Can I talk now?"

She nodded.

"Get me the hell off this wall. I want to fuck you."

Payton released the shackles at his ankles first. Rising to her feet, she rested her hands on one of the handcuffs that still bound his wrists. Pressing a soft kiss against his lips and her body against the hard line of his torso, she smiled into his eyes. "Did you like that?"

"I'll never forget it. This weekend is getting better by the hour." He kissed her back. "I love you," he murmured against her lips, loving the idea that her mouth tasted like him.

"I'm not done. You're still my slave, but I'm going to let you loose. Do you promise to still do my bidding?"

"If you want to keep playing, I'm in."

She let him loose. Andy shook his arms to get the blood running back in them, and then scooped her high into his arms. Payton squealed with delight.

"You're a bitch, Payton. I thought I might pass out at one point." He twirled her around with a laugh, and then stopped the spinning motion to kiss her waiting lips. When he was done, he pulled away and stared down into beautiful blue eyes. "What do you have planned next?"

"First we're going to eat something and give you a chance to…recharge your batteries. I might tell you then."

He carried her to a huge pile of satin pillows and laid her gently in the center. It wasn't long before he had the tray between them. Lifting the linen cover, his eyebrows raised with delight. Cold salmon, various cheeses, and a myriad of fruit met his eyes.

He popped a grape in his mouth and eyed her above the tray. "I suppose you're going to make me feed you now."

"Oooo, good idea. You won't get a piece of me until you do. Feed me, slave. But, first, get me a glass of wine." She reclined against a pillow and waited.

Andy rose and crossed to the decanter and goblets on a nearby table. She watched his firm stride as he walked away, the strong muscular line of his back, and the tight buttocks that were perfectly shaped.

"You have a great ass, Andy. I love your body."

He returned with a grin in place, stretched out with the tray still between them, and handed her a goblet. "You're starting to sound like me. I'm the one that says that all the time," he leaned forward and kissed her moist lips, "and I mean it all the time, too. You've got one of the sexiest bodies I've ever seen. You don't look like you're in your late thirties. Your great breasts and perfect ass remind me of a teenager. Don't get me wrong, though. You're no kid — you are pure woman."

Warming to the unasked for compliment, she sipped her wine. "Coming here was a wonderful idea. We should do it every anniversary. Just let our inhibitions fly away along with thoughts of work and kids. It would be just you and me, playing with each other and having orgasms like there was no tomorrow."

"Speaking of which," he stated as he ran a hand over the slope of her hip. "You haven't gotten the chance to get off."

She gently took his hand and forced it away from her pussy and to the tray. "Feed me first. I'll have my turn — and so will you again."

"I don't know if you'll be able to top that last one. Having you suck me was fantastic."

"Never underestimate the power of a woman," she promised. "Now feed me."

Chapter 19: The Overthrow

The last of the salmon and fruit was eaten before Andy knocked the tray off the pillows and pinned Payton beneath him in one fluid swoop.

"Okay, I've had enough eating. Tell me what you want me to do to you."

She batted her eyes at him and placed a finger on her cheek. "I don't know. I did think about taking a nap."

Andy grabbed her hands and dragged them over her head. He had her body trapped beneath him. "I locked all the doors," he whispered down.

She looked confused. "What are you talking about?"

"Your guards can't get in. I've decided I want my kingdom back."

Instantly, heat spread through her belly. A tongue wet her bottom lip. "I'll scream and they'll come running."

"Not if I keep you too busy to scream." He forced her mouth open wider and buried his tongue between her lips. It was sweet heaven for both of them as they explored the inside of one another's mouths. Tongues danced when they weren't nibbling swollen lips.

"Hmmm," Andy sighed against her cheek. "You taste like wine again. I think I want to taste your other sweetness." His lips traveled downward as he reached to cup a swollen breast.

Her hand rested on his shoulder and urged him to stop the delightful path of his lips.

Andy's head came up as he questioned her with his eyes.

"I know that you're more powerful than I am. I'm just a mere woman who tried to take your kingdom. Let's rule together and enjoy our lives forever." Payton was back in character.

Andy fell into the mood just as quickly. "How can I know that I can trust you forever. You might try to overthrow me in the future."

She sat up and used the palm of her hand against his bare chest to get him to lie on his back. "I haven't screamed yet, have I?"

His eyes narrowed in promise. "You will before I get done with you." They instantly widened, however, when she grasped his cock. He rose slightly on one elbow as his thighs dropped open.

Payton continued to stare into his eyes even as she felt him immediately grow hard in her hand. "Let me prove to you how trustworthy I am," she breathed out. "I want you to fill my body with heat. Now, lie back and let me show you."

When he was flat against the pillows, Payton smiled at him again, lifted her knee, and straddled his chest with her ass pointing toward his face.

The sight of her pussy dangling above his face drove Andy to grab her ass with both hands and massage her cheeks.

No words were necessary as she dipped her head and took his penis into her mouth. Spreading her knees further apart, she lowered her body to Andy's waiting mouth.

He licked her pussy once and waited. Payton's lips tightened around his cock, and she sucked harder between the gentle swirls of her tongue around his smooth head.

Andy pulled her ass closer, spread her pussy lips, and darted his tongue in and out of her. He felt her immediate response by the tightening of her fist around his erection and with more avid sucking.

Payton worked her hips above his searching mouth. She controlled the motion of running her clit back and forth across his tongue, knowing that an orgasm wasn't far away.

Andy continued to lick greedily at her pussy, and then inserted a thumb into her hole as he ground his mouth against her clit. He recognized his wife's body motions as she wiggled around his pumping finger. Payton was close. Andy was going to make her come time and time again before he was through with her. She could suck his cock all she wanted—it was his turn now to drive her insane with passion.

Andy withdrew his tongue from the pussy that bounced above his face, removed his thumb, and dipped two fingers between her lips and deep inside her.

Payton slammed against his hand. A second later, the pulsing of her orgasm was felt. Andy watched his fingers as they disappeared time after time into her vagina, loving that his wife was sucking like wild on his penis because of what he was doing to her.

As she collapsed on top of him, Andy rolled from beneath her and flipped her to her back. His hot gaze devoured her. "You're mine now, and I'm going to keep fucking you and playing with your pussy and sticking my cock in your mouth until you're weak."

Payton grabbed his shoulders and yanked his mouth down to her own. "I want it rough." She lapped at his mouth and squirmed beneath him. "Fuck me hard when you do it, Andy. Nothing else will do. Tell me what you want me to do and the kingdom is yours."

He straddled her chest, his stomach jumping around wildly when she opened her mouth. She took his entire length to the back of her throat, and then bobbed her head again, sucking and drawing the life from him. His hips pumped to the rhythm she set as perspiration beaded his forehead. Payton was a wild woman.

He jumped up and helped her to her feet before he came again. Lifting her into his arms, Andy hurried across the middle of the room to the narrow raised bed. Gently, but with force nonetheless, he bent her forward over the center, yanked her legs apart and entered her with a hard thrust.

Payton grunted at his urgency, and then grasped the handles screwed to the sides of the bed. She spread her legs further. "Fuck me, Andy. Make me come again."

He grabbed her hips and slammed her back onto his cock. Payton tightened her grip on the handles and met each thrust with determination as he continued to hold her firmly and fuck her wildly.

Payton's chest bounced against the surface of the bed, but she rocked against him with all her might. The feel of his cock slamming against her cervix only excited her. Hot sparks of fire began to build. "Yes! That's how I want it. Fuck me harder. Make me scream!"

Andy reached around her waist and stroked her clit with force as he continued to nearly lift her off her feet with each long thrust.

Payton's body burst into flames. She screamed against the flat of the bed as he pounded into her, each stroke intensifying her orgasm. "Oh, God!"

He fucked her until the waves of her climax disappeared, then withdrew, lifted her into his arms once more and carried her to the wall. Propping her against the padded surface, Andy dragged her hands upwards and easily locked the handcuffs around her wrists.

Payton's eyes were dark with desire as she stared at him — daring him to keep going. "Fuck me, Andy."

Rather than shackle her ankles, he cupped her ass and lifted her in the air and waited until she gripped her fingers around the soft leather straps attached to the wall. He guided her down onto his cock, taking most of her weight with his muscled arms and letting her back rest against the soft surface behind her.

Payton's breasts shook with each deep thrust into her pussy. She never took her eyes from his as he worked her hips up and down.

The thought that he might come never crossed his mind, so intent was he on watching his wife's face and waiting for her to find her own release again. As rough as he was with her body, he continually assured that she wasn't being hurt. He maintained a firm hold on her ass.

The sexual position was hot and exciting. Andy slid easily into her time after time. Payton not only felt his thick cock filling her, but felt the constant pressure of his erection grinding against her clit. Once again, she felt the first stirrings of another orgasm.

"Can you make me come again?" she managed to grind out through clenched teeth. "Are you sultan enough to prove you're stronger than me?"

Andy became motionless as he stared into her hot gaze and withdrew from her body.

"Andy…don't stop!"

"I don't intend to."

He dropped to his knees, yanked her legs apart and wrapped her thighs around his neck, while burying his tongue into her pussy.

Payton yearned to thread her fingers through the hair at his moist temples, but couldn't because her hands were still held captive to the wall. She glanced down to see the top of Andy's head buried between her legs. His broad shoulders shone with beads of perspiration.

He adjusted his position slightly, always assuring that his wife was comfortable, and two fingers joined his tongue.

Payton's head lolled against the wall to catch her breath. Gripping the straps tighter, she began to rock her pussy against his mouth, clamping her muscles tightly to keep his fingers inside of her.

Andy sucked her clit and vigorously finger fucked her.

"Oh, God…" Payton groaned. The hot waves started from between her spread legs and burned a path to her breasts.

In one fluid motion, Andy had his cock inside of her to feel the pulsing waves wrap tightly around him.

"Yes—" Payton panted beside his ear.

He stroked three times and impaled her on his erection as he came in wave after wave. Burying his head into his wife's neck, Andy breathed in the scent of her warm, perspiring body, the musky scented heat from their lovemaking, and knew he'd never love anyone like the woman who clasped her legs around his waist.

Andy dragged his mouth to hers and was met with warm lips. Using his knee to hold her upright against the wall, it took only a few quick flicks of his wrist and strong fingers to release her from the handcuffs.

Payton's arms dropped as she wrapped them tightly around his neck.

Andy carried her back to the pillows, laid her gently on her back, and then collapsed beside her. Pulling her closer, he tucked her damp forehead into the crook of his neck. Slowly, their breathing returned to normal.

A tired smile creased his face just before he fell asleep as her quiet words reached his ears.

"The kingdom is yours…"

Chapter 20: Andy's Ecstasy

Payton's eyes fluttered open. Knowing that the warm band of steel against her back was her husband, she wiggled her body deeper into his protective embrace and waited to see if the movement would waken him.

"It's about time you quit snoring." He pinched her butt.

Payton squealed and jumped from the bed in a flurry of tossed blankets. Rubbing her ass, she spun in his direction with her eyebrows slanted deeply over the bridge of her petite nose.

"You're a turd. I was all nice and comfortable, then here you go and be mean to me—especially when it's our last day here."

Andy stretched his arms, a smile resting on his mouth, and stared at her naked body. "How could I resist. Your ass was resting right in my hand." He yawned and threw his legs over the edge of the bed. "God, my muscles are stiff. As much as I would love to stay here for at least another week, I think even two more days would probably kill us."

His observation was so sincere that Payton burst out laughing. Leaping onto the bed, she grabbed him from behind and used her weight to knock him off balance and sideways to the bed. She scrambled up and straddled his stomach with a huge grin splitting her face. "Come on, you're not an old man!"

Andy reached up and cupped both breasts in his hands. "No, but you're aging me quickly with all your lurid demands on my body."

"Me? I'm making the demands? You're the one that wanted to come here because you weren't getting enough ass on a regular basis. Now, it's my fault because I'm having the time of my life?"

A giggle burst from her throat when he flipped her body to the mattress and pinned her beneath one muscular thigh. He dropped his mouth and teased her lips open to receive his kiss. "Mmmmm...Payton, my dear wife, as much as I want you, I've got to have something to eat. I almost hate to waste the time when the clock is ticking towards check out, but what's a guy to do."

Nibbling on his lower lip, Payton sighed and ran her fingers through the curls lying against the nape of his neck. "I hate to think of leaving, too. Promise me, Andy, that we won't let life get in the way again. Let's always be like this. I want to always be hungry for you. I want to always feel your passionate gaze heating my blood."

"I promise. Let's make a pact. As soon as things start to get away from us, either you or I have to grab it back for the other."

* * * * *

"Okay, wench, take your robe off. I want to see that beautiful body of yours." His eyes narrowed and a grin tugged at the corners of his mouth as his eyes swept her from head to toe. "Lady, you are one sexy woman. We've only got a few hours left. Want to come over here and play?" Andy patted his lap.

Payton placed her hands on her hips where she stood in the middle of the room and jutted her breasts in his direction. They had ordered a huge breakfast and now she felt energized and ready to take him on. It was going to be a morning to remember. "The thought entered my mind. I was just thinking of what we could do that's different." Her eyes darted to the cabinet set against the far wall. "You won't have an entire cabinet of sex toys at your disposal."

"Who gives a shit? The only thing we've used so far is that game the first night we arrived." He left his chair and stood before her with a few quick steps. Yanking her close, Andy sighed with enjoyment at the feel of her breasts pressed against him. "I don't need toys. I have these," he wiggled his hand between them and touched the mounds lying beneath the soft terry robe she wore, "and this," his hands quickly left her breasts and found her round ass, "and especially this." He snaked a palm around her hip, wiggled his hand through the folds of material, and inserted a finger into her. Payton's mouth dropped open. He couldn't help himself when he kissed her. "And the most beautiful mouth I've ever kissed."

Payton playfully pushed him aside, strutted past him, and poked a slender finger into his firm belly. "Last one in the shower is a rotten egg!" Payton bolted across the carpet and disappeared into the bathroom.

Andy tore his robe off and nearly tripped on the garment as he raced after her. He was hot for her again — evidenced by the hard-on that poked up in the air as he entered the bathroom behind her.

Payton was just slipping into the hot shower. Andy followed quickly, backed her up against the shower wall and laughed when she squealed from the instant contact with the cold tile. He wouldn't let her go though, and instead, trapped her between his arms and kissed her deeply. When he was through, he raised his head and watched her face.

Sultry eyes glittered up at him. "Even though I enjoyed that kiss, you're going to pay for that cold tile trick."

"You'll have to torture me then, I guess. Tell me what a bad boy I am."

She pushed him slightly away, then reached out to run her fingers across his firm chest. Her blue eyes chanced a glance down to his erection, and a wicked smile touched her lips.

A slow, sensuous walk of her fingers brought her hand down to his cock. She pushed him back against the tile of the far wall with her other hand and enjoyed his little gasp when his back touched the cool tile. Her fingers wrapped around the length of him as she stared into his eyes. Andy held his breath to see what would come next.

Payton ran her tongue slowly across her lips and eyed him closely. "You've been such a bad boy. It's time to make you do penance."

She used her hand on his cock and the other placed on his shoulder to guide him to the molded bench in the shower. Andy willingly obeyed, watching her every movement with anticipation.

Payton sank gracefully to her knees, and grasped his balls in her other hand. She continued to play with his genitals, never taking her gaze from his.

"Do you like how this feels?"

Andy's breath caught in his throat, so he simply nodded in silent response. He found it hard to believe that his wife was once again acting out a fantasy he had dreamed about many times. His eyes closed momentarily as he relished the feeling of her hand gently sliding up and down the length of his hard cock. He swallowed and finally found his voice. "I'm sorry for pushing you against the cold tile. I'll do whatever it takes to make it up to you—as long as you keep doing that." The pressure around his erection increased. He jumped slightly and opened his eyes again. "Payton—if you stop, I'll die."

He watched, mesmerized, when she bent her head and swirled her tongue around the tip of his penis. His stomach muscles contracted. She had never enjoyed giving him a blowjob before—not ever. It was one thing he had never asked of her. Now he relished the pleasure of her hot mouth around him for the third time in one weekend.

"Do you like this?" she asked, then nibbled on his cock, tasting the salty pre-ejaculate that bubbled across the tip.

"Jesus Christ, Payton..." his head fell back against the tile.

She smiled, feeling powerful and joyful at the same moment. It was because of her that Andy found himself in the state he was in now. Grasping his erection more firmly in her hand, she wrapped her mouth around his shaft and slowly slid down his hard length, wondering how this could have so sexually turned her off in the past. Since the blowjobs in the fantasy room, the taste of his penis in her mouth had occupied her thoughts constantly.

A whoosh of air left Andy's mouth. He reached out and gently guided her head as she sucked him. The swirl of her tongue around his swollen head nearly drove him mad. It was when she licked at the slit in the end to lap up the pre-ejaculate, then slid her lips over him again, that he began to fuck her mouth with a rhythmic motion.

Warm water pelted off his wife's back to spray small droplets erotically across his chest. He felt the beginnings of heat dart through his belly and pushed her head away. "You've got to stop or I'm going to come in your mouth."

Payton looked up at him. The desire that shone in her eyes shocked him. "I come in your mouth, don't I? I want to suck you until you come. I want to see what your face looks like when I do that to you."

She lowered her head, but never took her eyes from his clenched jaw. Her tongue caressed the length of his cock. Her hands continued to gently fondle his balls. Her mouth slid back up the length of him, nibbling, tantalizing, coming close to driving him over the edge.

Andy sat mesmerized when her lips circled the head of his penis. She began to suck gently, bobbing her head slightly each time she circled his width with her tongue.

Payton's hand moved to circle his penis with her fingers, and she began to stroke. She sucked harder and increased her tempo, and still watched him closely.

Andy's head fell back to rest on the shower wall. She could feel the motion of his hips as he pumped to the tempo she set. His fingers curled tightly around the shower seat.

She sucked harder. Her hand moved faster.

Andy arched against her hand with a throaty groan. Warm liquid spurted into her mouth. His eyes were closed tightly and his mouth hung open.

Payton leaned back, swallowed the semen in her throat and let him finish coming on her chest. She jerked her hand up and down his shaft until he was empty. The hot spray of the shower washed the semen from her chest as she waited for him to catch his breath.

Andy rolled his head, opened his eyes, and gave her a slack-jawed grin. "Jesus Christ, Payt. That was fantastic. I feel like a limp dish rag."

Payton stood, cupped her breasts with her hands, and leaned forward to rub them across his slick chest. Andy tipped his head and captured an erect nipple. He sucked on it, swirled his tongue around the tiny dart, then moved to its twin. "Christ, you have beautiful breasts."

His hand rubbed up her thigh and slid around to her pussy. He watched her face as his thumb came in contact with her clitoris. He could feel how wet she was when he dipped a finger between her folds.

Payton automatically spread her legs to give him better access. "God, Andy, that feels so good."

He played for only a few seconds, then stood. "Let's get the hell out of here."

Chapter 21: The Tease

Andy pulled her through the shower doorway, reached for a towel, and gently wiped the warm water from her quivering body. He patted her breast, her ass, and her flat stomach.

She simply smiled, second-guessing her earlier plans. Did she have the nerve to bring it up? Payton remained thoughtful when he took her hand and led her back to the bed. She laid down, reached out her arms, and Andy was wrapped in her embrace a moment later.

"I love you," she whispered against his mouth. "What else do you want me to do for you? I want to make you happy."

Andy wasn't about to second-guess the change in her. He planned to reap the rewards.

"What's left? You'll never be able to top that blowjob." He dipped his head and kissed her. "That was one of the most fantastic things that's happened to me in a long time. Thank you."

Payton rolled from his arms, stood beside the bed, and jutted out her breasts. Andy rolled to an elbow, completely surprised that she had left his embrace so quickly. He watched his wife reach up and pluck at her nipples with a sexy, wicked smile in place again. "I want to try something else. Pick something out from the cabinet. Ask me to do something that you've always wanted to see me do."

He stared at her and, suddenly, something came to mind. He grinned back. "What if it's too over the edge for you?"

"Try me."

Andy leaped from the bed and headed for the cabinet. A second later, he pulled out a box and handed it to her.

Her eyes widened. "A vibrator?"

"Yup. I saw this when we first got here. You've never used one before." One dark eyebrow lifted. "Have you?"

She laughed at his comical expression. "No, I haven't. But I thought about it this morning. This is exactly what I was thinking about when I told you to check out the cabinet."

"Ha! Great minds think alike."

"What exactly do you want to do with it? Do you want to use it on me or do you want to watch?"

"Use it on yourself. I wanted to watch you make yourself come."

A giggle bubbled in her throat. "There's a little of the voyeur in you, isn't there?"

He pulled her naked body next to his and nuzzled her neck. "Watching you make yourself come would blow me away."

She stepped away. "All right, I asked you what you wanted me to do, and I'll do it. You just sit back and we'll give it a try. In fact, I think you'll enjoy the show." She took the boxed vibrator from his hands, then stopped and raised her chin with a cagey smile on her lips. "Can I add something of my own?"

He nodded eagerly.

"All right. Come and sit on the bed with me. In fact, just sit upright on your knees."

Andy scooted across the room, climbed on the bed, and kneeled. He placed his big hands on his hips and waited with a huge grin on his face.

Payton unwrapped the vibrator and the lubricating jelly that came with it, then leisurely strolled to the edge of the bed to look at him. "Okay. I have a little game in mind. No matter what we do, you can't touch me with your hands or with your cock. I can touch you if I'm so inclined, but I'm off limits as far as you're concerned."

Andy smiled wider. "So, you've turned into a bitch again."

"Yup. One that's going to drive you to distraction."

Andy crossed his arms over his chest. "Okay, babe, let's see what you got." She excited the hell out of him.

Payton joined him on the king-sized mattress, leaned against the high footboard, and slowly sucked on one of her fingers. She brushed the vibrator across her heavy breasts, never taking her eyes from her husband's face while drifting a path across her stomach and down across her outer thighs with the tip of the sex toy. She kept her legs closed.

Andy's gaze followed the vibrator closely, waiting for her to open herself, but Payton continued to play along the outsides of her hips, then back to her breasts, then over to the curly mound nestled in the apex of her closed legs.

It was easy to see that the teasing motions were starting to affect Andy. His chest began to balloon slightly with each breath.

"Do you like watching me?" Payton purred.

"You know I do."

"But I bet you want to see more."

"No shit. Are you going to spread your legs?" Andy wanted to yank them open, but he enjoyed the game and would play by her rules.

"Hmmm, maybe—we'll see. You know, I think you need to move further away. I'm a little concerned you might... break... and want to touch me."

Andy crawled backwards, positioned himself again, and waited.

Payton slid to her back, careful not to open her legs, and then rolled to her side to hide her pubic mound from his gaze. She twisted slightly so her breasts would also be hidden and continued to rub the vibrator along the length of her thigh.

"I like the feel of this against my skin." She watched him closely for any reaction.

Andy sat tight-lipped. For a first timer with a vibrator, she was really getting to him.

Payton sighed deeply in exaggeration and circled her lips with the rubber tip. "I wonder what this will feel like inside of me."

"Not as good as me."

"We'll have to see." She sat up on her knees, turned from him, allowing her husband to only view her buttocks as they rested against her calves and the slender feminine curve of her back. Payton rubbed the vibrator about her shoulders to assure that Andy saw it. Then she slowly dragged it across the front of her body until it rested between her closed thighs. She turned her head to glance over her shoulder at her husband.

Andy's eyes narrowed.

Payton made a slow pumping motion with her arms, teasing Andy into thinking she was rubbing the vibrator against her clitoris. "Oooo, that feels good. Too bad you can't see."

His arms fell to his sides.

"No—you have to stay there."

"I wasn't going anywhere."

"Just making sure." Her brow furrowed in deep thought. "What would you like to see me do now?"

All he wanted to do was bang the hell out of her. Screw the vibrator along with the chance to watch her. His wife's teasing was getting the best of him. But, he sucked up his need with a deep sigh. "Do I have a choice in the matter?"

"Of course you do—as long as you don't touch me."

"I want you to turn around, get on your back, and spread your legs so I can see your pussy."

"It's really wet. I'm turning myself on."

"You're turning me on. Do it."

Payton smiled and rolled sensuously to her back, then spread her legs for his viewing.

Andy almost came on the mattress with just the sight. He was rock hard again with just the sight of her glistening folds.

"What now, loverboy?"

"Spread your legs farther apart and fuck yourself with the vibrator."

Payton flicked the ON switch. Instantly, a low whirring noise filled the room. She grasped the pulsating instrument with both hands and ran the tip down her slit, then back up again. Hot jolts swept through her stomach. She didn't know if it was the idea of sticking the thick vibrator inside her or Andy's look of yearning that settled in his eyes that turned her hot now.

She kept her eyes on him. "I don't think I'll even need any jelly because I'm so wet."

Andy agreed with her silently and clenched his jaw.

Payton inserted the vibrator and slid it all the way up her pussy, thrilled with the new experience of the pulses that stroked the inside of her vagina. She tipped it slightly to throb against her clitoris. Her head fell back with the wonderful sensation that coursed through her.

She nearly forgot Andy watching her as she began to pump against the vibrator, wrapped in the hot feelings that mounted as she fucked herself. She arched her hips and knew it wouldn't be long before she was rewarded with an orgasm.

She was right. She gasped as her muscles clenched around the thick length inside her, and she rocked until the hot flames subsided.

Her knees fell open as the last shiver raked her insides. Payton left the vibrator inside her as she massaged her breasts, then opened her eyes to spy Andy with fists clenched at his sides. Pre-ejaculate dripped from the tip of his penis.

"That was incredible. I want to fuck you, Payton."

Chapter 22: The Gift

She withdrew the vibrator, flicked the OFF switch and tossed it to the floor. Andy made a move in her direction. She quickly held up her palm. "No. Stay there. The rules were stated. You can't touch me unless I say it's okay."

"Come on, I don't know if I can do it. I want to be inside you." His erection throbbed with the thought.

"Well, you'll just have to wait." Payton was warmed to the idea of driving him out of his mind. She knew what the reward would be when she finally let him have her. Besides, she'd made the decision to allow Andy to do something to her that she'd always stopped before. He would see that waiting had been worth it.

She crawled close enough to him to feel the heat of his skin and kissed one of his nipples. Andy flinched and sucked in his breath.

"I love your body." She ran a hand down the bulging muscles of his arm and back up to caress his shoulder. "I know what it feels like to have you hold me in your strong arms. I know what it feels like to be kissed by you. You make me burn inside."

She pressed her lips to his cheek and quickly backed away when he turned his mouth to capture hers. His low growl met her ears, but she had to give him credit. He kept his hands to his sides.

Cupping her breasts, Payton rubbed the erect nipples against his broad chest as she had done earlier in the shower. Andy was breathing harder.

"Do you like that?" she asked while staring into his pained expression.

His eyes narrowed again. "I'm going to say to hell with your rules pretty soon."

"But that would take the fun out of it."

"I'm going to make you pay for this."

"That's what I'm counting on—but only when I say you can." She grabbed his erection, slid her hand down to the base and back up again; and then crawled away.

"Payton—" he growled out between raspy breaths. "How fucking long—"

"I'm thinking about letting you touch me with one finger."

He dropped his hands to the mattress and eagerly leaned forward.

"Not yet though."

"You're a rotten tease."

"But you love me for it, don't you."

He finally smiled. "You know I do. You make me hot to be inside of you. You turn me on like no other woman I've ever met."

The words melted her heart. She knew he spoke them from the depths of his soul, even though they were in the middle of her sex game. "I love you, too, Andy. I love you so much that I would trust you with anything." She wanted to kiss him, but knew it would be the end of the fantasy she had already played out in her quick mind.

Payton placed a hand on his shoulder. "Back up a little and give me some more room. I want to show you something."

Andy obeyed like a trained puppy.

175

Payton rolled to her hands and turned her ass in his direction to give him a complete view of her backside and her wet pussy. She arched slightly and looked over her shoulder again.

"You said you liked my ass."

"I more than like it."

"Maybe I'll let you touch it."

"Come on, Payton."

She reached for the tube of lubricating jelly and flipped it across the mattress in his direction. Sudden, surprised understanding of what she planned blazed in his eyes.

Payton swayed her backside back and forth before him. "I want you to lubricate only one finger. That's all you can use right now. If you're gentle, I might let you fuck me in the ass."

Another look of surprise widened his eyes as he rushed to pop the cover open. Andy spread the lubricant on one finger, and then used his other hand to make sure the digit was completely covered with the thick gel. He looked up expectantly, his eyes dark with desire.

Payton almost gave up the game. "Be gentle with me. Use only one finger at first. Make me ready for you, Andy. I can't wait to feel you inside me, but I want to take it slow."

Andy crawled between her spread knees and stared at her ass when she dropped her chest to the mattress and settled her head on a pillow. "I can't believe you're going to let me do this. I've wanted to for so long, but you always said no. I just gave up the notion completely."

She remained quiet, but he saw the smile on her lips against the pillow.

Andy squirted one more lump of lubricant on the end of his finger and reached out to rub it against her anus. Until now, this sort of sex was definitely off limits. But that was the other Payton. The one bent before him offered herself completely—and with total acceptance that he wouldn't hurt her.

Her anus was soft against his finger. Andy rubbed the gel around the edge of her rectum, and then slowly slipped the tip of his finger into her ass. Payton gasped into the pillow, but urged him on with slight movements against his hand.

He worked his finger further inside, amazed that nothing had ever made him this hot before. Her tight ass squeezed around his finger. His erection ached. Andy continued to slide the digit in and out, careful to follow the line of her rectum and not hurt her.

"How does that feel?" he whispered.

"Oh, God, Andy, like nothing I've ever experienced."

"I can't wait to stick my cock in you."

Her blonde head rolled on the pillow. Why hadn't she ever let him do this before? "Use two fingers now. Make sure I'm stretched."

He withdrew his hand and added lube to another finger. For good measure, he even squirted extra in her ass crack. As an afterthought, Andy filled his palm with lubricant and stroked his cock until it was covered. He was going to be damn good and ready when she finally let him enter her. There would be no waiting while he prepared himself.

A moment later, he was pumping in her again with one finger, and then slowly slipped another into her rectum. Payton reacted with a gasp and followed his motions with her hips. The finger fucking continued for another two minutes until she cried out.

"Andy, stick your cock in me! I'm ready for you. Don't make me wait any longer."

He grasped her hip in one hand and guided the tip of his dripping penis to her anus. Positioning his knees for better balance, Andy worked his cock inside her, slid as far as he could go, and then held her tightly against him with eyes squeezed tight.

"Don't move, Payton, or it'll be over if you do. God, you're tight."

She lay motionless before him, waiting for him to take the lead, afraid to tell him how she loved his cock in her this way because he might come before she wanted him to. She curled her fingers into the pillow and waited.

The telltale inhale and exhale of deep breaths as Andy fought an orgasm revealed his struggle. A full thirty seconds passed before she felt the pressure of his hands tighten at her waist. He began to stroke slowly.

She waited for his momentum to increase, then met each one. The strokes became faster and harder. Soon, her ass slapped against his upper thighs as the heat built again. Andy grunted each time he pounded into her, and she slid the length of his penis time after time.

"Andy! I'm almost there!"

And then it appeared. Flaming, intense sparks of heat burst inside her anus, raced through her clitoris, and burned a path from her belly to her breasts. Payton screamed out her husband's name with the intensity of the orgasm. It ripped through her body as Andy slammed her against him and impaled her on his pulsating cock.

He came in waves that caused his stomach muscles to clench, his heart to race, and his grunts to turn to strangled groans.

"Payton—" he ground out, "fuck...fuck—that was wild!" He withdrew from her ass and collapsed next to her on the bed. Both were slick with sweat and neither could say another word until they were able to catch their breaths.

No words were needed, however. Andy dragged her body close, slanted his mouth across hers, and drank in the sweetness of the inside of her mouth. Payton's tongue danced with his. The exploration of each other's mouth was as erotic as the sex they'd had over the last two days.

He couldn't get enough of her. The love that he'd always had for Payton multiplied with each hot kiss she returned. Eager hands left a path of fire as they traveled over her velvety skin, and Andy would be forever grateful he'd decided to do something to rekindle the sexual experiences of an earlier time in their marriage. He communicated that with his actions and murmurs of whispered love in her ear.

He wouldn't question what was responsible for the many reasons he loved Payton or how he had ever discovered someone like her in the first place. Just holding his sexy wife in his arms and knowing the pleasure she experienced was simply because of what he did to her body was enough.

Andy and Payton were ready to return home.

Chapter 23: Passion Ever After

Four months had passed since the two spent the wonderful weekend in Detroit. Both worked hard to find the private time to be together, but it became more and more difficult as each month passed. The kids constantly needed to be driven to various school functions, Payton received a promotion that seemed to occupy her every waking minute, and just life in general kept them on the run.

She was leaving work one Friday night, toting a briefcase full of files that she would need to go through before Monday. It was the last thing she wanted to do.

As she slid behind the wheel of her Blazer, Payton grasped the wheel and rested her forehead against the hard plastic warmed by the sun. Thoughts of *Sex & Love, Inc.* raced in her brain.

"God, I want to go back there," she whined quietly to herself. "No responsibilities, no kids…" Her head snapped up. A dawning smile creased her face. "Why in hell didn't I think of this sooner?"

She ripped open her purse, dug around until she found her cell phone, and quickly dialed Andy's mother.

"Hello?"

"Hi, Mary, this is Payton."

"Why, hello Payton. I didn't expect to hear from you so soon."

Payton's brow furrowed with a frown. What was her mother-in-law talking about?

"Mary, I hate to bother you with this, but do you think you—"

"Excuse me one minute, dear. George? Could you please check on Sara? She was standing next to me a minute ago and disappeared into the kitchen. Tell the boys it's time for dinner. Okay, Payton, sorry about the interruption. What did you need?"

Payton's brain swirled. She had just about been ready to ask Andy's mother to take the kids for the weekend. They were already at her house. *Andy must be visiting.* "Is Andy there? Could I talk to him?"

"Oh, no, dear. He's left already. Said you two needed to get on the road. I hope you have a nice weekend planned. He said you've been working real hard lately."

An even wider smile split her face. Payton looked heavenward and mouthed a 'thank you'. Apparently, Andy was one step ahead of her again. "All right, then. Well, thanks Mary for taking the kids. I guess I better get going."

"No problem, dear. You have a good time. I'll see you Sunday night."

Payton clicked the OFF button, dropped her phone on the seat, and peeled out of the parking lot.

* * * * *

"Payton..."

She rushed through the kitchen door. Andy sat on a stool by the snack bar. She raced across the floor and into his waiting arms. Andy lowered his lips and captured her mouth. The heat of his kiss built as he pulled her between his legs. His mouth slanted across hers and Payton responded with enthusiasm when his arms tightened around her tiny waist.

Andy ran his hands down the slim length of her back, cupped her ass and pulled her tighter against his growing erection.

Payton couldn't help but grind her mound against it. The memories of an entire weekend alone with him filled her senses.

"Jesus Christ, Payt," he murmured between hot kisses, and then brought a hand to her breast, "what if one of the kids come in."

"Don't pull that shit with me," she smiled against his warm lips. "I called your mother to see if she would take the kids over the weekend. Imagine my surprise when I discovered they were already there. Thank you, thank you, and thank you! I've been dreaming about this. God, I love you, and I love how we think alike." She leaned back and played with the front of his shirt. "Are we really going somewhere?"

"Nah, that was a little fib. I had thought about making reservations in Detroit, but didn't want to spend eight hours of my weekend behind the wheel of a car. I'd rather spend it fucking the hell out of you." He flashed her a sexy grin. "It's been too long since we've had two days alone."

"Then take me, Andy."

He rose from the stool and grabbed her elbow, intent on getting her through the kitchen door and up the stairs as quickly as possible.

She grabbed his arm, however, to halt his flight and molded herself against his body once more, then wiggled a hand between them. A second later, she stroked the outline of his erection through his slacks.

"Here, Andy, do it to me here. I can't wait until we get upstairs." She pulled at his belt to loosen the offending strip of leather between her and the penis she wanted to free.

"Christ, Payton, I'm goddamned glad I decided to dump the kids on my mom."

Payton's fingers worked furiously to free his cock. She finally had his zipper down and slid her hand into the slit of his boxer shorts. A second later, she held his hot length in her hand.

Andy growled his excitement and yanked her skirt up to her hips. Payton let go of his erection and grasped his shoulders for balance when he dragged her panties down her long legs. She was infinitely thankful she wasn't wearing pantyhose. Her leather sandals skidded across the kitchen floor when she kicked them off.

His large hands encompassed her waist and, a second later, she was perched on the edge of the breakfast nook table. Andy's finger immediately plunged into her pussy as he used his other hand to yank his pants and boxers around his hips.

"Christ, you're wet. Fuck...I don't know how long I can wait," he murmured as his hot lips seared a path across her collarbone. He inserted two fingers and pumped his hand wildly against her. His thumb ground against her clitoris.

Her flailing hand found his erection and she guided it between her spread legs. "Fuck me, Andy," she gasped. "Make me come!"

He needed no other encouragement. Andy grabbed a chair cushion and shoved it behind her on the table. He pushed her back and buried himself inside her a second later.

Payton gasped and met his thrusts, feeling the hot fire of desire spread through her belly. "Yes, Andy! Fuck me hard!" She clung to his shoulders and rocked against him.

He growled against her lips between strokes. "I can't wait for you, Payton!"

"Andy! I'm…"

Her pussy clenched around his shaft. Payton gasped as her head fell back. Andy plunged inside her, then joined her as wave after wave of cum let loose. His strokes slowed, but he continued to move inside her slowly. Muscular arms wrapped around her shoulders, and she was forced upwards to meet his lips.

Andy drank in the taste of his wife's lips, happier than he had ever been. Payton met his kisses, darting her tongue inside his mouth to search out the warmth she knew she'd find.

Heartbeats slowed until the kisses became soft and playful. Andy leaned back and stared at Payton's heavy-lidded gaze. She smiled her beautiful smile. It was only for him. He helped her to straighten further, assured that she was balanced safely on the edge of the table, and surrounded her bare hips with his hands.

His head shook slowly. "That's only a prelude to what's going to take place this weekend. I didn't hurt you, did I?"

Her smile stretched across her face. "I wouldn't have noticed if it did. Andy, I'm sorry it took so long to get home. I thought about this at every damned red stoplight, and then nearly ran over an old lady crossing the street!"

He burst out laughing as he pictured her driving like a maniac just to get home to have sex with him. Pulling her spread body back towards him, he nestled his wife intimately against him. "This morning, I made a decision. I wanted you all to myself. I've been at enough Little League games to make me gag. All I thought about today was getting you into bed with no interfering phone calls or kids whining. This was better than I planned, though. We never even made it to the bedroom." He chuckled and kissed her again.

"Are the kids really gone for the entire weekend?"

"Yup."

She wrapped her slender arms around his neck and was rewarded when he lifted her into his arms. Payton glanced up expectantly. "Sweeping me up to the boudoir?"

"Take a look around. You won't see these four walls until Sunday."

He adjusted her body in his grip and carried her through the doorway to the staircase across the living room. Before she knew it, they were in the master suite, where he unceremoniously dumped her on the bed with a chuckle.

Payton laughed out loud when he bounced down next to her, and then sighed deeply when he ran a hand up the inside of her thigh.

About the author:

Ruby Storm was born and raised in Minnesota and has lived there her entire life. Spending time in the outdoors is something she still enjoys immensely, whether it be camping or working in her garden.

Being an avid reader and relishing her state's history is what prompted her to begin writing seven years ago. Ruby and her husband of twenty-eight years (also her high school sweetheart) have three children and many friends and family who have supported her desire to write. Being captivated with it, she doesn't plan to stop any time soon. She also plans to have a long and sizzling relationship with Ellora's Cave.

Ruby Storm welcomes mail from readers. You can write to her c/o Ellora's Cave Publishing at P.O. Box 787, Hudson, Ohio 44236-0787.

AUTHORS IN ECSTASY

Bella Andre

Chapter One

Luke gave Claire one of his trademark smoldering glances, the kind that kept her and her vibrator company when she was alone in bed at night, dreaming of him. After ten years of platonic friendship, after a painful decade of hearing about every woman who had passed in and out of Luke's bed, Claire knew it was time for things to change.

Maybe her new confidence came from the three Manhattans she'd already gulped down. Maybe it was because they were celebrating her promotion to Senior Vice President of SF BankCorp, and she was giddy with her newfound power. Whatever the reason, Claire simply didn't care about anything else tonight, outside of the promise she read in Luke's eyes.

Uncrossing her long, supple legs, and then re-crossing them slowly for impact, she scooted to the edge of her barstool and leaned in close to Luke in the steamy bar. Keeping her eyes trained on his mouth, she found the courage hiding deep within herself and said, "If I have to look at your succulent lips for one more second without tasting them, I think I'm going to go crazy."

Luke's eyes didn't widen in surprise. And he didn't make things any easier for her by leaning in to kiss her. Instead he raised an eyebrow, puckered his delicious lips slightly in a half-smile, and said, "Prove it."

The heat between Claire's legs increased several degrees and her nipples grew hard beneath her sexy silk top. For once in her life it was time to feel, not think. Leaning forward until she was so close she could feel his breath on her lips, she reached up with her thumb and gently stroked Luke's bottom lip. A shiver ran through her, and she felt as if her nipples were going to break through the fine silk of her top. She wondered if anyone else in the bar had noticed how incredibly turned on she was, but she forced the thought aside. She wasn't going to ruin her one chance at seducing the only man she'd ever loved because of what some strangers thought.

She had imagined feeling his lips on her breasts so many times, just touching them with her fingers was almost enough to make her spontaneously come in her seat. His lips were almost rough to the touch, and she wanted to explore every square millimeter of skin, from the corner where his upper and lower lips met so exquisitely, to the incredibly sexy, yet masculine bow in the middle of his upper lip.

Part of her wanted to go as slow as possible, to savor the sensations already washing through her in waves. But the other part of her, the part that made her pussy lips drenched and hot, wanted nothing more than to straddle Luke, right then and there at the bar, to sink down on his cock one inch at a time until she was on the edge of the best orgasm of her life.

Lighter than a feather, Luke darted his tongue against her thumb. Claire groaned, practically in pain, her need for him was so great. Grasping her wrist with his strong, warm hands, he held the fleshy part of her palm up to his mouth and nipped at her sensitive skin. Claire was shaking now and hornier than she'd ever been. Her pussy was soaked, all without one single kiss. But then again, just thinking of Luke had always been enough to bring her right to the brink.

She was so caught up in her need, she barely heard Luke whisper, "Taste me." Trying to break out of her fog, she moved to obey his command as quickly as she could. Closing the distance between them, taking his breath as her own, she licked at the middle of his lower lip with the tip of her tongue, the same place she had already memorized with her thumb.

"What flavor am I?" Luke asked her, again so softly she could barely make out his words.

Her head was spinning and she could hardly speak. "I need another sample," she said, and captured his incredible mouth in hers, tasting every inch of him, relishing in the feel of his tongue against hers. In her wildest dreams, she never knew a kiss could be so hot. She'd give up her vibrator forever for a lifetime supply of his kisses. Lord knew, if he kept it up, she was going to be moaning so loud everyone in the bar would be forced to stop their conversations to watch the live sex show happening right in front of them.

Luke pulled away from her and threw a $20 bill on the bar. Grabbing her hand, he pulled her off the seat and dragged her through the teeming crowd. Her skin was so inflamed, every time her nipples rubbed up against some stranger she had to bite her lip to keep from crying out. In the back of her mind, she wondered if she should be embarrassed that she was feeling so incredibly sexual.

No, she told herself. I'm going to take tonight as far as it can go. Tomorrow I'll go back to being the straight-laced banker the world thinks I am. Tonight, I'm a sex goddess!

Luke got them out the front door in record time and into the balmy summer night. Within seconds damp air made Clare's silk top cling to her like second skin. Luke promptly directed them down the nearest alley, nearly running in his haste.

Claire was breathing hard, but not from their quick pace. She knew what was about to happen, and on the verge of every single one of her dreams coming true, she was working hard not to hyperventilate in fervent expectation. Turning down another alley, this one even darker and narrower than the first, Luke stopped abruptly and pushed her against the cool brick wall. Reaching his hands under her shirt, he cupped her full, high breasts and squeezed her nipples while he leaned his head down to devour the pulse of her neck with his mouth and teeth.

"Luke," she moaned, *wrapping one of her long legs around him, trying to pull him in closer to her. She pleaded, "Fuck me now, I can't wait another second."*

He reached down to her short skirt and pulled the hem up to her hips. His hands searched for her panties to take them off, but all he found were moist, pink lips, readier for him than they had ever been.

"You're not wearing any panties," he growled into her mouth, consuming her lips once again as he slid two fingers into her pussy. "You're so wet," he said reverently against her lips, the bulge in his pants growing even more huge against her thigh.

Claire ground her hips into his hand, on the verge of exploding, and began to scream as an orgasm ripped through her. Luke covered her mouth with his, taking in her scream, muting it with his tongue.

As wave after wave coursed through her, Luke unzipped his pants and pulled out his cock. Wrapping her hand around it, he said, "I want you to guide me into you. Every single inch."

Claire's eyes widened. She always suspected he was big, but even in her wildest imaginings she couldn't have come up with this. His cock had to be at least ten inches long and two inches in diameter. Her dildo wasn't even this big and for a brief second she worried that she wouldn't be able to take all of him.

Luke must have sensed her reluctance, because he said, "Don't worry, baby. You're so wet I'm going to slide right in."

Grabbing her ass with his hands, he added, "Wrap your legs around me." Doing just that, suspended in mid-air, she positioned the tip of his cock at the entrance to her lips. Waiting for barely a second, wanting to remember the sensation of his cock entering her for the first time, she slid his head around on her lips, on her clit, until he was drenched with her juices. She could tell he wanted to plunge himself into her as hard and fast as he could, and she admired his restraint and the way he let her pace their lovemaking.

Slowly, painstakingly, Claire slid the first inch of him into her, and as the walls of her vagina stretched to accommodate his cock, she felt herself on the verge of another orgasm. Trying to contain her need, she slid in another inch and felt herself slipping and sliding along Luke's skin. Drenched in sweat, Luke managed to keep his hold on her, holding her up against the wall, poised on his cock as if she weighed no more than a fly.

Unable to wait another second, she let gravity pull her down and she fed the last eight inches of his cock into her pussy. Nothing had ever felt so good to her in her whole life and she fell into the second biggest orgasm she'd ever had as Luke squeezed her ass cheeks while lifting her up and down, sliding his cock in and out of her.

Pulling his head back to look deep into her eyes, he said, "I've always loved you," and then pumped into her, all the way to the hilt, rocking back and forth rapidly as he shot his seed deep within her. Claire went straight from two orgasms into three, even as her heart filled with the deepest joy she'd ever known.

Charlie saved his file and rubbed the tired muscles on the back of his neck with his hands. "Too bad real life can't be like my books," he muttered, trying to remember when the last time was he'd actually had sex.

"Ancient history," he grunted as he got up to take a shower. He had another blind date tonight, but he didn't have any higher hopes for this one than the multitude of other dates he'd been on in the past five years.

In fact, he wouldn't be surprised if all of the single women in San Francisco had been spreading the word about him, to warn each other off, in a show of female solidarity.

He let the scalding stream of water pulsate against his chest as he tried to shake off his depression. "She's out there. I know she's out there," he said aloud, his words reverberating against the tiled shower walls. Drying off and dressing quickly in chinos and a polo shirt, he slipped on his solid-platinum watch and grabbed his wallet and car keys.

Right on time he pulled up to the café and was pleased when he saw the cute blond sitting alone in a booth by the window. Getting out of his car, he walked up to her and held out his hand in greeting.

"Hi. I'm Charlie. Are you Sophie?"

The blond nodded happily. "I sure am," she drawled in a light Texas accent.

They ordered white wine and chatted as they sipped their drinks, beginning the process of getting to know each other better. Charlie could tell that Sophie liked what she'd seen so far. She wasn't so bad herself, and he hoped that she would be more open-minded than the last thirty or forty women he'd dated.

"So," she asked coyly, "what do you do all day? Your friend Bob didn't tell me much about your line of work. Is it something top secret?" she asked hopefully, all the while eyeing the platinum band of his watch, taking in the expensive Ralph Lauren label on his polo shirt, and the faded leather of his $500 Italian loafers.

Charlie smiled engagingly. "I'm a writer."

"Ooohhh," she said. "How exciting. What do you write? Mysteries? Action?"

"Actually," he said, striving for a confident tone, "I write erotica."

The silence was deafening. Not bothering to hide her sneer, his blind date said, "You're a porno writer?"

Charlie cleared his throat. "No, I write sensual romance. Women make up 99% of my audience. It's really quite…"

But before he could get another word out, his date stood up, said "You pervert!" and splashed her entire glass of ice water on his face. Then she grabbed her purse and stomped out on her four-inch heels, her tight little ass wiggling in outrage all the way down the street.

Charlie wiped the shards of ice off of his face and chest, while the waitstaff openly laughed at him.

"Wow. That's a first," he muttered to himself as he stood up and headed for his car. Usually his blind dates were satisfied with looking scandalized and making excuses about getting home early because the babysitter called with an emergency. At the very least, he had to give Sophie points for originality.

But no matter how he tried to frame the situation, he was sure of one thing: he wasn't getting any closer to finding the woman of his dreams.

Chapter Two

Evan laid Sara against the silk sheets and stood back to admire the way the firelight danced off of her creamy skin. She was the sweetest girl in the world, and he'd been waiting years for this moment.

Sara's cheeks were rosy and she nervously licked her pink, delicious mouth. "Are you going to take your clothes off too?" she asked him innocently.

Evan smiled and kneeled at the side of the bed between her legs, sliding her body across the silk sheets so that his face was mere inches from her sweet vagina. He didn't want to frighten her any more than she already was, but he was having a hell of a time trying to rein in his passion.

It pleased him immeasurably to know that Sara was a virgin, and that she had been saving herself for him, for their wedding night. He had waited so long for this night, for her to finally grow up. Of course, even though he had spent the past several years walking away from their chaste kisses and straight into cold showers, he had been with his fair share of women. But he always knew, no matter how good the sex was with these other women, he was simply releasing pent-up steam and honing his skills for the one woman who really mattered.

"I am, sweetheart," he said, stroking her hand lightly with his own. "But first I want you to experience deep pleasure."

"Oh, I have Evan. Your kisses are incredible," she sighed, trying to sit up so that she could kiss him again.

Getting up onto one knee, he leaned towards her and captured her mouth in a passionate, scintillating kiss. "Kissing is only the beginning," he said, promise in his eyes.

Sara opened her mouth into a darling "o" and blushed prettily. "Should I be doing anything?" she asked hesitantly, and Evan was touched by how much she wanted to please him.

"Oh my darling," he said, pushing his hands into her silky blond hair. "Just lay back against those pillows and I'll do the rest." Kissing her again lightly, he said, "And remember, there's nothing to be afraid of, because I love you and this is how I want to show you my love."

Sara followed his instructions and lay back against the pillows. He ran kisses down her neck and got caught up in worshiping her breasts.

He marveled at the sensual picture she presented. Her nipples were rosy and had formed into tight buds as he neared them. Even the swell of her breasts had a delicate pink flush, proving that she was as aroused as he was.

Cupping her breasts gently in his large hands, Evan ran his thumbs over her taut nipples and blew warm air across them. Sara gasped and he bent down to rain soft kisses all over her mounds, making sure he stayed away from the place she needed him to touch most. It wasn't until she was writhing on the bed in torment that he took pity on her and slowly took one nipple into his mouth, swirling the nub with his tongue, tasting her on his lips.

At that moment, Sara arched her back into him, pushing her breast even more deeply into his mouth and he nearly lost control of himself, more ready than ever to rip his clothes off and mount her like a stallion. Pulling from a deeper well of control than he knew he possessed, he continued to give loving attention onto her other breast, making her moan with pleasure.

Barely managing to pull himself away from her breasts, he nipped and kissed her flushed skin across her tight belly, while running his hands up and down her quivering thighs. His attention was soon wholly focused on the soft, wet mound before him.

Her blond, curly pubic hair was wet with her juices, and her scent was intoxicating. He ran his open hand down her stomach. Lightly, he slid his finger between her lips and then slowly into her incredibly tight pussy.

"Evan," she moaned, her head thrashing back and forth on the bed.

"Oh baby," he said, his voice thick with lust and emotion. "You have the sweetest pussy." He saw her eyes widen and slipped his finger back out, and stood up partway to kiss her again. "You're so beautiful. Am I making you feel good?"

Blushing again, Sara replied, "I've never felt like this before. Is it normal?"

Evan laughed softly and brushed the hair out of her eyes. "What we have is amazing, baby. Trust me," he added, "and I'll take you all the way to heaven."

Sara swallowed, and then said, "I do trust you."

Laying her back down, he knelt between her legs again. This time, he couldn't help himself, and he leaned in and tasted her wetness with his tongue. She nearly bucked off of the bed, and he held her thighs firmly with his hands to keep her pussy right where he wanted it – in his mouth.

He plunged his tongue into her several times before focusing on her swollen clitoris. Taking it into his mouth, he swirled his tongue around once, slowly. Then, taking the utmost care, he swirled it again. At a snail's pace, he teased her clit, savoring every moment of his fantasy becoming real.

Sara grabbed his head to push his face down harder into her mound and he knew she was on the verge of coming. He abruptly changed tactics and flicked her clit rapidly and firmly until she was crying out with joy, her spasms taking over her body for a long while.

Evan stood to remove his clothes as quickly as possible. Even the mere friction of fabric against his penis was almost more than he could bear, and he wanted to divest himself of his clothes and sink himself into Sara as soon as was humanly possible.

He was greatly pleased when Sara pushed herself up into sitting position and began to rip off his clothes in haste. But once they had pulled off his slacks together and were taking off his boxers, she stilled.

Looking up at him, she said, "I'm afraid, Evan."

Cupping her face in his hands, kissing her thoroughly, getting her used to her own sweet taste, he said, "I promise you, it will only hurt the first time. Only until you get used to having me inside of you."

Sara nodded and slowly reached for the waistband of his boxers, pulling them down his hips with excruciating slowness. When his shaft sprang free she gasped.

"You're so huge!" she exclaimed.

Evan chuckled softly, thrilled that she was so impressed with his cock. "And I'm all yours," he said as he took her small, soft hand in his and wrapped it around his shaft.

"Mmmm," Sara said. "You're hot too." She ran her hand up and down his length, getting used to the feel of him.

But Evan couldn't take any more teasing, so he gently pushed her back into the silk sheets and pulled himself up and over her, careful not to lean too much of his weight onto her. Placing the head of his cock at the entrance to her vagina, he gently probed her wetness.

The way Sara was writhing underneath him made him want to ram into her without waiting even one more second, but he wanted her first time to be perfect, so he governed his lust. Pushing in no more than an inch, then two, he heard her swift intake of breath and felt the barrier that guarded her most precious gift.

Poised above her, gazing deeply into her eyes, he said, "I never want to hurt you again," and then forced himself to push past her barrier, until he was practically touching her womb. She cried out softly in pain, but within moments he knew her virgin's muscles had adjusted to the feel of him as she began to rock her hips back and forth in an age-old rhythm of love.

Her body eagerly swallowed his cock and Evan lost all control, pumping hard and fast into her. Beneath him, Sara met every thrust and together they cried out in a magical simultaneous orgasm.

For Evan and Sara, their wedding night was the beginning of a lifetime of love, better than anything they could have ever conjured up in their dreams.

Candace finished reading the final words of her chapter and looked up at the faces of her new writing group expectantly. The silence was heavy in the library meeting room. She couldn't miss the shocked expressions on the faces of her fellow writers.

Several people cleared their throats, and to get the ball rolling Candace said, "I'd love to get some feedback on the ending of my story. I just wrote it yesterday, so it feels pretty fresh to me."

Sixty long, painful seconds ticked by before one of the older ladies spoke up. "Candace, I'm not sure about the, ahem, appropriateness of the passage you just read us."

"The appropriateness?" Candace exclaimed. "It's erotica, for god's sake. I'd say a sex scene is pretty damn appropriate." She searched the eyes of the other members of the group for some support, but found none.

Exasperated, she said, "I thought I made myself very clear with all of you before joining this group. I write erotica. Sexually explicit romantic fiction. That means there's sex in it. And you all said you were okay with it."

Right as a man and woman excused themselves from the room, a forty-ish man spoke up. "I thought it was an excellent passage, Candace. You perfectly captured your hero's deep feelings for the heroine."

"Thank you," Candace said, flashing a smile at him, but before she could feel better about her evening, an old biddy who had just contributed a story about her cat said, "I will not stand for such smut! I think we should take a vote right now. Who here wants to listen to this trashy porn?"

Only the middle-aged man half-raised his hand, giving Candace a sheepish grin, and she had the awful feeling that he was only voting for her because he thought she was easy.

Looking smug, the ringleader asked, "And who wants her to leave immediately?"

Everyone else raised their hands while their eyes shot daggers at her.

"Fine," Candace said, calmly slipping her papers back into her leather satchel. Swinging it up onto her shoulder she stood and left the room without a backwards glance.

She was none too surprised when she heard footsteps behind her in the hallway and turned to see her one supporter hurrying to catch up with her.

"Candace," he said, slightly out of breath. "I feel terrible about this."

"I'm sure you do," she said, a slight twinge of bitterness lacing her words.

"Even though this didn't work out, I was hoping that, ah, maybe I could take you out for dinner next Saturday."

Candace acted like she was considering his words carefully. Forcing a coy look onto her face she asked, "Is that all you want from me?"

Giving her a sleazy smile, he leaned in until she could smell his bad breath, and said, "I'm game for helping you try out some of your new scenes, any time you want."

Candace worked hard to keep her hands firmly at her sides. He wasn't the first guy she'd wanted to slap, and he wouldn't be the last. From between gritted teeth she said, "I don't know why every guy who meets me thinks all I want to do is fuck his brains out simply because I write erotica. Because I wouldn't have sex with you if you were the last man on earth."

Clearly upset by her slam, he looked her up and down and disdainfully said, "Then maybe you should stop begging for it, you slut," then ran back down the hall to the meeting room, slamming the door behind him.

Standing in the hallway, stunned by her latest bad experience, Candace heard the distinct sounds of lovemaking coming from the women's bathroom. A minute later, the two people who had left the room right after she read her Chapter emerged, clothes in slight disarray, and sneaked back off towards the meeting room, thinking no one was the wiser.

Candace smiled momentarily. "I guess that means it was a good chapter," she said. But then, falling despondent again over the difficulties of her new writing direction, she added, "At least some people are having a good night."

Trying not to be too down about the events of the evening, she headed out for her car and another lonely night curled up on her couch with a paperback, where she could dream about having a perfect life, like the characters in her favorite books.

Chapter Three

Candace stood underneath the huge "Sensual Writer's Conference" banner and took a deep breath. As soon as she walked through the double glass doors she would officially be entering into her new life. Instead of continuing to write young adult stories, where sex was never allowed to enter into the storyline, no matter what, today she was officially going to make the jump into the world of erotica, where the only limit was how far a writer wanted to go. Practically nothing was forbidden.

Now, if she could just muster up the nerve to walk through those damn double doors.

She tried not to be too hard on herself. After all, anytime anyone made a career change they were bound to have some butterflies in their stomach. Unfortunately, what Candace was feeling went far beyond butterflies. More like huge ravens flying around inside of her, picking at her innards.

A middle-aged woman brushed past her and hurried inside the conference hall. Candace knew it was now or never—time to either bite the bullet and commit to doing the work she loved, or to wimp out by continuing to write the same old stories she'd been pumping out since college.

"If she can do it, I can do it," Candace told herself firmly. She squared her shoulders, fluffed up her orange curls with one hand and set off for the door.

Candace was so focused on her goal, on making it past the threshold of her current comfort level, she didn't see the attractive, muscular man who was just about to step through the doorway. They collided as Candace bumped into him in a particularly graceless way, the full-body impact knocking them both to the floor. Candace tried to catch her breath as she lay in a heap atop the stranger.

Absolutely mortified by her clumsiness, Candace scrambled to get up off the man, but not before she became aware of the firm muscles of his butt, back and shoulders rippling beneath her.

Overcome by both embarrassment and a rare jolt of lust, she blathered on and on without being able to stop herself. "Oh! I'm so sorry! I can't believe I didn't see you and then I walked right into you and then I fell onto you and now we're on the ground and are you okay?"

Pushing himself up on his palms and then spinning around so that he was sitting on the cement floor, the stranger gave her a devastating smile. Brushing the dust off of his slacks, he stood up and said, "I'm just fine, thanks."

Candace was bowled over by the dimple in his left cheek and could do little else but gape at the man standing in front of her. "And besides," he added with a mischievous glint in his eyes, "who wouldn't want to have a gorgeous woman lying on top of him first thing in the morning?"

Candace felt her cheeks turn pink, and she covered them with her hands, hoping to cool them down.

Looking slightly repentant, he said, "I hope I haven't made you uncomfortable. I'm just joking around. You looked like you were heading into the Coliseum to face the lions for a minute."

Candace dropped her hands from her face and gave him a small smile. "I just feel like such an idiot for knocking you over like that."

The blond hunk held up his hand to stop her from lambasting herself any further. "I can't stand to hear you insult yourself. Especially since I don't even know your name yet." Holding out his hand he said, "I'm Charlie."

As the warmth of his skin covered her cold hand, she relaxed for the first time since she'd parked her car that morning. "Candace. It's nice to meet you."

She could tell he was trying to put her at ease as he picked up her leather bag and handed it to her. "Is this your first conference? I've never seen you here before."

Candace nodded. "Is it that obvious that I'm a newbie?"

Charlie shook his head. "Nope, that's not it. I'm just pretty sure if I'd ever met you before, I'd have remembered you."

Candace blushed again and silently admonished herself to cut it out. "I'm sort of new to this genre."

"To erotica, you mean?"

She nodded. "I'm really excited about making the switch from young adult fiction to sensual romantic fiction, but I guess I'm feeling a little overwhelmed today by it all."

Charlie smiled. "I know exactly how you feel."

"You do? Are you new to erotica also?"

"Nope. I've been going at it," he stopped and cleared his throat. "What I mean is, I've been writing erotica for a little over five years now. I can honestly say it is the most enjoyable, challenging writing I've ever done. But when I first made the switch from crime to erotica, it was pretty daunting."

While he talked, Candace thought there was something vaguely familiar about Charlie, but she couldn't quite put her finger on it. In any case, although she was greatly enjoying talking with him, she was worried about monopolizing his time.

Rather briskly she said, "Thanks for the pep talk, Charlie. But I don't want you to feel like you have to baby-sit me all morning. I'm a big girl. I'll be all right."

Giving her an enigmatic look that set her heart pounding like a drum in her chest, Charlie brushed off her concerns. "You know what, Candace?" he said, her name rolling off his tongue like warm butter. "I'd like nothing better than to show you around the conference hall and to introduce you to some of my friends and colleagues." Leaning in closer to her he added with a wink, "Not that I don't think you're capable of taking care of yourself, of course."

This time, instead of blushing at his double-entendre, Candace laughed. "Thank god I'm starting to get your sense of humor," she said. "And by the way, if you're going to be my chaperone, why don't you call me Candy? The only people who ever use my full name are either my mother or my elementary school teachers when I really got into trouble for something."

Clearly unable to stop teasing her, in a rough undertone Charlie asked, "Did you get into trouble a lot, Candy?"

Candace swallowed and stared into Charlie's deep blue eyes. The flash of lust she had felt when their bodies had collided was jumping inside of her full-force now.

Forcing herself to remember to be cautious, to remember how badly she'd been hurt, a shadow passed over her eyes.

Shrugging, she finally replied, "More times than I can count."

If Charlie noticed her swift change of demeanor, he didn't let on. Looping his arm through hers, he said, "I'm going to take you in now. But I'm warning you to be prepared for lunacy. We're a naughty little bunch, you know, us erotica writers."

Shaking off her painful memories, Candy smiled up at Charlie. "Lead on, oh wise one," she said in mock subservience. "Lead on."

Charlie directed them into a crowded common room, which had at least a hundred different information booths set up inside. Candace gaped at the displays all around them and started to wonder if it was too late for her to make her escape.

Seeming to sense her growing embarrassment in that incredibly perceptive way of his, Charlie held firm to her hand. "Now just remember," he said, leaning down to whisper in her ear, "there's nothing to be embarrassed about with these folks. We're all in the business for the same reason—because we love it. No one's going to look down upon you or call you a pervert today, I promise."

Shivering as his breath gently blew against her ear, she looked up at him, a question in her eyes. "How did you know people have been giving me a hard time about writing erotica?"

Charlie gestured to the group of people in the room with them. "Every one of us has had to deal with misconceptions at one point or another." With a grimace he added, "And I'd be lying to you if I said it's all a bed of roses, even after five years."

Suddenly, Candace was overwhelmed by the clear picture of the two of them, entwined together on a bed of rose petals. As warm heat pooled between her legs, she forced the vision from her head.

Thankfully, he didn't wait for her response and led them up to the first booth by the door, which, to Candace's dismay had the most comprehensive display of dildos she had ever seen amassed in one place.

Actually, considering she had never even gotten up the nerve to walk into an adult bookstore, they were the only dildos she had ever seen outside of a magazine ad.

"Candy, this is Albert. He's an old-timer around here, and frankly, without him, none of us erotica writers would be worth a damn."

Candy managed to muster up a smile for the gray-haired, bearded man, and reached out her hand to shake his.

"Don't be shy, missy," he barked at her. "Feel free to wrap your hands around any one of these babies to find out what they really feel like. I've got rubber. I've got really life-like skin. I've got hard dildos and soft dildos and dildos with vibrators attached. They come in a range of colors, including day-glo green with florescent pink stripes, if you're really looking for something to spice up a scene."

Candace wanted nothing more than for the ground to open up and swallow her whole. She had never been so uncomfortable in her entire life. What made her think she could write erotica, she wondered frantically. For god's sake, she had never even been able to have an orgasm during sex. And she certainly had never used a vibrator, or any kind of penis-like dildo to get herself off. Considering how naughty she felt when she used the stream of water from her hand-held showerhead to bring herself to orgasm, she now had to face just how far over her head she was.

"Albert is a walking guru of sex toys. Thank god he's willing to share his knowledge or I'd look like an idiot in more books than I'm willing to mention."

Candace nodded mutely, knowing words were beyond her at this point. Not letting her run off, Charlie held fast to her hand. "We'll talk to you again later Albert," he said as he directed them to another booth.

At first glance, this one looked to be far tamer than Albert's booth, with a simple display of hardcover books for sale. Candace breathed a sigh of relief.

Introducing her, Charlie said, "This is my friend Candy. Candy this is Steve Holt. He's pretty much a hero around here."

Laughing, Steve said, "Only second to you, buddy." Turning to greet Candace, he said, "Welcome to the wild and wacky world of erotica. Unbuckle your seatbelt and enjoy the ride."

Candace laughed and gave silent thanks that everyone was working so hard to put her at ease. Of course, she knew that meant she was probably walking around with a panic-stricken look on her face. Telling herself she was doing her best in a new situation, she said, "I'm beginning to sense a theme here."

But when she caught sight of the cover of Steve's latest book, she almost gasped aloud. Depicted on the cover were two women in sixty-nine position along with the title, *Sixty-Nine Kinds of Love*. Knowing she was trapped in a full-body flush, with Charlie's hand tucked in hers, all she could think about was what it would feel like if his head was buried between her legs, his tongue lapping at her clitoris. No matter how hard she tried to clear the sexy vision from her mind, she just couldn't.

Fortunately, the two men were busy catching up with each other, and hadn't noticed her reaction to the sexy book cover.

"So, how's the new book going Charlie?" Steve was asking him.

"Pretty good," Charlie replied, running his free hand through his golden blond hair. "Although I'm having some trouble with my character's motivations, but I'll figure it out in time."

Steve laughed and said to Candace, "I swear to God, this is the only author I know who wants to know what his characters ate for breakfast in high school. Most of us are content to be able to do a character sketch for their past couple of years."

"Wow," Candace said to Charlie. "You sound pretty thorough."

The look Charlie gave her was so hot she felt seared to the bone. At least to her panties, which were beginning to feel distinctly moist between her legs. "I am," he said hoarsely and then blinked hard a couple of times.

Clearing his throat, Steve said, "Oh, I almost forgot. There's a woman here from the Chronicle and she wants to interview you about *Morning Dew*."

Candace gasped. "You wrote *Morning Dew*? You're Charlie Gibson?"

A faint flush stole across his face. "That's me."

Too stunned to keep the words from falling out of her mouth, she said, "You're the reason why I wanted to get into erotica." Realizing her sentence had come out all wrong, she tried to backpedal, saying, "What I meant is that I absolutely love your books. They move me more than anything else I've ever read!"

Charlie looked incredibly pleased. "Really?"

Cutting in, Steve said, "You're not the first person who became a convert after reading his stuff. At least half of the people in the room did the very same thing."

Suddenly, Candace felt incredibly foolish. "And here I am, taking up all of your time, when so many people must be dying to get a word with you." But Charlie refused to relinquish her hand.

Right then, an attractive, medically enhanced brunette, whose tits were each the size of Candace's head, sidled up to Charlie. "I was just over at the mentoring table and they told me you don't have anyone under you yet." Licking her lips for impact, having stressed the word 'under' as if it was a magical spell she could weave around him, she pouted and added, "They said you had the final word on who you were going to work with." Walking her long, polished nails up his arm she said, "So, are you free for some lessons?"

Candace wasn't sure if her mind was playing tricks on her, considering her gut was teeming with jealous bile, but she thought she saw Charlie flinch and back away from the silicone Amazon.

Turning to her, with a cunning smile on his face, he said, "Actually, Candy has already snatched me up."

"I did?" she said, before she caught the pleading look Charlie was pinning her with. Trying to recover from the shock of being singled out by the man she respected more than any other writer of erotica, she smiled and slapped him playfully on the arm with her free hand, trying to look like she was just joking around.

"Of course, I did. I'm just teasing you." Then she turned to the Amazon-bitch and said with false syrupiness, "Actually, I tackled him the minute I saw him walking through the doors to make sure he'd be all mine."

Glaring at them both with fire in her eyes, the Amazon spat out, "Your loss," at Charlie and then went in search of new prey.

Charlie led Candace into a semi-private corner of the room. "I'm really sorry about that back there. If you don't want me to be your mentor, I understand perfectly."

Candace blinked in confusion. "I don't even know what my mentor is supposed to do."

Giving her a reassuring smile, Charlie said, "All of the established writers sign up to work with a new writer. You know, to show them the ropes."

Candace's brain was assailed with visions of Charlie tying her up to golden bedposts, while she writhed underneath him and begged him to fuck her as hard and fast as he could. She shook her head, wondering when the hell she had started to have such incredibly vivid sexual daydreams.

Looking up at him, suddenly shy, she said, "I can't think of anyone I'd rather work with."

And just like that, she leapt head first into the unknown, with the most sexually potent man she had ever encountered.

Chapter Four

Charlie paid the delivery boy from the *Love You With Flowers* floral design shop on Chestnut Street in the Marina and then watched him get back into his delivery truck and drive away. He picked up the surprisingly heavy cardboard box of red, pink, and purple rose petals, placed them on the floor of his foyer, and closed the front door with a soft click. He leaned his forehead against the back of his front door and closed his eyes.

At least a hundred times in the past week, ever since he had coerced Candace into letting him be her mentor, he had told himself not to fuck this up. From the first moment he met her, in the instant that she had landed atop him in the conference hall, he knew she was special.

"Don't fuck this up, Charlie," he said aloud and listened to his words bounce off the shiny pine flooring and the expanse of windows that flooded his house with light.

Unfortunately, every time he thought about Candace he got lightheaded and his heart started beating to a heavy-metal rhythm within his chest.

He thought back to their phone call, the Monday after the erotic writer's conference and groaned, remembering how lame he sounded as he outlined his mentoring plan to her. He banged his forehead against the door several times as his words flooded back into his brain.

"Thanks so much for offering to work with me, Charlie," she had said.

He had said, "You know what? I think we're both going to get a lot out of this." But then as he realized how smarmy he sounded, he backpedaled. "What I mean is there's nothing more enlightening than trying to teach another person what you already know. It's a good chance for me to see if I actually know what I'm talking about, or if I've just been faking my way through my last eight books."

Belatedly, Charlie realized he was going on and on about utter nonsense so he added, "Does that make sense?"

His palms got slick and sweaty on the handset of his cordless phone as he waited for her response. Trying to put him at ease, she said, "I know exactly what you mean, Charlie. And by the way, I've been thinking we should probably be upfront about things."

"What things?" Charlie asked, so suddenly nervous his heart was going clackity-click and he could swear he heard a heavy metal soundtrack in his head.

"I want you to know that you don't need to worry about the vocabulary you use when we're talking about work. I know you're a complete gentleman and that everything we do during our lessons is purely professional." She cleared her throat and then added, "Even if we do happen to deal with things like dildos and kinky sex in our profession."

Charlie forced a chuckle, but inwardly he felt like the world's biggest scum. Sure, his intentions were honorable. He was going to teach Candace how to write great erotica. But he couldn't deny the fact that in the privacy of his imagination he had already devised twenty different ways he wanted to make Candace scream with pleasure.

But no matter how strongly he felt about her, he had decided to put the lid on his desire until their mentoring sessions were through—jumping her bones during their lessons would be a complete betrayal of her trust. He only hoped it didn't kill him in the meantime.

"Good," he'd said. "I'm glad we are being completely upfront about everything right from the start. I knew you were the right person to work with."

"Frankly, I was afraid that Sheba Queen of the Sluts wouldn't have left you in one piece by the time she was done with you. I had no choice but to save you by offering up myself."

Charlie let himself savor the vision of Candace tied and bound to an altar, naked and gleaming, in sacrifice for him, before he said, "I appreciate that. More than you know."

"So, what's on the agenda?" she asked him, and just like that his entire body broke out in a sweat as he unfolded the piece of paper he'd written their lesson plan on.

Trying to keep his voice light, he said, "I've broken our mentoring sessions into five different lessons. Lesson one will be how to set a romantic scene."

"That sounds great. I love the way you paint pictures in your books."

"Thanks," he'd said, and then swallowed loudly as he prepared to continue spelling out his list of lessons. Lesson one was the easy one, and he knew things were only going to get harder from here. Especially if the rock-hard bulge in his pants was any indication.

"Let's see, for lesson two I thought we'd work on varying positions." Oh shit! What had he just said? "I mean, we'll take a look at...uh, you know study the different ways that..."

Suddenly he couldn't think of any way to rephrase the sentence that wouldn't sound like he planned on screwing her brains out the minute she walked through his door. Thankfully, she reminded him in a gentle voice, "Charlie, you've got to stop worrying about offending me."

"Okay," he said, but his trepidation must have been clear in his voice, because she said, "Say fuck ten times to me."

"Huh?"

"Just say it," she demanded.

"Fuck, fuck, fuck, fuck, fuck, fuck, fuck, fuck, fuck, fuck."

"Good. Now say, 'I want to lick your juicy pussy.'"

Charlie choked on an intake of breath, but he did as she asked. He repeated, "I want to lick your juicy pussy." Even as he imagined how amazing she would taste, he braced himself for her disgust, expecting her to say, "You're scum and I never want to talk to you again."

"Feel better now?"

He took a moment to gauge his feelings and realized, much to his surprise, that his palms were dry again and his heart rate had returned to near-normal. Candace, in her sly way, had forced him over the hump of his anxieties. Yet again, he was impressed by what a clever little piece of work this delectable woman was.

"Thanks for that, Candace. You definitely have a knack for dialogue. And now that I've decided to stop being such an idiot, here are the rest of my lesson plans." He spoke quickly and didn't pause between lessons. "Lesson three — using toys. Lesson four — the joy of sex in exciting locations. Lesson five—how to use role playing to really up the ante."

He knew if he gave himself even a second to think about her reaction he'd start to make an even bigger ass of himself than he already had, so he barrelled ahead. "So, how about we start next Saturday at my house on Lombard? Noon?"

"Great," she'd said and hung up as soon as he gave her his address.

Now here he was, on the big day, with noon quickly approaching. Through great force of will, Charlie stopped banging his head on the door, stopped torturing himself with thoughts of what a dweeb Candace thought he was, picked up the box of rose petals and walked into his guest bedroom to finish preparing the classroom.

Charlie had decided the best way to teach Candace how to set a romantic scene was to show her one in real life. He knew, however, that using his master bedroom for any of these lessons was a very bad idea. As it was, in the past seven days he had beaten off to the picture of her he had in his head so many times while lying in his bed and while showering, as soon as he walked into his master bedroom it was practically a reflex for him to reach for his cock and start pumping it in his hand.

Standing in the doorway of his large guest room, he surveyed the space with a critical eye. He had draped the four-poster queen-sized bed with Indian silk. In his writer's mind, he could see two lovers deep within their own world, sheathed in the exotic silk.

He had covered the mattress in red plush velvet, and underneath the luxurious cover, he had put red satin sheets. To top it off, a dozen pillows fought for space near the head of the bed.

Charlie had never been particularly interested in interior design—although he felt that he had done a nice job with making his house a comfortable and cozy reflection of himself—but as he went from store to store in Union Square, as he ran his fingers lightly over the fabrics, he realized that he was, in fact, greatly enjoying himself.

His enjoyment, he thought ruefully, may have sprung from his intense desire to see Candace wrapped in the silks, velvets, and satins he purchased.

Or, more to the point, his even more intense desire to *unwrap* her.

He tried to shake the image of Candace naked with her legs spread wide open before him, begging for him to ram his cock inside her. He needed to focus on the task at hand. He had draped the windows with shimmering translucent red fabric, shot through with gold thread. Then he'd brought light back into the room with candles of varying sizes and colors, which he had placed on every possible surface.

On the bare wood floor in front of the rock-framed fireplace he had laid a chenille rug. It felt so good to the touch in the store he couldn't resist buying it. He wondered if Candace lay face down on the rug and rubbed her breasts across it slowly, what would the soft fabric feel like brushing against her nipples?

The rose petals were the final touch. Checking his watch and noting it was a quarter to twelve, he bent down, opened the large box and reached into the mass of flower petals.

To his great satisfaction the scent of the roses wasn't overpowering. As he had hoped, the flowers lent an alluring air of sweetness to the room.

In fact, it was just the right scent to mix with the sweet smell of endless, overpowering, passionate sex.

Closing his eyes again for a moment, still squatting on the floor with both hands deep within the box and covered with rose petals, Charlie told himself, "Get a grip, man!" He unclenched his teeth, stood up, and began to throw the rose petals to the floor, on the side tables, on the antique chest, and on the velvet-covered bed.

When the box was empty and rose petals beautifully littered the room, he started a fire in the fireplace and then painstakingly lit each of the candles. Once he had a flame on every candle, he stood in the doorway of the bedroom and smiled. The room had a sensual vibe and fairly glowed with romance, just as he had hoped it would.

The doorbell rang, jolting him out of his pleasant trance. His palms went damp again and he half-laughed, half-groaned at how ridiculous he was being. All he and Candace were going to do was look at the room, study its romantic elements, and then do a writing exercise using the room as the setting for a story.

No big deal.

Charlie walked down the hall towards the front door and told himself to pretend he was working with Steve Holt. Why should he be nervous? They were just a couple of writers doing research for their craft.

He opened the door and all of his good intentions came crashing down upon him.

The only thing he was cognizant of was her smell, the pulse he saw moving under the soft skin on her neck, and the way the breeze was moving the tips of her red, curly hair around on the tops of her luscious breasts. An image of her pubic hair, red and curly and moist with her come and his saliva, popped into his head and he knew he was in deep, deep trouble.

By the time he remembered to say, "Hi! Come inside," he had no idea how much time had gone by since he'd opened the door. Thirty seconds? Five minutes? Time was a blur to him.

How could he treat her like one of the guys when she was a walking, breathing orgasm waiting to happen?

* * * * *

Candace walked into Charlie's foyer and tried not to betray her nervousness by giggling, babbling, or checking to see if her hair was out of place. Instead, she plastered a big smile on her face and squeezed past Charlie and through his front door. He hadn't moved aside very much to let her into his house, but she had to admit she didn't mind rubbing up against him, not one bit.

He was just as gorgeous as he had been at the conference, with the highlights in his blond hair picking up the sunlight that streamed in through the windows. She took in the snug fit of his well-worn jeans and his thick denim long-sleeve shirt. She couldn't keep her eyes from straying to the light brown chest hair that peeked out through his shirt. Salivating at the thought of seeing his chest—which she knew she'd never get a glimpse of in this lifetime, but a girl could dream, couldn't she?—Candace wished he had left a couple more buttons undone.

Charlie's bare feet were the icing on the cake. Candace had never seen such sexy feet before. She had never even known feet could be sexy. Until now. His feet were tan, with well-manicured toenails and a light dusting of hair. Suddenly, she saw herself naked and ready for him, straddling his big toe and...

No! Candace stopped herself from taking her daydream any further. What was happening to her, she wondered, as she swallowed past her dry tongue. Despite her newfound career, she had never had very many sexual thoughts, let alone ideas involving a strange man's toes! But now everything she saw made her think about Charlie's cock and fingers and tongue.

Her mind was turning into an X-rated pay-per-view channel.

Trying to force her thoughts away from the incredibly dirty things she wanted to do to each and every part of Charlie's body, and wishing he would just say something already, she tuned into the details of his house. It was crazy, but Candace felt that Charlie was even more potent, even more intoxicating when he was within the walls of his private environment. His home, like the man himself, was masculine and yet warm all at the same time.

"So," she said in a bright voice to break the awkward silence, "this is your house, huh?"

As the words left her mouth, Candace turned pink and had to fight the urge to run out of his front door, down his steps and back into her car. Could she have sounded any more like an idiot?

Charlie's eyes seemed to refocus in on her and he said, "Yup. Sure is. Glad you could come."

"It was my pleasure."

He smiled at her and she melted under his gaze. She knew she had a serious case of hero worship, but this was worse than she had bargained for. *Don't make a pass at him under any circumstances*, she told herself in a firm inner voice. *He's your teacher, and you should be grateful that he is taking any time out of his busy and illustrious schedule for you*, she added with a flourish.

She noted he looked a little uncomfortable as he said, "I've set up a classroom of sorts for us. It's down the hall." But when he comfortably added, as if she were a buddy from his baseball league, "Let me pour you a glass of chardonnay," she decided his discomfort was just a figment of her imagination.

Her mind was playing tricks on her. More likely than not she was projecting her own uneasiness onto him.

She followed him into his kitchen. "You have a beautiful home."

He turned to smile at her as he uncorked a bottle of white wine. "Thanks. I love this house. It's a big change from my last one."

"How so?"

Candace hoped her question didn't seem like she was prying, although she acknowledged that she definitely was. By the time their lessons were through, she wanted to know everything she possibly could about Charlie Gibson. She was already tucking all the little details of his clothes and his furnishings away into her memory for safekeeping and leisurely review on lonely nights. Who knew, she might even buy herself her own personal dildo if she was feeling really brave.

"I got to design this house from the ground up. And I, uh, didn't have anyone telling me she hated my ideas this time around."

He handed her the wine glass and said, "That's probably a whole heck of a lot more than you wanted to know, isn't it?"

She laughed and patted his hand. "Trust me, I know exactly how you feel."

But as she felt a tremor pass through her from simply touching his hand, she immediately pulled back and said, in a shakier voice than she intended, "Should we get started with things, Mr. Mentor?"

He nodded. "I've set things up in the guest room. Follow me."

She followed him out of the kitchen and down the hallway. When he opened the door to the guest bedroom she was overwhelmed with the potent scent of roses. Her heart started to beat double time so she joked, "Are we going to write a story about the florist and—"

Her words stopped altogether as she rounded the corner and stepped fully into the room.

She gasped. "This is amazing!"

Candace wanted to rub herself on all of the luxurious fabrics draped across and above the bed. She wanted to feel the rug under her toes. She wanted to wrap herself in rose petals.

Turning to Charlie, she said, "Did you do all this for me? For our lesson? You shouldn't have gone to all the tr—"

He smiled at her and cut her protest off. "You know what? I really enjoyed creating this room. And now that I've seen the effects of if myself, I think I'm going to leave it as a nice surprise for my houseguests. Although, I probably won't see much of them 'cause they'll be so busy going at each other."

Candace forced a laugh and started worrying in earnest as Charlie sat down on the chest at the foot of the bed and motioned for her to sit next to him.

"I think you need to take off your shoes and socks to fully appreciate this room."

She knew he was right and she was certain that he wasn't the least bit interested in her, so she set her wine glass down on the mantle of the fireplace, then sat down next to him and removed her shoes and socks.

Playfully she said, "Should I take anything else off?"

Charlie's eyes got wide for a moment and then he grinned wolfishly. "I suppose you'd better, otherwise, how are you going to write about the feel of the material brushing across your heroine's skin?"

"Oh, do you really think I should?" Candace said, some panic creeping into her voice. But then, as she looked around the room at the candles and the fire and saw the velvet and silk beneath her, she decided, what the hell. Not giving herself the chance to think, she pulled her v-neck sweater over her head, leaving only a skimpy tank top covering her torso.

"Okay," she said impishly, vowing to let herself be carried away by the mood for once in her life. "I'm undressed."

Charlie looked her up and down. "I'm not sure I'd call you undressed, but it's certainly a start."

Suddenly, something inside Candace clicked into place. Or broke down completely. She wasn't sure which. But the new voice inside her was loud and clear.

She spoke quickly, before she lost her courage. Before she came to her senses. "Charlie, you know how we agreed that everything that went on during on mentoring sessions was going to be strictly professional?"

"Yeah?" he said, drawing out the word as a question.

"Well, it has just occurred to me that it's one thing for me to appreciate this room as a writer." She paused and then said, "But it's another thing entirely for me to experience it as a woman."

She saw Charlie's Adam's apple move in his throat and clenched her hands into tight fists at her side. She didn't know how she was going to manage it exactly, but she wasn't going to be a wimp and back down. Not here. Not now.

For the first time in her life, Candace was going to go for what she wanted. She reached for the button on her jeans and Charlie's hand shot out to grab hers.

"What are you doing?"

She half-grinned at him, but she knew she was far too nervous for it to look like a smile. More like she was baring her teeth at him. "I'm taking off my clothes."

He blinked at her in confusion. "Oh."

Candace tried not to let his utter non-reaction to the idea of her taking off her clothes bother her. She wasn't here because he thought she was a sexy woman. She was here to learn about the art of erotic writing. And if she had to do it on her own, by god, she was doing it.

She stood up and unzipped her pants. As she lowered them to the ground and pulled her legs out of each pants leg one at a time she looked up at Charlie, who was still sitting in stunned silence on the edge of the chest. "The fact is, I have never experienced the sensation of silk sliding against my skin. I've never lain naked in front of a roaring fire. I've never rubbed my nipples against satin."

She looked at him imploringly. "These are all things that I have to do or I'll never be able to write about characters who know what these physical sensations feel like. Can you understand that?"

Charlie nodded.

She stood in front of him in her skimpy tank top, knowing her nipples were jutting out and she forced herself not to flinch, not to run, and not to cover up. She hooked her thumbs into the thin straps of her silk thong undies and said, in a soft but firm voice, "I won't pressure you into joining me, Charlie. I'm sure this is all pretty old hat to you, but it's all brand new to me. So I could sure use some help if you were willing to instruct me." Lowering her eyelashes to cover her eyes, she licked her lips and then made eye contact with him again. "In a purely professional way, of course."

"Whatever happens inside the classroom stays in the classroom?" he asked in a calm, detached voice.

A little shiver worked itself up Candace's spine. Trying to sound as unaffected by her near-nakedness in an incredibly romantic room with the most potent man she'd ever met, she said, "You got it."

In the blink of an eye, Charlie replaced her hands with his on the sides of her thong.

With a new gleam in his eyes he pulled her closer to him, so that her muff was mere inches from his mouth.

"Let the lessons begin."

Chapter Five

Charlie hooked his thumbs under her panties and slowly pulled them down to her thighs. Her pussy was pink and so hot he could feel the heat emanating from it, practically scalding his face. Her auburn bush had been waxed and trimmed into a Brazilian style—mostly smooth and glistening skin with just the barest patch of hair in the middle. Her lips were plump and he was more glad than he could ever say that she had just given him permission to touch her, to taste her, to spread her legs wide open and plunge into her until he had quenched the sexual need that had ridden him hard from the moment he'd met her.

Pushing her panties down around her knees, he pushed her thighs apart and her lips separated slightly. He slipped the index finger on his right hand into her tight, dripping cunt a couple of inches. She moaned and wiggled her pussy against his finger, so he pushed it even further inside her until his palm was cupping her entire vulva and his thumb was covering her swollen clit.

He lifted his thumb and blew softly on the swollen flesh. Her vagina clenched around his finger, and he wondered just how close she was to coming. He blew on her clit again and slid his finger in and out of her pussy. Just as he had suspected, she was a powder keg waiting to explode. Sensitive to each spasm of her slick yet powerful pussy muscles around his index finger, he bent his head down an inch or two and barely touched the tip of his tongue to her firm, throbbing flesh.

She screamed out and pressed her cunt against him, begging for a tongue fuck. Grasping the back of his head with her hands, she ground his face into her pussy, crushing herself against his lips and teeth.

Charlie knew what she wanted, even as she thrashed onto him. Slipping his middle finger into her pussy to join his index finger, he continued to slide his fingers in and out of her in a slow, steady rhythm. He gripped her firm, round ass in his left hand and pointed his tongue so that all she felt against her clit was the hard tip. As if he were typing the same letter over and over on a typewriter, as if she was the page he was making his mark on, he moved his tongue steadily up and down on her clit as she cried out with pleasure.

Finally, the pulsing of her muscles around his fingers slowed and Candace's body went limp. The muscles in her back and butt cheeks tightened up as she tried to pull away from him, but he wouldn't allow it. She might not have known what she was getting into when she made her "let's get naked because we're professionals" comment just minutes earlier, but now, whether she liked it or not, he would decide when they were finished.

After all, he was the teacher.

And she was the very promising new student.

Quickly, he put his arms around her trim waist and threw her onto the plush bedding, face down. As her body hit velvet, it was as if flowers rained from the sky. Several rose petals landed on her ass, thighs, and calves. Charlie moved to blow warm breath up her legs, removing each of the rose petals one by one until all that remained before him was her naked, creamy skin. With every breath, Candace whimpered her pleasure.

She started squirming, but when she tried to turn around, he quickly moved to straddle her, leaning over her back to cup her full breasts in his hands through her tank top. He whispered in her ear, "I'm going to take off your shirt now so that you can feel the velvet rubbing against your nipples."

She stopped squirming and in a voice so quiet he could barely hear her she whispered, "Okay."

Charlie sat back up with a leg on each side of her thighs, the huge bulge in his Levis pressing into the curve of her ass. He grinned as he slid his fingers underneath the hem of her tank top. He liked to hear her quick agreement. It made him feel like he was running the show. After years of women making him feel like he wasn't worth their time due to his choice of profession, after years of women using him only for his huge bank account, Charlie savored the sensation of being in complete control of a woman's body and soul.

Knowing he had already given her intense pleasure so quickly only served to up the ante. She was still nineteen orgasms away from matching the number of times he had exploded with her name on his lips in the past week. Before lesson one was through, he wanted her in the double digits.

Her breath quickened as he slowly rubbed his fingers underneath the hem of her shirt, along her rib cage. With infinite precision he dragged her cotton shirt up her ribs until it caught on her breasts, which were much larger than he had thought a week ago at the conference.

If someone had asked him to guess her cup size he would have confidently said she was a B-cup, given her small frame. But now, having held her globes in his hands, even only for a moment through her thin, damp cotton shirt, he knew himself for the fool he was.

Candace was definitely a D cup. At least.

Slipping his hands between the plush velvet coverlet and her shirt, he hooked his thumbs up under the hem of her shirt and tugged it up over her tits. As he pushed the shirt past her nipples and the tips of his fingers covered her tits, he heard her rapid intake of breath and almost came in his jeans. He was already breathing like he had run a marathon.

"Put your arms up," he whispered into her ear and as she obeyed him he slid the tank top off of her body and threw it to the floor.

Candace turned her head to face him, but he already had a plan of action and was not going to let her deter him. Putting his hands on her rib cage, he lifted her torso slightly off of the bed so that her nipples were just barely touching the velvet.

"I'm going to rub your tits against the cover, slowly, focusing all of your attention on how good it feels."

She nodded, just barely, showing him she understood. He pressed his groin into her ass, which pressed her mound into the velvet. He separated her legs with one of his and her juices soaked through the denim covering his legs. Roughly, so she could feel the coarse fabric pull and tug against her tender lips, he moved his thigh up and down against her.

Tightening his hold on her ribcage, he lifted her torso up high enough that her nipples floated just above the velvet cover. "I want you to concentrate on your nipples right now. Your breasts are the only thing in the world that matters. Forget about my thigh rubbing against your lips." She groaned and tried to protest, so he squeezed her ribs tighter in his strong hands.

"Do as I say," he said forcefully. "It's for your own good."

Candace's body tensed underneath him for a split second before her hips started to buck wildly against his leg. She was coming again, convulsing helplessly against his leg. His mouth curved up into a steamy look of satisfaction as he drove his thigh against her pussy and gave her what she wanted.

The fierce rocking of her lower body blew dozens of rose petals off of the bed, into the air and onto the floor. The mingled scents of her pussy, her pleasure, and the rose petals were a fragrance he knew he would never be able to forget.

But he still hadn't forgotten his goal. Before they left the room, before lesson one had come to its incredible, unforgettable end, he wanted her to realize just how sensitive a woman's breasts were, so that she could write powerful sex scenes in her books that left no part of the female body unexplored.

He almost laughed aloud as he realized what a poor job he was doing of fooling himself that he cared one whit about her writing skills at this moment as he lay over her, his fingers mere inches from her tits, his leg practically jammed up inside her cunt.

They could offer him the fuckin' Pulitzer Prize right now and he wouldn't care. Frankly, what he was doing in his guest bedroom—what he and Candace were doing together—had nothing to do with writing and everything to do with sex. And he wanted Candace to experience sex in its most heightened form. With him.

Still holding her rib cage in his large hands, he began to slide her torso ever so slightly back and forth, so just the tips of her breasts were rubbing up against the velvet fabric on the bed. He thought about turning her over and taking her tits into his mouth and sucking them, nipping them until she was crying out again, and he barely kept his own needs reined in. But what kind of teacher would he be if he changed the lesson plan mid-way just because his cock was about to explode in his pants?

He heard her whimper again and he knew she had fallen ever so slightly back down to earth from her explosive orgasm, so he leaned forward and whispered again in her ear, "You're going to come again, sweetheart. Any minute now, you're going to feel the way the velvet caresses your rock-hard nipples. You're going to realize that your breasts are the center of your body."

She started to say, "Charlie, I," but he cut her off saying, "Shh. I don't want you to talk to me. I want you to feel." Then he wrapped his left forearm around her waist, while still rocking her breasts gently side to side on the velvet comforter, and ran the fingers of his right hand down from the bottom of her rib cage, down along her flat stomach, which convulsed as he lightly touched her skin, to the top of her mound.

"Uh uh uh, Candy," he admonished her when she strained to move her clit closer to his finger. "What did I tell you?"

"My breasts," she gasped.

He smiled and moved his fingers down a millimeter. "That's right. If you keep doing what I want, I'll keep doing what you want."

A small sob left her throat, and he knew she was close, so close that if he so much as touched the tip of her clit with his fingertip she'd explode again in his hand. He moved his left arm slightly. He was still holding her torso suspended from the bed, but now every time he slid her body to the left side on the velvet her breast slipped into his palm.

"Charlie!" she moaned and again he had to fight the urge to rip his jeans off and split her wide open with his cock.

He kept his palm open at first, so that all she felt on her nipple was the callused skin of his open palm. "Are you focusing on your breasts and only your breasts right now?" he asked her in a low voice.

He saw her nod her head and rewarded her by moving his right hand another millimeter towards her clit. Even though he was no further than the top of her slit, her juices were soaking his hand, so he rubbed his fingers around in circles on the slick skin of her well-waxed mound.

Then as he slid her left breast into his palm again, he held her still and pinched her nipple between his fingers, rubbing it between his thumb and middle finger. At the same time he plunged his hand down into her wet, hot cunt and ground one finger and then two and then the tip of a third into her.

She screamed "Charlie!" and the muscles of her pussy clenched as they tried to hold his fingers hostage.

When she was still so far gone, still so entranced by the waves of pleasure washing over her, he took advantage of her pliability and effortlessly rolled her over onto her back.

Looking at her luscious breasts for the first time, he gasped at her perfection, at her beauty in the candle-light, surrounded by the deep hues of the silk, satins, and velvet furnishings.

Her breasts were lush melons and he knew immediately that they were entirely real, with no silicone added. Having felt one of them in the palm of his hand, he knew how deliciously heavy they were. His mouth watered as he anticipated tasting them.

Don't get ahead of yourself, Charlie, he warned himself. He had to stay on track with his lesson plan. *All in good time*, he told himself. *All in good time.*

Candace's eyes were just starting to open and she was trying to refocus them on his face, when he slipped a length of richly patterned silk fabric off of the bedpost. He quickly grabbed her right wrist and tied one end of the cloth around it and the other end about the bedpost. He slid yet another length of fabric around her left wrist and tied that one up as well.

"You're such a good student we're moving straight to lesson two."

Her eyebrows scrunched down in an unspoken question as he splayed her legs and tied up both her ankles to the nearest bedpost.

"Varying positions is lesson two."

He tied the final bow on her left ankle, then lapped once at her very wet, well worked vagina, with his tongue. She tried to buck up into his mouth, but he had tied her just tight enough that she couldn't move more than an inch or two off of the bed.

He took one of the thin pillows from the headboard and slid it underneath her perfect ass.

Breathing hard, he said in a low voice, "I just want to look at you for a few moments before we take this any further."

* * * * *

Candace's head was spinning. She had definitely surprised herself when she decided to take off her clothes during the lesson. But after coming three times in rapid succession with a virtual stranger, in his guest bedroom, during her mentoring session, she was more than surprised.

She was stupefied.

She was flabbergasted.

And damn it, she was still horny as hell. Hornier than she'd ever been her entire life. And this was how she felt after *three*, count 'em, *three*, mind-blowing, soul-shaking orgasms.

Candace could hardly believe it when the first "Big O" had rocked through her. During a decade of lackluster sex, she had never, ever had an orgasm with a man in the room. The only paltry orgasms she had ever managed to bring upon herself were with the tip of her middle finger swirling her clit—usually after reading one of Charlie's books. But that was neither here nor there, so she left that thought to dissect later when the man himself wasn't looming over her with an unholy gleam in his eyes and her come all over his hands and clothes. She couldn't believe how quickly she responded to the barest touch from Charlie's tongue, from his finger inside her swollen labia.

And then again with his muscular thigh between her legs.

And then again with one of his hands on her breasts and one between her legs.

Oh god, she thought to herself, *he must think I am a total slut. Just like that other woman with the huge fake tits who wanted him to be her mentor.*

She looked down at herself and realized he had tied her to his bed. *I'm no better than that bitch from the conference. And now he knows.* But worse than having her hero know what a slut she was, was that *she* now knew what a slut she was.

Suddenly wanting to be as far away from her embarrassment as possible, far away from Charlie's probing fingers, from his tongue and his all-seeing, all-knowing eyes, she laughed nervously and said, "Charlie, I feel like I'm all spread out for you like you're Jesus and I'm The Last Supper."

He was still kneeling between her legs, clothed in his Levis and light blue denim shirt, and she could see where her come had stained the fabric near his wrists and along his right thigh.

She was so embarrassed she wanted to die. *Right here, right now, God, you can take me. Please!* What she didn't add to her plea, although she wanted to, was, *Now that I've experienced pleasure like this, it's all right for me to go. At least, I know I've truly lived in this man's arms.*

He didn't laugh at her lame joke about the Last Supper. Instead he leaned over and lapped at her pussy once more. She felt all of the remaining blood from her head and the rest of her body rush between her legs, straight to her clit. If she weren't so damn embarrassed, she would have begged him to lap at her just a couple more times.

One more touch and she'd be over the edge into oblivion.

For the fourth time in the past hour.

She was Candace Whitman, for god's sake. A girl who had gone to Catholic school with ruler-thwapping nuns. A girl who still turned bright red every time she thought about the astonishing array of dildos on display at the erotic writer's conference.

But before she could make any more feeble protests about how ridiculous it was for him to have her splayed open and tied up like some sort of sex slave on his four-poster bed, surrounded by rose petals and a hundred candles, Charlie slid another length of silk fabric off the four-poster bed frame. Slowly, as if he knew how much his every move tortured her inflamed libido, he twisted the thin fabric into a tight cord.

Then he stood up and began to walk around the side of the bed. She wondered, somewhat wildly – hopefully too, much to her ongoing chagrin over what an utter and complete slut she was turning out to be – if he was going to whip her with the tip of the fabric. She knew it would hurt. But then, she knew Charlie would make it feel good too. And then he could kiss it all better.

Instead, he took the fabric and covered her eyes with it, lifting her head slightly so that he could tie the fabric in a knot behind her head.

Candace had never felt more powerless.

And she had never been so full of anticipation in her whole life.

Firmly tamping down on the logical part of her brain that said their lesson had gone too far, way too far, she let her senses take over. She listened to the crackling fire, the sound of Charlie's footsteps on the wood floor and then the carpet. She smelled the potent scent of rose petals mixed with her own come and the faint scent of vanilla from the candles. She tasted her own musky desire on her lips.

Feeling silk slide around her ankles and wrists, holding her hostage, for the second time in her life, for the second time in one short, sunny afternoon, Candace gave herself up to a greater power.

The power of a good fuck.

And wondered why she had never let herself experience it before.

Chapter Six

Charlie had watched the play of emotions work their way across Candace's face as he'd turned her over on her back. Feelings of self-doubt and self-consciousness were the reasons why he had wanted her face down for his initial onslaught. It was so much easier for her to let herself go if she forgot anyone was watching.

From what she had already said to him, from all of the nervous signs she tried to conceal from him, he knew how badly Candace wanted to experience incredible heights of lust and passion. He knew she wanted to learn what it was to fuck and be fucked so hard and so long that the tender, slick skin between her legs was raw from it. And to still want more, even when pain was beginning to get all mixed up in the pleasure.

Knowing she was a beginner in the sensual arts, he was going as slow as he could with her. Putting her face down. Showing her how strongly she could react to the simplest, lightest touch. Letting her hide from her embarrassment. He wondered who had taught her that sex was dirty, but knew it was a conversation they would have later, down the line, when she had accepted what her body wanted from her.

Oddly enough, while Charlie was no sexual novice — he'd had his fair share of hot one night stands and had been sandwiched between more than one woman during the past five years since his divorce — he had never wanted to fuck anyone this badly. Ever.

Not even when he was a fourteen-year-old virgin used to beating off to Playboy, and was finally ready to sink himself into the pussy of one his mother's friends who had come on to him, did he feel this out of control. It was taking every ounce of restraint within him, and then some, to keep from thrusting his cock into Candace and yelling her name out.

At the same time, he had never wanted to give anyone as much pleasure as he wanted to give Candace. He felt like he could make her come a hundred times and then a hundred more, and though his cock would surely be turning blue by then, he would gladly give up his own sexual release just to see her achieve hers.

Without knowing just how or when it had happened — was it the minute she walked through his door, or was it when they spoke on the phone, or maybe it was when she had accidentally tackled him at the conference — the teacher had become the student.

Charlie would have been amused by this realization were it not for how painfully she aroused him. She was innocent, she was confused, she was unknowledgeable, yet her body had the answers from all the way back to Eve.

But they weren't done with her lessons yet and he knew the only way to keep her imprisoned in her own sexuality, the only way to show her how many ways she could feel good, was to take control away from her. So he tied her up and blindfolded her, praying all the while that he was doing the right thing. Hoping that he wasn't pushing her too far.

As he tied the knot around the back of her head and felt her soft red hair caressing the backs of his arms, he noted with satisfaction that the tension was leaving her body, almost as if she had made the decision to give in to everything he was offering her.

He stood up and picked up one of the candles from the dark-pine bedside table.

"I want you to tell me if I'm hurting you, Candy," he said.

She swallowed once, then twice, then licked her lips, nodding her agreement.

He blew out the candle and then kneeled at the side of the bed. With infinite precision he poised the candle over one of her thighs and tilted it so that the barest amount of hot wax dripped onto her skin.

Candace hissed out a stream of air between her teeth as the wax made contact with her skin.

Immediately concerned, Charlie covered the patch of skin with his hand and said, "Did I hurt you?" If he had, he knew he would never forgive himself.

"No," she whispered. Her voice sounded heavy. Drugged.

Charlie breathed out an enormous sigh of relief, but he couldn't help but worry that he had crossed a dangerous line.

Instead she surprised him. "Do it again," she whispered.

His heart flip-flopped in his chest and swelled with something he couldn't quite name. He replaced his hand with his lips as he kissed her softly on her thigh, right above the now-dry vanilla wax. Reaching for another candle, he blew out the flame and slowly dripped a trail of hot wax up the inside of her left thigh, enjoying the sound of her moaning as the wax came closer still to her wet, hot pussy, enjoying watching her try, futilely, to move her sopping mound closer to his hand.

Again he followed the line of quickly drying wax with his tongue and his teeth as he nipped at her skin.

"Charlie, Charlie, Charlie," she whimpered with every touch of his lips to her skin, and Charlie wondered what the hell he was doing still fully clothed while a sex goddess was tied to his bed.

He reached for another candle and told himself to chill out. There would be time enough for him to pump into her wet, tight hole, but not before he gave her more of what she so desperately needed.

So he dripped wax along her stomach, and kissed his way along her rib cage, until his face was so close to her breasts he couldn't hold off any longer.

When he gently touched the tip of his tongue to one of her nipples, she nearly broke the silk binds off of her wrists.

"More!" she urged him.

"Please!" she begged him.

Obeying her wishes, he took her nipple into his mouth and sucked her areola in as well. He wanted to be gentle, but he was too far gone himself to hold anything back. In the back of his mind he hoped he didn't bruise her, but he knew she wouldn't care even if he did, because she was moaning, "Yes! Just like that! Yes!"

As if he had a timer in his head, Charlie knew her fourth orgasm was long past due. And if he played his cards right, he thought he could move her from four to five in rapid succession.

Laving his tongue back and forth over the hard nub of her nipple, he moved his index finger into the cleft of her pussy and just as he touched her incredibly swollen clit he bit down slightly on her left nipple.

She screamed again and Charlie sucked as hard as he could on her breast while ramming his finger in and out of her feverishly.

"Your cunt is so hot," he said, unbelievingly, and knew that by the time he stuck his cock in, it would be scalding.

Thinking of all the heat pooling in her juicy cunt gave Charlie an idea. He took the long, slim pillar candle and slid it into her vagina, just a little at a time. By the sound of her moans, he knew she was still coming, and easily turned on enough for whatever he wanted to slip between her legs

In the midst of her orgasm, Charlie removed his lips from her breast and joined the candle in her wet hole with his tongue on her clit. Even as she was resurfacing from her explosion, he felt her clit twitching again beneath his tongue. He could feel the candle jerk as the muscles of her vagina clenched.

She screamed out, "Oh my god! Charlie. I'm coming again!"

When the spasms that rocked her had subsided, Charlie untied the silk bindings around her arms and legs. Leaving the blindfold on, he picked her up in his arms. Her body was completely limp from her five intense detonations and slick with a faint sheen of sweat.

Gently, he carried her over to the chenille rug in front of the fire.

She wrapped her slim arms around his neck and as she sank into the deep rug, softly pressed her lips to his.

Charlie was unprepared for their first kiss, and even the merest touch of her lips on his was more than he could handle. Roughly he pulled the silk fabric away from her eyes and stood up, pulling off his jeans and shirt as he did so.

In a few seconds he was completely naked and kneeling on the rug between Candace's legs. He paused briefly, knowing it was longer than he could stand to wait, but he'd kill himself later if he didn't have this image of Candace burned into his brain forever. He memorized every gleaming, creamy, perfect inch of her incredible body, her luscious breasts, and wet, soft vagina in the flickering light of the fire. He pushed her legs open wide, bent her knees so that she could take him into her and reached for one of the condoms he had placed at random in the room, just in case he should get as incredibly lucky as he was right now.

Her eyes followed his movement, and she shook her head.

"No. I want you like this." She reached out tentatively to touch the skin on his penis with the tips of her fingers. "I want to feel you inside of me. Skin to skin."

Charlie wanted it too, more than anything in the whole world, but he was torn. Candace broke into his confusion and said, "I haven't been with anyone in over a year. So you don't have to worry about me."

He shook his head and grinned ruefully, "Me either."

"Thank god!" she exclaimed and then laughed as she reached for him and pulled his head back down. As their lips touched, her laughter died in her throat.

"Fuck me, Charlie. I need to feel your cock inside me." Her words were punctuated by a firm squeeze of her fist on his throbbing shaft. For a moment, he was afraid he was going to spurt all over the creamy skin of her belly.

Reluctantly, Charlie took a final kiss from her, sucking her lower lip between his, and he then reared back up, kneeling between her legs. More than anything, he wanted to watch as his cock slid into her pussy, just like the candle, but this time it would be his own throbbing flesh and blood pumping into her. His hard, thick shaft was about to make her scream her pleasure.

Spreading her lips with his fingers, he angled the tip of his cock into her soaked labia and probed her entry with the very top of his head.

She was not the only one wet with come. The head of his cock was slick with his sperm, slick with his intense desire to blow inside her womb.

He slid his cock up and down from her clit to the opening of her anus and back again. He knew she was going to come again, and he wanted her to do it before he got inside her, lest the convulsing of her muscles send him to his own end too fast.

Reaching his hands up to her breasts, he fondled the huge globes, rolling her nipples between his fingers, cupping her breasts. His cock was his weapon of delight on her pussy and within moments her eyes drifted shut and her neck arched. Her hands held fast onto his ass as she came against him.

Taking a deep breath, he slid into her an inch. She was so tight, which he already knew from how snugly she held onto his fingers when he pushed them inside of her, he wondered how he was going to make it one more inch, let alone the next eight.

He grasped for control, not wanting to blow his wad before he had sheathed his entire shaft inside her. More than he had ever wanted anything his whole life, he wanted to feel Candace's slick heat wrap around his cock, her tight muscles milking him dry.

Gritting his teeth, he slid his hands underneath her hips to cup her butt cheeks in his hands, and he slid in another couple of inches. She began to buck into him while using her own strength to pull his cock into her.

"Charlie, you feel so good," she moaned.

Charlie began to say, "Candy, you've got to let me move slow here. Or else..." but let his words drift off as she smiled a teeny little smile at him.

She lay back against the rug, rubbing her hands up and down his thighs. "I wouldn't want to disobey the teacher," she said, her voice a husky whisper of need. "You might have to bend me over your knee so that you can spank me," she added, her voice thick with desire.

A vision of himself spanking Candace's sweet ass as she cried out on his lap gave Charlie no choice but to plunge as deeply into her cunt as he could go. Mindless with the need to ravage her, to blow his seed as deep within her as he possibly could, he dragged her legs over his shoulders and rammed into her again and again.

Joined to him in the most elemental way, Candace's hips bucked wildly, taking him all the way inside of her and then forcing him back out along her slick canal. She cried out his name, begging him to send her over the edge, but the roaring in his ears was so loud, he could hardly make out her words. He thought he tasted blood in his mouth, so he knew he must have bitten his tongue in his crazy rush to savage her.

Breaking through his fog, he heard Candace's impassioned sob, "Oh Charlie, oh god, yes, yes, there, now!"

As her vagina clenched and sucked around his shaft, he crashed into her tight pussy one last time. Gripping her hips against his, they pounded back and forth in perfect rhythm. The muscles in his prick released and he emptied out all of his seed into her womb.

And as he collapsed on to her, with his heartbeat sounding louder than a bass drum in his ears, he said, "Sweetheart, you are definitely an A+ student."

Chapter Seven

Sunday morning, less than twenty-four hours after the most mind-blowing sex of her life, Candace sat in her cozy home office at her cherry wood desk with her laptop open to a blank Word file. She stared blindly at the cursor as it blinked at her.

"What happened to me yesterday?" she asked herself for the hundredth time since her lessons with Charlie had come to an end the previous day. Her breath fogged up her computer screen, but she didn't notice. She couldn't see anything beyond the images in her head of her writhing beneath Charlie, of Charlie plunging into her, of his fingers wet with her, touching her, making her scream out his name again and again.

She couldn't for life of her figure out how she had managed to put her clothes on, find her way to the front door, get in her car and drive home. Less than twenty-four hours later, she looked back on the entire experience and could barely make out the details of the scene through the thick sensual haze that blanketed her memories.

It was as if she was looking into a forbidden realm of pleasure, where only the privileged, where only the elite were allowed to participate. And since Candace knew she had never been one of those elite, her brain bewildered by the entire experience.

She had hardly slept the night before. Every time she closed her eyes she could swear she felt the imprint of Charlie's tongue between her legs, and when she gingerly touched herself she was wet. So wet that she couldn't resist touching herself some more. She couldn't resist thinking about everything he had done to her body. Everything he had done that made her feel so damn good.

She didn't know exactly how many times she had masturbated during the night. Five times? Six?

As soon as Sunday morning had arrived, bright and shiny through her windows, she dragged herself out of bed. She put on her robe, made herself a hot cup of strong coffee and sat down at her desk.

Candace had never let another human being control her before. Always, even when she thought she was in love, she held a part of herself back. Kept a part of her soul safe.

But with Charlie, surrounded by rose petals, candles, and sumptuous fabrics, she had given in to his every touch. If he had stopped touching her, stopped tasting her at any point, she would have begged him for more.

Disbelieving still, she shook her head and tried to make sense of her feelings. After she caught her last boyfriend cheating on her, after he had made it perfectly clear that it was her fault for being a prude, for being cold and lifeless in bed, she accepted that she was never going to know true passion. Even worse, she believed she wasn't good enough for the bastard and all the men who had come before him. They all wanted to fuck her boobs, but didn't give a shit about her heart.

But now that Charlie had pleasured her more ways in one afternoon than she had ever felt in the first twenty-eight years of her life, she wondered if it was because they had a deeper connection than just bodies.

"I'm in love with him," she whispered to herself, stunned by the discovery. But then again, how could she not be in love with him, she asked herself. He was the perfect man in every way.

She sighed and told herself to get over it. Just because their mentoring lessons had spiraled way out of control—Candace hadn't forgotten that it was entirely her own idea to take off her clothes—he was probably thinking how she was just another fan, another wannabe writer who wanted to get into his pants.

"I'm not in love," she said aloud. "I'm in lust. Big difference."

Feeling a little better, a little saner, Candace took a sip of java and suddenly words began to dance through her mind. She shook her head, but they refused to go away.

"No," she said aloud. "I can't write this. I won't write this. I promised!"

But as the words continued to appear in her mind, one after the other in beautiful succession, she accepted she had no choice but to type them into her computer.

Jolene was a good girl. She was the kind of girl a boy took home to his mother and said, "I'm going to marry her, Mom." They took one look at her angelic blue eyes and smooth golden hair and knew she was pure as driven snow.

Jolene had spent her entire life with nuns. In Catholic school uniforms. When she was a little girl, she thought every other little girl got ready to go to school in the exact same way she did, automatically reaching into their closet for the blue and white plaid jumper and white cotton shirt. She thought the only clothes in the world were white cotton knee socks and black patent leather Mary Janes.

Mary, Jolene's mother, was pleased with how well-behaved her daughter was. They were more like sisters than mother and daughter, and Mary thought Jolene told her everything. But if Jolene ever had secret thoughts in her pink and white ruffled bedroom late at night, under the covers with a flashlight, reading the latest Nancy Drew mystery about a mysterious boy who kidnapped her and gave her forbidden kisses, she never told her mother about them.

The day Jolene turned twenty-one, she was offered a full-time position playing piano for the church. For the first time in her life she was torn. She loved the nuns with all of her heart. Growing up in the safe environment of her private school had brought her nothing but happiness, but lately she had begun to feel a yearning inside of her that grew stronger every day.

Unbeknownst to her teachers, to her parents, and to her few chaste and respectful boyfriends, Jolene had been sneaking off to the used bookstore downtown and spending her allowance on books.

Jolene had long ago outgrown Nancy Drew. Her fingers trembled as she read Judy Blume. And then Jude Deveraux. And then Kathleen Woodiwiss.

Jolene would have sworn that no one liked sex, that her parents had copulated only to create her and then settled back in their separate bedrooms as soon as her father's sperm sunk into her mother's egg.

In these books she saw a far different reality and knew it was something she had to experience for herself. Before she agreed to marry one of the boys who wanted her only as a wife and mother. Before she agreed to spend the rest of her days playing piano in accompaniment for the little girls as they sang their hymns.

Bravely she told her parents and the nuns that she was going to spend some time in the city. She told them she was going to work with a local church there – which in fact she was, part time – and they were all so proud of her. Her parents found *her an apartment and paid for six months' rent and didn't worry about their precious daughter. Why would they, when she had never given them even the slightest bit of trouble.*

Jolene Mackenzie was a good girl.

Zane stood behind the bar and wiped another glass dry, sliding it beneath the counter in preparation for opening the bar. His bar.

He still couldn't believe "Piano Man" was his. Every time he pulled up underneath the neon sign on his Harley, he got a rush. But as he wiped down the brass counter one more time, he frowned at his reflection. If he didn't find a great piano player, and fast, "Piano Man" would be a laughingstock among piano bars. Unfortunately, the last five guys he had auditioned stunk.

Hell, he could play better than them, and he could barely read a note.

Someone from outside pushed the door open slightly and a shaft of blinding light hit Zane across the forehead.

"Excuse me," he heard a timid little voice say.

"We're closed," he said gruffly. "Come back at five."

But the girl disobeyed him and walked through the door.

Zane looked at her in disbelief. The last time he'd seen someone as prim and proper as the young girl standing before him, he was in church looking at a nun. And lord knew he hadn't set foot in a church for well over a decade. Maybe two.

On second thought, no nun ever had such gorgeous blue eyes and a mouth he could imagine wrapped around his dick.

"I said we're closed," he said, glaring at her. It was pissing him off the way his dick was perking up just because some meek, blond girl, barely out of pigtails, was walking across the floor toward him.

"*Are you the owner?*" she asked him, as if she hadn't heard him tell her to leave twice already.

He glared at her, trying to scare her away, but when she kept staring at him with her huge, blue eyes, and held her ground, he nodded. "*What's it to you?*"

She held up the want ads. "*I'm here to apply for the piano job.*"

He snorted. "*You?*" He threw his head back and laughed in her face to drive the point home. "*Honey, this ain't no church, and you certainly ain't no piano man.*"

Her face set in a mulish expression. She turned away from him, but instead of walking back out the door, she walked towards the small stage and sat down at the piano.

"*I'm auditioning,*" she said, and he knew she was trying to be brave, but even in the dim light of the bar he could see her hands shaking.

He looked down at his jeans and cursed the huge bulge in the front of his pants before taking several menacing steps towards her. But before he could forcibly grab her by her skinny little shoulders and throw her out onto the sidewalk, she opened the *Blue Book of Jazz* and *Pop* standards and began to play.

He stopped in his tracks. She played thirty seconds of one song and then flipped the page and played thirty seconds of the next. Zane sank down into the nearest chair.

The little choirgirl was incredible. The piano player of his dreams. Shit! He couldn't have her in the bar. Every man in the place was going to start having dreams about laying her sweet little body over the front of his thighs, pulling up her pleated skirt and...

"*Stop!*" Zane said loudly, almost more to himself than to her, but this time she obeyed him.

"*I want the job, sir,*" she said in a calm but firm voice.

"No. The bar is called *Piano Man,* not *Piano Woman.*"

"That's sexual discrimination," she pointed out.

He rolled his eyes. "You're not good enough."

Her eyes shot fire at him. "Yes I am!"

Suddenly Zane had a thought. "How badly do you want this job?"

She lowered her long eyelashes and then looked back up at him. "I want it."

Slowly, Zane got up from the chair and sauntered over to her. Sitting down next to her on the piano bench, he said, "I'm willing to make you a deal." He saw her swallow and then she licked her lips.

"I'm listening," she said as she removed her slender fingers from the keyboard and clasped them primly in her lap.

He bent his head over hers until their lips were touching and then he slipped his tongue into her mouth, dying to taste her. "This is what I want. Are you willing to give it to me?"

Her eyes grew even wider, but she nodded.

"Whenever I want?"

She nodded again.

"However I want?"

This time she smiled at him and reached out her hand to shake on the agreement. "I'm Jolene," she said in a voice as sweet as honey. "What's your name?"

That first night, Jolene played the piano like she had never played it before. She knew she was still on shaky ground. Besides, she was so excited and nervous about the terms of her contract with Zane, she needed to blow off her energy at the keyboard or she'd go crazy.

All night she had watched him out of the corner of her eye. In her fantasies, she had never created any man as incredible as this one. Six feet tall, and all muscle beneath his worn jeans and tight black t-shirt, his teeth gleamed white against the dark tan of his skin. Stubble covered his jaw line and his shoulder-length dark brown hair and piercing green eyes made him look so much like a pirate that Jolene felt as if he was living in the wrong century, on the wrong continent even.

At the end of the evening as the last customer walked out, he locked the door and then joined her on the stage again.

"Stand up," he said as he sat down on the piano bench.

She did as he asked and tried to get her knees to stop shaking. Pulling her so that she was standing between his knees, he reached around the back of her skirt and popped open the top button, then slid the zipper down until her skirt fell into a heap at her heels.

She looked around the bar at the hundred tea-light candles glowing, at the fireplace roaring, and knew that all of her fantasies were about to be made real.

He hooked his fingers into the edges of her cotton panties and slowly slid them off, over her ass and down her smooth, untouched thighs. Jolene had to fight the urge to cover herself from him, and she barely managed to keep her hands clenched at her sides.

Before she knew it he had moved his hand between her legs and slipped the index finger of his right hand into her vagina. She gasped even as she felt her muscles convulse around his thick, long finger.

Jolene was scared. She had barely even touched herself there in the shower! But she was so excited her fear hardly seemed to matter. She strained against his finger and he pushed it so far inside her his palm covered her and his thumb was pressing on the sensitive flesh at the top of her vagina.

She knew from her books that it was called the clitoris, but she could hardly think the word to herself.

"Your clit is so swollen," he murmured, his mouth less than an inch from the cleft between her legs.

She liked the way clit sounded coming from Zane's mouth and she forced herself to say the word out loud. "My clit has been swollen all night," she murmured.

He groaned, then lifted his thumb off her clit and blew softly on the engorged flesh. Her vagina clenched around his finger and as he blew on her tender clit again and slid his finger in and out of her vagina, she closed her eyes and started to see a rainbow of colors. Her legs were shaking uncontrollably now, but not from fear. She was trying to crest the tallest hill she had ever encountered, and she needed Zane to help her over it.

She put her hands on the back of his head and pressed his mouth to her. "Thank god," she cried as he worked his tongue and his teeth over her inflamed flesh and clasped her buttocks with his strong hands.

Jolene's world exploded in a blaze of fireworks. Now that she knew what awaited her on the other side, she knew she would never be able to go back to the perfect world she had come from.

Jolene Mackenzie wasn't a good girl anymore.

Candace looked up from her computer screen and realized she had been writing all morning. She reread the beginning of her new story and smiled.

Evidently, Charlie's lessons had inspired more than her underutilized libido. His incredible lessons had stimulated her mind and imagination as well.

But then as she remembered their promise to each other to keep whatever happened in Charlie's "classroom" inside the classroom, she was assailed by guilt.

A bad little voice inside Candace's head said, *Don't worry, honey. He'll never read your book. He'll never find out that you and he are the live action figures playing out your sex scenes.*

Candace had never written so fluidly before. What's more, she had never been so inspired to continue with her story, to find out what was going to happen with Jolene and Zane.

I can't stop now. The words reverberated in her skull, so she said them aloud, announcing them to herself in her empty office. "I can't stop now. I *won't* stop now!" she proclaimed and gave up trying to win the battle to be the good girl she was supposed to be.

"Being good has always been my problem," she muttered, thinking how very close to the truth her new heroine Jolene was. And then Candace smiled again thinking about all the different ways Jolene was going to be bad, and couldn't wait to get the story finished.

Candace spent the rest of the afternoon typing away at her laptop computer, working hard to get every nuance and every emotion of her first two lessons with Charlie just right on the page.

And as she did so, Candace began to forget that she had ever lived a life without pleasure.

Chapter Eight

Charlie stood up from his desk and walked into the guest bedroom of his house. He hadn't been able to work since Saturday, since the day his whole life had been turned upside down by a redheaded vixen who didn't even know the power she wielded. He needed to call her, but as it was, he was still too chicken to dial her entire number without hanging up.

He hoped she would still talk to him. After the way they had parted on Saturday, after she stood up, put her clothes on mechanically, and then turned to him with a plastered smile and shook his hand, saying "Thank you very much for the lessons, Charlie," he wasn't sure if he had done the right thing with her at all.

His conscience was bothering him more than he wanted to admit. Above and beyond the fact that he was worrying he might have taken advantage of her, was the undisputable truth that if he were with her again, he knew he wouldn't have one single qualm about making her scream his name out, over and over again.

He was still upset that she had left after only seven orgasms, when he had planned to give her at least ten. He supposed, somewhat ruefully, the three times he took care of himself that night after she had left practically made up the difference. Nonetheless, he would rather have Candace coming in his arms or on the tip of his tongue, than his hand and his memory making him shoot all over the shower walls.

The phone rang and Charlie picked up the cordless handset on his shiny black and white kitchen island.

"Charlie Gibson."

"Hi Charlie. It's Candace. How are you?"

Charlie nearly dropped the phone he was so surprised by her phone call. "Um, uh, I'm fine. Great. Super." He thwacked his forehead with the back of his hand for sounding like such an idiot. "How are you doing?"

He heard her laugh across the wireless phone line and the choking sensation around his heart eased up a bit.

"I'm great Charlie. Really, really great. I wanted to thank you for your excellent lessons on Saturday."

"You do?" he asked and then tried to cover his gaffe by saying, "What I mean to say is, I wasn't sure if — "

Thankfully Candace cut him off before he could make an even bigger ass of himself. "I loved every second of it, Charlie. And you know what, I've been writing better than ever."

"That's great," he said to her, and meant it. He hadn't written worth a shit since Saturday, but he didn't care at all. All he wanted was to see her again, but he was afraid he'd be coming on too strong, that he'd be too obviously sniffing after her, if he suggested moving onto lesson three.

"Anyway," she said, "I was wondering if you'd be up for lesson three?"

Her matter of fact, professional tone confused him, again. Didn't she know what was bound to happen again when they got in a room together? But he was so glad she wanted to see him again, he pushed the thought aside.

"I certainly am," he said, trying to sound as detached as she did.

"Should we meet at your house again? Or mine perhaps?"

"Actually, this time I was thinking we would meet at a restaurant."

"A restaurant?" she said, her misgivings sounding clearly in her voice. "To learn about sex toys?"

He chuckled softly into the phone. "Don't you trust your mentor, Candace?"

She was silent across the line for a couple of seconds and he knew she was thinking it over. *Say yes*, his brain urged her telepathically.

"Yes I do, Charlie," she said.

"Great," he said. "Do you know where Oceanview Restaurant is on the edge of Golden Gate Park?"

* * * * *

Candace was shocked by Charlie's suggestion. She had been shocked ever since she and Charlie had hung up that morning.

When she had boldly called him, she was completely sure she was going to have no problem rolling with whatever Charlie was going to throw at her. In spite of her misgivings after their first two lessons, she couldn't suppress a shiver of delight as she imagined him using a dildo, or something even more creative, on her during this lesson.

She couldn't help the flicker of disappointment when it didn't look like that was going to happen. There was no way he could ply her with a dildo in a restaurant, was there?

Besides, wasn't learning about having sex in new locations lesson four, not lesson three?

She checked her makeup and outfit one last time before stepping out of the car. She didn't want to look as if she was trying to seduce him, but then again, she wanted to look as sexy as possible.

On Saturday at his house, he had seen her under forgiving candlelight and fire glow. As the sun hadn't set yet and he was going to see her in full daylight, she wanted him to think she was pretty.

She had dressed a little more risqué tonight than she usually would have for a date. She shook her head. *This is not a date*, she reminded herself again. He was her mentor and she was his apprentice.

If she read anything more into it than professional education, she was going to end up with a broken heart. Candace figured she already had enough of those as it was.

Nonetheless, she had dug out a gold-sequined tank top from the bottom drawer of her dresser and paired it with a flirty black skirt, which brushed the tops of her kneecaps when she walked. She had swept her ginger curls up onto the top of her head with a gold clip and wore small gold-hoop earrings on her lobes. The final touch to her outfit was a pair of frivolous spike-heeled black and gold sandals that she had never had the nerve to wear before.

She left the parking lot and walked up the pathway to the beach. Charlie was waiting for her on the steps to the sand, looking out to the Pacific Ocean. She noticed he had a plastic shopping bag in his hand and shivered, wondering what was inside of it.

She put her hand on his arm and he turned around to face her with a huge smile on his gorgeous face.

"Candy," he said, "You look amazing."

She blushed. "Thank you. So do you."

He looked better than ever, which was really quite a feat considering how incredible he had looked the two other times she had been with him. He had dressed up slightly, wearing navy blue light-wool slacks and a pink pin-striped long-sleeved Ralph Lauren shirt.

He slipped her hand into his and was moving towards the front door of the restaurant. She pulled back slightly, saying "I'm curious about what you've got in the plastic bag."

Charlie turned and smiled at her. "I was going to wait to give it to you until we went inside, but now's as good a time as any, I suppose." He opened the bag so that she could look into it.

"A pair of panties?" she said and looked up at him in confusion.

He nodded. "I want you to put them on."

"Now?"

"Once we get inside, go to the restroom and change out of the panties you're wearing."

Candace felt her face turn red. "And then what?"

He shrugged. "And then we'll eat and enjoy each other's company." He handed her the bag, then pulled her back up the steps towards the restaurant.

"Let's go inside. I'm starved," he said, and she had no other choice but to follow him.

Candace wondered how it was possible for her pussy to already be soaking wet when all she had done was say a few sentences to the guy. He was turning her into a walking orgasm, for god's sake.

They stepped into the foyer of the beautiful restaurant and he whispered in her ear, "I think the bathroom is just down the hall to the left." A shiver ran down her spine as his breath stroked her cheek and she obediently headed off to the ladies room, plastic bag in hand.

Once in a stall, she took a deep breath and wondered if she should cut bait and run before she got in any deeper than she could handle.

But then she thought about the hundred pages she had already written of her new book and how well it was going, and she knew that a true professional should be willing to give everything to her work, to try anything if it had the potential of enhancing her art. So after listening carefully to make sure no one else was in the bathroom, she slid her red silk panties off of her bare legs, folded them neatly, and slid them into her gold hand-purse. Gingerly opening the plastic bag, she pulled out a black thong.

"Is this it?" she whispered to herself in the bathroom stall, as she turned it this way and that, poking her hand back into the bag to see if there was something else.

Wondering what the big deal was about the thong, and knowing it was bound to be something good if Charlie was behind it, with her heart racing, Candace slipped her feet into the thong. Settling the panties up on her hips she let her skirt fall back down over her hips to her knees.

Wadding up the plastic bag into a ball, she stuffed it into the garbage can in her stall and stepped back out under the fluorescent lighting above the sink. Taking one last look at herself in the mirror, she thought she looked pretty confident considering how jumpy she felt. She grabbed her purse from the counter in front of the mirror and pushed the bathroom door open.

She rounded the corner and headed back into the entryway, careful to walk slowly so she wouldn't trip in her very high heels and make a fool of herself. She looked up and saw Charlie watching her carefully and she gave him a little grin. He reached into his right pocket with his hand and suddenly she felt her vagina tingling.

She stopped dead in her tracks, propped herself up against the wall with her left hand and closed her eyes, trying to determine what had just happened to her.

She felt as if she had just sat down on a vibrator! Not that she would know firsthand what that would feel like, since she didn't own any self-stimulants, but she couldn't disregard the quivering sensation between her legs.

How could that be, she asked herself. Comprehension dawned on her and she opened her eyes to meet Charlie's gaze.

He looked like a lion who had just captured a milk truck.

He held his hand out to her as he met her halfway down the hallway and said, "Good. I'm glad you did what I asked you to do. Now let's go eat."

"Eat?" Candace asked him, her voice squeaky, off its normal pitch. "We're really going to eat?"

The next thing she knew, the hostess was seating them at a table by the window, and Charlie was ordering drinks for them.

"This is a joke, right?" she asked him, half-hoping he'd say, *Yes, go put your regular panties on and then we'll head back to my place so I can fuck your brains out*, but mostly hoping he'd press the button on his little remote control again to send her into orbit.

"There are a lot of strangers in the room with us, aren't there?" he said rather wickedly.

Her mouth fell open. She quickly moved to shut it, intent on keeping her cool even though this third lesson of theirs was already moving far beyond their last lesson, far beyond her realm of comfort, far beyond anything she ever thought to encounter in her lifetime.

And here I thought I had experienced everything with him on Saturday, she mused silently as she pretended to study the menu. The words were a blur, and when the waiter came to take their order she couldn't seem to open her mouth. Thankfully, Charlie ordered for them both.

Candace was on pins and needles as she waited for the next surge of energy on her pussy lips, as she waited for Charlie to gratify and simultaneously embarrass her across the table. Her vagina was already incredibly wet, just from seeing Charlie, from the one jolt he had already given her, and from the sensual promise she read in his eyes.

"So, how was the rest of your day?" he asked her innocently, as if he didn't hold the control to her entire world in the pocket of his wool slacks.

She opened her mouth to reply, but her mouth was as dry as her pussy was wet. She reached for her water glass and as she lifted the cool rim to her lips, Charlie put his weapon of pleasure to use again.

The sensations that washed through her vagina were so intense she nearly dropped her glass. Suavely, Charlie reached for the glass and slid it from her fingers back to the table without spilling a drop. She gripped the edge of the table and rode the waves of pleasure her panties were giving her under her skirt.

Charlie let off his cunt controller—as she was beginning to think of it now that she knew the absolute power he wielded over her—a second later when the waiter dropped off two glasses of champagne and two small salads. Candace looked around at the other diners in the posh restaurant and wondered if any of them had noticed her writhing in her seat. From the expressions on their faces, she didn't think anyone had, thank god.

Charlie speared a crisp slice of tomato and held it out for her across the table. "Taste this," he said, and she noted he was holding the fork with his left hand, so she shook her head.

"No thank you," she said as formally as she could under the circumstances.

He took his right hand out of his pocket and put it on the table. "Look, both hands are free now." He held out the tomato slice again. "I want to watch your teeth and lips take in this plump, juicy tomato," he urged her and this time she acquiesced.

But as she began to open her mouth to slide the sweet fruit off of his fork, the buzzing on her clit began in earnest. This time, she was too close to the edge to fight off the explosion.

A low sound came from her throat, and she clenched the edge of the table so tightly the skin on her knuckles turned white.

"Let it go," Charlie implored her softly across the table.

Candace closed her eyes and let the waves of intense pleasure suck her into the abyss once again. Little whimpers escaped from her mouth, no matter how hard she tried to hold them back. She was dimly aware of Charlie's intent gaze as he watched her come.

Just as her orgasm had rocked all the way through her, turning her completely inside-out, their waiter approached their table with a concerned look on his face.

"Is everything all right here?"

Charlie let off the controls and looked expectantly at her, waiting for her answer. She smiled tremulously at the waiter. "Yes. Thank you. Everything's fine," hoping he would just get the hell away from the table and leave them alone.

Instead the waiter said, much to her ongoing chagrin, "I was afraid that something was wrong with your salad. The look on your face while you were eating was—"

Their young waiter seemed stuck on searching for just the right word to describe the public agony of her sexual release, so she jumped in and said, "It's just that the tomato was *so incredibly good.*" She hoped her performance was a believable one.

Finally, he smiled at her and bowed a little, saying, "Good. Great. Your main courses should be out in just a few minutes," before he walked away.

"You really are an A+ student," Charlie said as she touched at the corners of her mouth with her napkin.

She looked up at him and couldn't decide if she was furious with him or falling harder for him than ever before. She decided to keep things light until she decided.

"And you are quite the inventive teacher, aren't you?"

He raised an eyebrow and slid the small remote control across the table.

She looked at him in surprise. "Why are you giving this to me?"

He reached for it again, saying, "I'm happy to take it back if you want," but she grabbed it a split second before he did.

"No. I think it's better if I've got this with me for the rest of the meal." She slid the remote control onto her lap and put it underneath her napkin.

He laughed and ate a bite of his salad, washing it down with a sip of champagne before saying, "When I tell you to, I want you to press the on button."

"Are you crazy?" she asked, positive she could never do such a wanton thing. After all, it was one thing for him to drive her wild in public, but it was unthinkable for her to do the very same thing to herself!

He stared deeply into her eyes, his pupils slightly dilated, his breathing heavy and slow. "Now."

She stared back at him, willing herself to stay strong, to stick to the only sense of herself she had ever known, and shook her head once.

"I said now," he repeated in a clear, firm voice.

"No," she said as her heart raced straight to her throat and got stuck there.

"I'm only going to say it one more time," he said, his voice and face devoid of all expression. "Push the button right now."

And this time, she knew she had no choice but to obey him, although she wondered how he would punish her if she disobeyed him. But right now, she didn't have the strength for disobedience. Considering she was on the verge of coming just from the sound of his voice, she figured she may as well go for the whole damn thing. For that matter, she didn't want to look too deeply into the fact that she desperately wanted to press the button, that her finger had been trembling over the on button ever since she slipped it beneath her napkin.

So she took a deep breath that quickly turned shallow, pressed the button and turned the machine in her panties on. As she did so, Charlie said in too low a voice for anyone but her to hear, "I want you to keep your eyes open. Look at me while you're coming. And keep holding down that button no matter what else happens."

Candace felt hot, slick liquid pool between her legs as she digested his words. So she trained her eyes on him, and every time she was tempted to shut him out, to experience this radical pleasure all by herself, he said, "Open up, Candy. Open up." And so she lifted her heavy lids and instinctively widened her legs underneath the table, opening everything up for the man she was falling for heedlessly.

Candace was on the brink of bursting when the waiter arrived with their dishes. She was tempted to turn off the machine purring away in her labia, she began to lift her finger off the button, but Charlie's eyes held her in some sort of magnetic pull, so she continued to hold the switch down.

As she continued to detonate in her seat, the waiter set down their plates and then since they were obviously ignoring him, he stepped away from the table again without a word. Charlie whispered, "You're so beautiful," and it was enough to make her close her eyes and fall back into her chair, holding onto the remote for dear life as she fell deeper and deeper into the void.

When she finally resurfaced, it took her several long moments to figure out what had happened, to remember where she was. All she knew was that Charlie was with her, as he had been for every one of the best sexual releases she had ever experienced.

She took in his broad grin across the table, and the expectant, slightly nervous look on his face suddenly made her want to shout out with happiness.

"Wow," Charlie said. "That was more intense than I thought it would be." He looked a little worried as he said, "Are you angry with me?"

"Nope," she said matter-of-factly. "It was a great lesson. At least as good as one and two." Taking a sip of champagne she leaned closer to him across the table and said, "I have to tell you, I can't wait to find out what you have planned for lesson four."

Finally, the look of surprise on Charlie's face turned into laughter and he relaxed back into his chair.

"You certainly are full of surprises," he said with obvious appreciation.

Candace just smiled a new I'm-All-Woman-So-Watch-Out smile. She waved the waiter over to their table.

"Could you pack up our food into a doggy bag and leave it up at the front desk?" she asked him sweetly. "We just remembered a meeting we need to be at right away." Reaching into her purse, she threw a wad of twenty-dollar bills onto the table and stood up.

She held out her hand to Charlie. "Come with me," she said in a husky voice.

He rearranged the enormous bulge in his trousers and slid the chair back to stand up. Candace folded her small hand into his large, warm one and a shiver ran up her spine.

She was being so naughty! She hardly recognized herself as the woman she'd been for the past twenty-eight years.

Stepping outside into the ocean breeze, laughter bubbled up through her. Kicking off her shoes, she pulled Charlie along towards the grove of trees several hundred yards from the restaurant. They walked in silence until they reached the small forest.

Candace ducked her head to get under the branches of the nearest cypress tree and stepped inside to find a small clearing of soft, white sand in the middle of the circle of huge trees.

She turned to Charlie, who had followed her into the center of the grove, and put her hands on either side of his gorgeous face. Standing on her tippy-toes she tilted her neck to nip at his lips with her teeth. She tasted the salty breeze on them with her tongue.

"Candy," he groaned, wrapping his large hands on her ass, pulling her against his erection, grinding her against him.

She sank to the sandy floor and he descended with her, their lips and tongues still entwined in a sensuous dance.

"You didn't actually think I was going to let that huge cock of yours go to waste, did you?" she asked him, mirth twinkling in her large brown eyes as she unzipped his pants and pulled out his throbbing penis.

Rolling him over onto his back, she crawled up on top of him, stroking the velvet skin on his cock as she did so. He reached up under her skirt and roughly pulled the motorized thong from her hips. She moved her legs to help him get the panties off.

"Fuck me, Candace," he said compellingly, his voice full of need.

She licked her lips and with great concentration kneeled above his cock and guided it into her wet hole with her hand. "Charlie!" she moaned as he slid deeper and deeper into her.

He leaned up to kiss her. As their lips found each other, she began to ride him with a ferocity that was more than he could handle after already watching her explode twice in her seat at the restaurant.

Her tight, slick cunt sucked his cock so thoroughly he knew he was going to blow. Wanting to take her with him he slid his hand up under her skirt and pressed his thumb against her engorged clit.

"Oh god, you feel so good, don't stop!" she cried as he simultaneously pounded in and out of her and swirled her taut nub.

Together, they fell into a gulf of intense pleasure, kissing each other frantically, thrashing heedlessly against each other as they climbed higher and higher on the soft sand floor of their private love shack.

Chapter Nine

Candace shook his hand and said, "Thank you for a wonderful lesson," then got into her car and drive away.

Charlie stood in the parking lot and watched her leave. He was unaccountably disappointed. He had hoped that maybe they had progressed beyond the handshake now; hell, he thought they had progressed beyond a handshake the minute she started stripping off her clothes and he had pressed his tongue to her eager clit.

He ran his hands through his hair and walked out onto the beach, sitting down on an old log. He knew what was happening to him and it scared the shit out of him.

Good old Charlie Gibson, writer extraordinaire of erotic romance, who hadn't had a serious girlfriend since his messy divorce five years earlier, was falling in love.

And he didn't have a clue how to tell the object of his affection how he felt.

"So much for being good with dialogue," he muttered into the wind and let the waves carry his words away.

* * * * *

Candace drove home from the restaurant Monday night still wearing the remote controlled thong, with the controls stashed neatly in her little purse along with her silk panties. A balloon of joy was swelling up inside of her chest.

Being with Charlie made her feel good. Okay, so being with him made her pussy feel incredibly good, but it was more than just the sexual rush she got whenever he was near her.

When she was with Charlie, she felt like the best of her was actually breaking out. The walls that she had built up around her heart to protect herself from pain were falling, one by one, and even though she was frightened about what lay ahead, she wasn't sorry that she had embarked on this crazy ride with Charlie.

My mentor, she thought, and laughed wickedly, thinking about how upset Sheba, Queen of the Sluts, would be if she knew just how hot and hands-on Charlie's version of mentoring actually was.

But in addition to all of the personal revelations Candace was having, she also felt more inspired to write than she ever had before. And as soon as she parked her car and let herself inside the door, she headed straight to her office and booted up her computer.

Pausing for just a moment to gather her thoughts, she began to type furiously, the words coming out as fast as a hard rain.

Jolene felt her innocence falling off of her in thick sheets. Every time she exploded in Zane's arms, she changed just a little bit more. But still, twenty-one years of Catholic School training was hard to get rid of, no matter how powerful her orgasms were, no matter how much she loved the feel of his thick cock between her legs.

All day, she had been working with the local Catholic church, helping the choir get ready for their annual performance, and she couldn't help but wonder if she had fallen in with the devil.

It wasn't the first time this thought had occurred to her. Surrounded by all of the pure, untouched young girls and the solemn nun who was conducting the practice, Jolene felt dirty. As if she didn't deserve to feel the way she felt when Zane was in the room with her.

No, it was worse than that. All she had to do was think about Zane, think about his full lips, the way his stubble scratched her breasts, the tender skin on the inside of her thighs, and her panties instantly got wet.

That kind of thing only happened to bad girls. And although Jolene had made a conscious decision to stray from the path of perfection, she wondered if she had strayed too far.

Now, as she stood in front of the door to "Piano Man", she was tempted to turn and run as fast as she could back to the life she used to live.

Suddenly, the door flew open, and Zane's large, muscular body filled the frame. "Why are you skulking around outside?" he asked irately. "You know I don't like you hanging around by yourself in this neighborhood."

Jolene scowled at him. It felt so good to give in to her natural emotions instead of always caging her responses in politeness.

"Ha! That's a good one," she replied in a snotty voice. "I'd like to know how anyone on the street is going to do anything worse to me than the things you've already made me do!"

His eyes narrowed at her sarcastic comment and roughly he grabbed her by the arm and hauled her inside. Pushing her up against the wall, he shoved one of his leather-clad thighs between her legs and pinned her arms up against the wall.

"Are you actually telling me that you think I made you grab my head so that you could rub your cunt all over my tongue?"

She whimpered as his hands tightened on her wrists. She was aware of the huge bulge in Zane's tight leather pants pressing up against her hip, and she couldn't believe how much she wanted him to unzip his pants and plunge into her until she couldn't see or breathe or even speak.

"Do you expect me to believe that I made you so sensitive that the slightest touch of my tongue on your clit makes you scream? That I'm to blame because you are so hot and ready all the time all I have to do is slide into your pussy an inch and you lose control?"

The way he growled the questions at her, Jolene was almost afraid to respond. Frankly, she wasn't sure what the right answer was anymore.

But before she could say anything, he cursed and shoved away from her. "I got a present for you."

Jolene's face lit up and she started to move towards him, saying, "You did? Can I see what it is?" but the look he gave her was so fierce she instinctively backed up against the wall again, as if she could hide in between the studs that held the building up. Rationally, she knew he would never hurt her – he was too gentle, too intent on giving her pleasure – but by the look in his eyes at the moment, she wasn't sure she knew him at all.

He walked behind the bar and pulled out a plastic bag. "If I give this to you, do you promise to do exactly what I tell you to do?"

Jolene laughed and sassed back at him, "When have I not done exactly what you've told me to do, boss?" She felt like she was back on solid ground as she waited for him to give her the present.

He tossed the bag over the counter at her and she caught it right before it knocked over one of the tea-lights on a table. "Can I open it right now?"

He shook his head. "Go to the bathroom, and when you come back out to play, I want you to be wearing what's in the bag."

She cocked her head at him in confusion. "You bought me clothes? What's wrong with what I have on?" she asked as she gestured to her sky blue cocktail dress.

"Nothing," he replied, "as long as you have a thing for nuns." He shook his head. "Just go. The bar's about to open."

As he turned back to getting the bar ready for the busy evening ahead, Jolene headed for the bathroom. Barely staving off her curiosity, she walked into the ladies room and locked the door behind her. Opening up the bag all she saw was an itty-bitty scrap of black fabric and wondered just what kind of game Zane was playing with her.

"He can't actually expect me to put this on!" she exclaimed as she picked up what looked to be a pair of underwear. She had heard about thongs but had never worn a pair of them herself. They seemed much too slutty and besides, they didn't seem the least bit comfortable.

She wondered what Zane would do if she didn't put the thong on. "He'll never know," she whispered, but at the same time, she knew he never did anything without a reason, and the rapidly emerging bad-girl in her wondered what his reason was.

At the least, she knew he would make her feel incredibly good when the last customer had left for the night and it was just the two of them. She still blushed at the thought of how she had let him penetrate her with the mouth of a beer bottle the previous night. Not that it didn't make her scream with joy, of course, it was just that the whole thing seemed a little crazy.

Jolene was pretty sure that being with a good girl like her was a new experience for Zane, even though she was getting to be more and more of an ex-good-girl with every night she spent at the "Piano Man". By the looks of the women who threw themselves at him night after night — trashy hair, too-tight jeans, caked-on makeup — she figured the only reason he was with her was because she was a novelty.

If his reaction to finding out she was a virgin that first night was anything to go by, he was definitely in uncharted territory. After his release, she could have sworn he was about to apologize to her for taking advantage of her, but she couldn't stand to hear him say he was sorry about the best thing that had ever happened to her, so she kissed him before he could say the words.

She refocused on the thong she was holding between her thumb and index finger. "What the heck," she said. "If he wants me to wear a thong, I'll wear a thong. And he'll be the only person who knows." It was a little exciting, she thought, for him to know she was hardly wearing any underwear underneath her ankle-length dress.

She slipped off her white cotton panties and pulled the small slip of material up around her hips. It felt as if there was something firm tucked up around her vagina lips, and she shrugged, figuring all thongs came with plastic in the crotch, for extra support, perhaps?

She walked back into the bar and handed Zane the plastic bag. He opened it, and when he saw her white cotton underpants lying in the bottom of the bag, he smiled. Jolene headed for the piano to warm up, and when she sat down on the piano stool she was distinctly aware of a pressure against her clitoris. She stole a glance at Zane, and wondered if this is what he had planned for her, but he was on the phone and didn't so much as look at her.

Jolene smiled a small smile and felt the tips of her breasts tingling behind her white cotton bra. Now that she knew Zane wanted her to play piano all night for his customers with a solid reminder of what was to come later pressing against her already swollen flesh, it took a great deal of effort for her to concentrate on playing scales to warm up her fingers.

An hour later she was playing the chorus to Billy Joel's "Piano Man", which had just been requested by one of the regulars, when she felt something funny happening between her legs. She missed a note and then quickly covered with a vamp up the ivory keyboard to make it sound like she was playing Billy's song wrong on purpose.

Then she felt it again, a quick jolt of energy pulsing against her clit. She looked up in confusion, but she didn't lose her place in the song this time. Zane was standing behind the bar watching her carefully.

What the heck is wrong with these panties, she wondered as she played into the last rousing chorus of the song. Suddenly, the buzzing started up again between her thighs, but this time she knew that somehow, some way, Zane was manning the controls to her cunt.

As a huge orgasm overtook her, as her nipples grew rock-hard and incredibly sensitive, as her clitoris grew engorged by the stimulation of the vibrating thong, she played louder and louder, faster and faster, hoping the booming piano would mask the whimpers that escaped her as wave upon wave of pleasure shook her to her very core.

When the orgasm had finished ripping through her and she played the final line of the song, she paused for a moment to catch her breath, staring unseeingly at the song sheets in front of her.

She now knew two things for sure.

Zane Michels was, indeed, the devil.

And she, Jolene Mackenzie, had most definitely strayed onto the path of evil.

Candace saved her document and looked up through the window of her office just as the sun was rising in the night sky. She slumped back against her chair feeling equal parts pride and remorse.

On the one hand, she was writing the best damn erotica of her life! But on the other hand, with every page she wrote she felt guiltier and guiltier about abusing Charlie's trust. The problem was simple: She may have promised not to reveal the content of their lessons to anyone, but once the words started to come to her, she couldn't stop herself.

It was just how she felt when she was with Charlie.

Completely, utterly out of control.

* * * * *

The phone rang loudly three times and Candace sat straight up in bed, the covers falling to her waist. *Why am I still in bed at 5 pm,* she wondered as she looked at the clock by her bedside.

Then, in a rush, memories of sitting in the restaurant coming violently while Charlie watched closely, flooded into her head.

I need to stop thinking about him all the time, she admonished herself. *I'm starting to act like an obsessive fan, and I need to cut it out ASAP!*

She threw back the covers, grabbed a silk robe from her closet and walked into her kitchen to make herself a cup of coffee. While she was sleeping the mailman had made his delivery and she picked up the pile of bills and magazines and took them into the kitchen with her. The words EROTICA CONTEST caught her eye and she pulled the leaflet out from the stack of envelopes and read:

Do you have an erotic manuscript that would knock our panties off? If so, you should enter the 15ᵗʰ annual Erotic Writers Contest. If your manuscript makes it to the finals, your book will be read by a panel of top editors. A secret celebrity judge will present the winner his or her award, along with a $10,000 grand prize check! Enter now!

Candace usually threw contest solicitations out, but that was because she knew she didn't have something that could win. The wheels started turning in her head.

"No," she said aloud in her empty kitchen. "I can't do it. It's not right."

The wicked little voice inside her said, *Come on Candace. You know you've got a winner on your hands. Charlie will never know.*

She tried to ignore the voice, but it just got louder, saying, *This is the entire reason he agreed to be your mentor. Charlie wants you to become a better writer. After all, isn't that the only reason why he's sleeping with you?*

Candace wanted to argue, she wanted to tell her nasty inner-voice that Charlie was sleeping with her because he cared about her, but in her experience, that was never what was really going on.

Suddenly angry at all of the ways men had used her via false pretenses over the years, she exclaimed, "I don't owe him anything! He's just my mentor, we have a strictly professional relationship, and I need to enter this contest to further my career."

Using her past hurts as her guide, tapping into her failed love affairs to try and cover up the strong feelings she had for Charlie, she picked up her phone and dialed his number.

She needed to schedule lesson four, and fast. After all, she had a book to finish and there was only one way she could get the experience she needed.

In Charlie Gibson's arms.

Chapter Ten

Charlie was pleased that Candace had called him to arrange lesson four so quickly. *Maybe she likes me a little bit after all*, he thought to himself.

The only problem was, he hadn't quite figured out an appropriate site for their lesson on sex in new locations. Dodging her questions on the phone, he told her he'd pick her up at noon on Thursday and surprise her with their destination.

He ran through the options again in his head. A sex club was too predictable, and there was no way in hell he'd let anyone else get his hands on Candace. Doing it in his car, parked out over a beautiful vista, was too much like being in high school. Having a quickie in a dark alley on a busy street was straight out of his latest novel, so that was out of the question.

With only fifteen minutes to go until he was supposed to be at Candace's house, he still hadn't come up with a good location for their lesson. "Where is the one place she'd never think about having sex?" he asked himself in frustrated tones.

Then the answer came to him in a flash, so he smiled, grabbed his keys, and hopped in his red Z3 BMW convertible, turning up Aerosmith so loud he could feel the bass drum vibrating in his seat.

* * * * *

"The zoo?"

Candace turned to him with a look of utter surprise.

Charlie paid for their tickets and followed her into the park. "Yup," he said, nodding happily. "The zoo."

She shook her head and chuckled. "You have got to be kidding. I'd like to know one thing that's sexy about the zoo."

He pulled her close and said, "You," before kissing her hard on her lips. Grabbing her hand, he said, "Let's go ride the train around the park."

Candace raised an eyebrow, but followed after him. "You're the teacher, so I guess you know best," she said, but he could tell by the sound of her voice that she thought he was completely nuts.

The zoo grounds were deserted at noon on a Thursday and as they walked hand-in-hand, Charlie thought again how much he loved being with Candace. She was funny, witty, smart, and incredibly passionate. For a moment, he almost wished they were done with their lessons so that he could finally tell her how he felt about her, without feeling like a total jerk for taking advantage of their teacher/student situation.

But then he thought about what he had planned for the day and grinned. No, he certainly didn't want to give up any of the time he'd be spending exploring Candace's body. And he sure as hell wouldn't trade the satisfaction he'd already received from showing her how to let herself go, how to explode with every fiber of her body and soul.

They walked past the tiger and lion cages, stopping to admire the brawny beasts, finally arriving at the miniature train depot. One of the small amusement park trains was on the track waiting for them to board.

Each of the cars of the train was just big enough to seat two people, except the miniature lion cage, which was barely big enough to fit four people.

"Wait here for a second," Charlie said as he went up to the ticket taker and said a few words to him while covertly slipping him a hundred dollar bill.

Mission accomplished, Charlie was grinning ear to ear when he waved Candace through the gate.

She started to step into one of the small, uncovered cars that was shaped like a baby elephant, but he redirected her to the lion cage. The bottom half of the car was completely covered with plastic, with only the upper half of the car open to the outside through thick plastic bars. Unlike the other cars, this one had a roof on it that blocked out the sunlight.

"We're going to ride in this one," he said, and he thought he saw a tiny hint of a smile appearing on the corner of her luscious lips as she crawled into the small space. When she bent over, her short skirt flipped up and revealed to him her tight, round ass, and smooth pussy lips peeking between her slightly parted thighs.

His cock went instantly hard. His innocent student hadn't worn any panties at all!

He stood on the outside of the cage, holding onto the bars and cleared his throat, finally managing a husky, "Did you forget to put something on this morning when you were getting dressed?"

Candace blushed and said, "I might have forgotten a couple of things, actually."

Suddenly he noticed she wasn't wearing a bra either. He could discern the faint outline of her areolas beneath her light pink tank top. As he stared at her chest in continued amazement, her nipples grew hard and pronounced, and it was all he could do not to rip the thin fabric off of her body and suck at her nipples like a hungry newborn.

He rearranged his pants to accommodate his throbbing bulge and climbed in after her. Once he was inside the cage and had latched the gate closed, he gave a thumb's up to the conductor and the train began to move slowly on the tracks.

"You seem a little nervous today," he said as he rubbed his thumb in a circle over the palm of her left hand.

She nodded, but didn't quite meet his eyes. Finally she looked up at him and said, "You're right. I am nervous today." Then she laughed and said, "Which is crazy! You'd think I'd be perfectly calm around you after the three lessons we've had so far, wouldn't you?"

Charlie nodded absentmindedly as he kneeled in the small floor space between her legs. "I'm a little nervous too," he murmured as he slowly slid his hands up from her ankles, to her knees, to the outsides of her thighs.

"Lift up," he said softly and as she did so, he slid his hands underneath the curve of her ass, cupping each of her butt cheeks in his hands. Her head fell back and she moaned softly. He'd left her skirt still covering her body, even though he wanted nothing more than to bury his face between her legs, hoping the waiting would intensify her arousal.

Even though his hands were on her ass, she was already so wet her juices were soaking his fingers. Gently he slipped his pinkies into her dripping cunt and her moans grew louder. Her hands moved to circle the back of his neck, to pull his face down to her impatient clit.

"Hold onto the bars," he demanded. He saw her warring with herself, but then she reached out and grabbed the bars with her hands.

"Good girl," he whispered as he bit the hem of her tank top and pulled it up several inches to uncover the skin on her flat stomach. He laid several kisses across her belly, and then on her pelvis through the thin fabric of her skirt.

Her nipples jutted out to him and he couldn't resist their beckoning. One at a time, he put the thin straps of her tank top between his teeth and slid them down her shoulders, uncovering first one lush globe and then the other. He moved his hands closer to her pussy and slid several fingers in and out of her.

"Charlie, I don't think we should," she began to say, and he cut off her protest with a hot kiss, roughly taking her tongue into his mouth, forcing it to mate with his own.

"I'm in charge of this lesson," he said sternly when he finally pulled away from her slightly bruised lips.

She said, "I know you are, but," and he kissed her again, gently this time just on the corners of her mouth.

"Won't you trust me, sweetheart?" he asked her, his tone now gently cajoling.

She smiled tremulously and he returned his attention to her succulent tits, finally bared in all their glory. He rubbed his face across them, letting her nipples slide in and out of his mouth, driving his tongue across them, forcing whimpers from Candace with every stroke.

Finally looking up from her breasts, he noted that the train had taken them into a deeply forested area, which was far more private than the open tracks they had traveled upon thus far. As he slowly pulled his hands out from beneath her ass and reached for the hem of her skirt to lift it up, she whimpered, "Yes, Charlie. Please!" and opened her legs wide so that he would have easy access to her swollen cunt. He ran the tip of his thumb up and down her moist folds, steering clear of her most sensitive spot. She tried to maneuver her hips so that he'd be forced to touch her clit, but he teased and circled, all the while avoiding the one place that was dying for his touch.

He slid one finger into her and took one of her huge tits into his mouth. He sucked her nipple in the same rhythm as he moved his long finger in and out of her.

Candace's head thrashed back and forth and she let go of the bars to wrap her hands around the back of his head, holding him tightly to her breasts. He could feel the tension in her body, felt the muscles begin to convulse around his finger, and knew she was about to explode.

Hastily he removed his finger and, with his lips still sucking gently on one of her breasts, Charlie moved to a sitting position on the hard plastic seat behind him, bringing Candace's body with him, so that she was straddling his hips, her knees on the seat.

Her slender fingers moved to unbutton and unzip his khaki slacks, until the full length of his hard shaft sprang free.

She wrapped her hand around the hot length of him, positioning herself above him so that the head of his penis was just at the entrance of her incredibly wet lips.

And then, with a sound of deep satisfaction, Candace lowered herself down onto his enormous cock, taking in each and every inch.

Charlie was overwhelmed by the sensation of her tight, wet pussy enveloping him. He looked up from her breasts, and pulled her head down to capture her mouth in a hot, tongue-thrusting kiss.

Candace was in charge of their lovemaking as she rode up and down on Charlie's cock, milking it with her tight, throbbing muscles.

"I can't hold on anymore," he gritted out through clenched teeth and as he began to come, she began to scream, her muscles convulsing around his cock. He drained every last drop of his seed deep within the woman he loved. He covered her scream with his mouth and as they rode towards ecstasy together, their lips and tongues mated in a frenzy that matched the mating of their bodies.

As their convulsions came to an end, they kissed, their caresses growing tender and soft.

"Candy, I," Charlie began to say, but right as he was about to declare his feelings for her, regardless of their mentoring, the train left the trees and emerged back into the daylight.

Quickly, Candace slid off his lap, pulled her tank top back up over her breasts, and slid her skirt down over her thighs. After she did so she looked at him with undisguised amusement and said, "You might want to zip your pants back up."

He surfaced from his daze and made his fumbling fingers obey his commands to tuck in his shirt. Just in time, he fastened the button of his pants as they arrived back at the station and came to a stop.

The station attendant unlatched the door to their cage. "Enjoy the ride?"

Candace looked at Charlie with a twinkle in her eye and said, with a fairly straight face, "Oh yes. More than you can ever imagine. In fact, it's safe to say, I'll never look at the zoo the same way again."

And with that, she headed out the gates back towards the lion cages. Both Charlie and the young zoo employee watched the perfect curve of her ass swing from side to side as she walked.

Charlie slipped the kid another $100 bill and said, "You really have a great ride on your hands here, kid. You got a girlfriend?"

The boy nodded his head speedily on his skinny neck and Charlie said, "I definitely recommend the lion cage." He followed after Candace, thinking yet again what a lucky man he was.

Chapter Eleven

When Charlie dropped Candace off at her house, she was torn between inviting him in and running to her computer to write down the next scene in her book. But before she could ask him inside for a drink, he looked at his watch and said, "I've got to get going. Thanks for a great afternoon," and sped off, leaving her standing on the sidewalk in front of her house feeling more than a little bereft.

The truth was, no matter how much she tried to pretend she didn't have feelings for Charlie, no matter how much she wavered back and forth about the emotional extent of their relationship, she now knew with 100% certainty that she was in love with him.

After their incredible sex play on the mini-train at the zoo, they had spent the rest of the day eating cotton candy and hot dogs, riding the elephants, and admiring the baby tiger cubs that were brought outside during their feeding. With every minute that passed in Charlie's company, Candace fell harder and harder for him.

He was funny, gorgeous, brilliant, and the most sexually intoxicating man she had ever encountered. Candace was sure she would never meet anyone again who would make her feel so incredibly good, so wonderfully happy.

All of that only served to increase her guilt over her deception. Every time she wrote another scene with Jolene and Zane, she was elated by how far she'd come as a writer. But at the same time, another part of her was horrified by her dishonesty.

To a moan, every scene mimicked her encounters with Charlie.

She went inside her house, sat down in front of her computer and booted it up, holding her head in her hands, trying to figure out some sort of compromise she could live with.

What if I tell him about the story after we've cemented a strong relationship with each other outside of his mentoring?

If he wanted to have a real relationship with her, then by the time she told him about the story she had written, he'd just laugh and kiss her, telling her she was silly for even worrying about it in the first place.

She wasn't going to keep it a secret from him forever. Just until she entered the contest and got some feedback on her writing. Just until she and Charlie communicated with each other about their feelings.

Feeling slightly better about what she was doing, she opened up her document and typed the words she had been writing in her head all afternoon.

"You ever been on a motorcycle?"

Jolene looked up from the piano keys at Zane who was standing by the front door of the bar. "Are you kidding? I've never even been in a convertible," she replied.

"We're gonna open a little late today," he said, gesturing for her to come to him. "Let's go."

Zane held the door open for Jolene and tapped his booted foot impatiently while she serenely closed the lid on the grand piano, stood up and walked towards him.

He led her around the back to his Harley and handed her a helmet. She swallowed nervously and didn't put the helmet on.

"I'm not so sure about this," she said, but he was already on and had revved up the engine.

"You'll be just fine," he said, "just keep your arms wrapped tightly around me."

Jolene felt like she had no choice but to do as he asked. It was always that way with Zane, she mused. Him telling and her doing.

"One day the tables are going to turn, Zane," she said, but he couldn't hear her over the rumbling of his engine.

She slipped onto the seat behind him and wiggled her hips tightly up against his muscled rear end and thighs. She ran her hands up and down his chiseled abs through his t-shirt and reveled in his extraordinary masculinity.

And then they were off, flying down the streets of San Francisco. The wind whipped at her hair and with her body wrapped around Zane's, she felt perfectly in tune with the world around her. Every person who walked by them seemed to be smiling. The sky was bluer. The sun was hotter.

Of course, her pussy was completely soaked. It was such a frequent occurrence, she had stopped wearing panties altogether. As it was, whenever she was with Zane he was always ripping them off of her in his haste to thrust his huge shaft into her or to press his lips to the sensitive nub between her legs.

She had only worked for him for a month, but already she knew she wouldn't have it any other way. Zane was a drug she never wanted to get off of, no matter how wrong anyone thought he might be for her.

She had gone home once to visit her parents, and she couldn't believe how hard it was for her to pull her hair back into a ponytail and sit quietly at dinner. All night while she was with her parents she wondered what Zane was doing, wondered what he would have done to her at the end of the evening after he locked the door to his bar.

After catching her in a daydream more than once, her mother pulled her aside in the kitchen to ask if anything was the matter. Jolene knew she had to get back to the city right away, back to the man whose caresses had become as important to her as breathing.

Eventually, the road dead-ended into Golden Gate Park. Zane slowed down the bike and drove into a thickly forested, deserted area. Jolene shivered with anticipation, hoping Zane was going to start touching, licking, and biting her soon.

I am a slut, she thought. Wholly and completely a slut. But by now, after so many nights of falling to pieces in Zane's arms, she was too far gone to care about something that would have bothered her deeply in her past life.

He pulled off his helmet and his shoulder-length dark brown hair whipped gently against her face in the wind. She took off her helmet and shook out her long blond hair, trying to finger-comb the knots out to no avail. Still balanced on the bike seat she leaned her head back and closed her eyes, letting the gentle breeze wash over her.

Zane stood up and got off of his bike, turning around to face her as he straddled the seat once again.

"Oh!" she exclaimed nervously when she opened up her eyes. His face was directly in front of hers, his eyes hot with need.

He bent his head down and captured her lips in a sweet kiss. Reaching under her skirt, he ran his hands slowly up her calves, past her knees, up to her thighs.

When he finally reached her hips, he stopped kissing her and gave her a searing look. "You're not wearing panties," he said.

She gave him a half-smile, saying, "I was wondering when you'd notice."

He growled and kissed her again, hungrily, slipping his large callused hands beneath her ass, lifting her up off the seat and onto him. She felt the thick bulge in his pants and reached for the button of his jeans.

He chuckled softly. "We're in public, you know," he said.

Unable, unwilling to stop herself, Jolene worked at his fly. "Isn't that the point, Zane?"

By then she had his pants undone and as his shaft sprang free into her hands, she was pleased to find that he wasn't wearing anything underneath his jeans.

As she stroked the satiny skin of his huge cock, he groaned, saying, "What did you do with my little nun?"

Jolene wriggled onto Zane's lap and gasped as his hot flesh probed her pussy lips, stretching her open to fit all of him inside. Finally, after she had taken in all nine inches of him, after he was sheathed to the hilt within her, she looked him in the eye.

"I love you Zane," she said, and then instinctively rode up and down on his cock, faster and faster as her orgasm swelled up to overwhelm her.

Zane kept the bike steady while she took him in and then slid him out until just the tip was still within her. He pulled her down on him again, so deeply she could feel his balls press against her ass cheeks. At the feel of him swelling impossibly bigger within her, she went over the edge, crying out his name as her inner muscles clenched and milked him hard.

He buried his head in her long hair and roared, "Jolene!" as he shot inside of her, crashing his hips into hers as hard and deep as he could.

They held tight to each other until their heartbeats returned to normal, and then he slid her off of him and zipped up his jeans. Without a word, he handed Jolene her helmet, put his back on, and started the engine.

Jolene blinked back tears. When they were joined together she realized she could no longer deny how much she loved Zane and was unable to hold back the words.

But now they were heading back to the bar and he hadn't said anything. Not, "I love you too," or any kind of comment at all in response to her open and honest statement of her feelings for him. With a sinking feeling low in her belly, she wondered if she had done the wrong thing.

Maybe, she thought with sudden sorrow, loving the devil is nothing more than a one-way trip to hell.

Candace finished writing her new scene and as she reread it, she had a spark of insight about the piece of the puzzle between her and Charlie that she had been missing all along.

It was one thing for her to learn to enjoy taking pleasure in Charlie's arms—lots and lots of pleasure!—but it was another thing entirely for her to lead the way.

Her path was suddenly crystal clear and she wanted to jump for joy. Lesson five was going to be different than the previous four lessons, for one big reason.

She was going to be the teacher this time.

Decision made, she grabbed her car keys, and locked the front door behind her. If everything went according to plan, she wouldn't be coming home tonight.

* * * * *

Charlie sat in his living room and stared blankly at the TV. "I'm such an idiot," he told himself, taking a large swig from the beer he'd pulled out of the six-pack by his side.

"She was going to ask me to come inside, probably to her bedroom, and I act like a sixteen-year-old boy!"

He shook his head at his stupidity. He couldn't believe how nervous he got around Candace whenever it came time to wrap up their lessons. He was still afraid she'd say, "Thanks so much for everything, and by the way, I never want to see you again, you pervert."

He wanted so desperately to tell her he was in love with her, even though he had only known her less than two weeks. But no matter how he tried to frame it in his mind, he felt like a total cad for bringing such powerful emotions into their mentoring sessions. As it was, the fact that they had mind-blowing sex during each of the lessons was a little weird, but at least they had an upfront agreement about it: Whatever happened during their lessons, stayed in their lessons.

If only they had made some sort of agreement about their emotions. Something like: If I fall in love with you, I can tell you how I feel and you'll say you love me too.

Charlie sighed and flipped the top off another bottle. Getting drunk was the sucker's way out, but since that's what he was, he drank up.

A knock on his door startled him out of his not-quite-drunken-enough stupor. He plopped the beer bottle down, sloshing sticky liquid all over the coffee table, and dragged himself to the door.

"Probably some kid trying to sell candy bars," he muttered as he turned the doorknob.

"Hey Charlie!" Candace said, as she stood on his doorstep looking more glorious than any angel ever had. "Could I come in?"

He nodded and stepped aside dazedly.

She was still wearing the short yellow skirt and pink top from their jaunt to the zoo. She looked tastier than ever, especially since the zippy night air had puckered her nipples up beneath her thin cotton tank.

Still in his foyer, she turned to him with a determined look in her eyes, and said, "I was thinking about lesson five, and all of the wonderful lessons we've already had. I think we need to shake things up a little bit for this last lesson."

"So, for lesson five, which I believe you told me was going to be about role playing, I'm going to be the teacher and you're going to be the student."

Charlie's cock stood up at attention as he took in her words. He was speechless, stunned that she had magically appeared on his doorstep, mesmerized by her beauty, and bowled over by how she wanted to reverse their roles.

Not waiting for any response from him, she walked out of his foyer and down the hall, until she reached the door of his master bedroom. She looked over her shoulder and said, "You don't want to be late to class, do you? 'Cause I hear the teacher spanks her students when they're bad," and then disappeared into his bedroom.

By the time he snapped out of his fog and ran down the hall to the goddess who awaited him, Candace was nowhere to be found in his bedroom. Hearing the water running in his adjoining bathroom, he peeked his head into the doorway and saw a blessed sight.

Candace was leaning over his enormous spa bathtub, setting the water temperature and jets, completely naked.

He reached for the hem of his t-shirt to pull it off over his head, but she whipped around and said, "Keep your clothes on."

He stopped with the shirt mid-way up his torso. "Huh?"

She walked up to him and pressed her full breasts up against his chest. "You heard me. I want you to keep your clothes on until I tell you otherwise," she said, and then spun around and gingerly dipped a toe into the hot water. Slipping into the tub, she stretched out fully, with her nipples jutting proudly out of the water. They puckered tightly as cool air blew across them.

"Soap me up," she said, and Charlie immediately gathered up a small washcloth and a bar of herbal soap off the holder by the sink.

"Kneel on the bath mat," she directed him, and again he did as she bade. Then she crossed her legs in the tub and wiggled the toes on her right foot. "Start here," she said.

Incredibly aroused by the way she had taken charge of their lovemaking, Charlie thought his cock was going to explode in his pants. He wet the small, soft terry cloth towel, slid it over the bar of soap until it foamed, and rubbed it over the arch of her foot, making her moan with pleasure.

He worked the cloth diligently up her right leg, leaning over the rim of the sunken two-person tub to touch every inch of her smooth skin, running the cloth past her kneecap, across the top of her thigh. And then, just as he got to the apex between her legs, he stopped, lathered up the towel and started with her left foot, mirroring his actions on her left side.

"Wash my cunt, student" she said as he got closer and closer to her mound.

Charlie held back a grin and obeyed her again, pressing the cloth firmly into her pussy lips, rubbing it back and forth over her clit, watching her nipples grow engorged as she got more and more aroused, watching the pulse in her neck beat wildly as she closed her eyes and arched her back.

"Yes! There! Don't stop!" she cried as she began to come underneath his hand, beneath the small towel he rubbed forcefully against her.

He wanted to kiss her, but he knew she was in charge of this lesson, so he continued to rock her pelvis in the palm of his hand until her breathing returned to normal and she opened her eyes again.

"Take off your clothes and get inside the tub," she said evenly. He was surprised by how controlled she was, considering she had been screaming and writhing just moments before.

He quickly stripped off his t-shirt and jeans and then stepped into the warm water. He stood in the tub, his cock thick and hard and ready to plunge into Candace's dripping cunt. As he watched her eyes take in his arousal, a thick spurt of come spilled from the tip of his penis.

"Don't you dare come until I tell you to," she said as she kneeled in the tub and while he was still standing up, she took the head of his cock into her mouth and lightly ran her tongue over it, tasting him.

Then she slid more of his penis into her mouth and he felt his head pushing up against the back of her throat. She sucked against his shaft while she held his balls in her hands.

"Candy, I won't be able to," he began to say when he didn't think he could take it any longer, and she took her sweet lips off of his cock and pulled him down into the tub.

"Do me doggy," she said, and turned over so that her breasts were pressed up against the cool tile surrounding the tub and her ass was flared up from the rim.

Charlie kneeled behind her and said, "If the teacher insists," as he reached one hand around between the tile and her torso to cup and squeeze her breasts and the other around to swirl her swollen clit.

And then he did what he'd wanted to do since the beginning of lesson one, and rammed his cock hard into Candace's pussy.

His balls were swinging into her thighs and she reached around to cup them in her hands. "Harder, Charlie. Harder!" she demanded as she pushed her ass tighter to his hips, wiggling and moaning.

He couldn't remember the last time his cock had been so distended, so engorged. As he felt his cock begin to contract, he pressed his palm against her swollen, firm clit and pumped his hand against her mound.

"Oh god, Candy, you're so hot, so wet," he groaned as she screamed, "Harder, there, now!" in ecstasy.

The water was cold by the time she wrung the last drop of come out of him. They untangled their bodies and got up to take a shower. As he soaped her up, he kneeled between her legs, asking "Are we done with all five lessons now?" But she didn't get a chance to answer because another huge orgasm overtook her.

As he dried her off with a thick towel, she smiled at him and said, "Thanks for the five great mentoring sessions," and kissed him softly on his lips, letting her tongue merge with his.

Pulling back from her mouth, Charlie said, "Candy, there's something I need to tell you," at the very exact time she said, "Charlie, there's something I've been meaning to say to you."

They laughed and kissed again. "You first," he said, and tried to get his heart to stop pounding so damn hard in his chest as he waited for her to speak.

Suddenly looking shy and unsure, she forced herself to look into his eyes and said, "First of all, I want you to know how much I've enjoyed working with you this week."

He smiled and waited for her to finish. "And even though I know these were just supposed to be lessons for me to write better erotica, the truth is..."

Her words fell away and Charlie swallowed hard once.

Taking a deep breath she started again. "The truth is, Charlie, I'm in love with you."

Charlie had never been happier. He put his arms around her waist and spun her around in a circle in his large bathroom, their towels falling into a heap on the floor.

Breathless with joy, he said, "Candy, I love you too, and it's been killing me not telling you all week."

She reached her hands up around the back of his head and kissed him passionately. He swept her up into his arms, walked into the bedroom, and laid her on his bed.

Where she belonged.

* * * * *

"Nothing is ever going to come between us," Charlie said thickly and Candace covered his mouth with hers before he could see the guilt and worry in her eyes.

I'll tell him about the story soon, she promised herself as she sank deeper into the comfort of Charlie's arms.

Chapter Twelve

Candace thought back on the incredible night she and Charlie had spent together and smiled, happier than she had ever been. She had taken charge of her own sexuality for once in her life, and told the man she loved how she felt. And to add to the perfection, he felt the same way!

He had wanted her to spend the weekend with him, and she was tempted, but she wanted to finish her story first so that she could overnight it to the judges. Making an excuse about some errands, she promised to be back in his bed by the evening, for another all-night fuck session.

Sitting down at her desk, Candace knew exactly how her story needed to end.

Zane watched Jolene play the piano and reminded himself again that his relationship with her would never last, that they came from different worlds, that he would eventually tire of her body.

He laughed out loud at how bad a liar he was. He was full of shit. Any fool could tell that he was completely, irrevocably, ridiculously in love with the angel-faced girl who sat so primly at the piano in his bar and played jazz standards with all her heart.

The girl who looked like a nun, but fucked like a she-devil.

As he served a trio of overly made up, cheaply dressed women sitting at the bar trying to get his attention, he winced and thought about how they used to be just the kind of women he would take home and fuck. Now, just the thought of being with any woman but Jolene disgusted him.

He hadn't known the meaning of good sex until the first time his tongue laved her clit, until the first time he sank his cock deep into her tight, virginal pussy as she screamed his name, her muscles tensing around his shaft.

By the time the bar closed that night, he had never been more ready to lock the doors and take Jolene into his arms. But when he looked around the bar for her, she was nowhere to be found.

"Damn it!" he said, angry at her for leaving him alone when he needed her most. Walking into his office, he found a note on his desk, so he picked it up and read, "Zane. I've never stolen anything in my life, but I took the keys to your house and I'll be waiting there for you, if you want to join me. Jolene."

He stroked the prickly stubble on his chin and wondered what she was up to. They had been in his house only once, on the way home from the bar, before he dropped her off at her apartment. *She knows damn well we only fuck here, in the bar,* he thought angrily.

He didn't want to take her to his bed where he had screwed so many other, meaningless women. Jolene was special. And so much hotter than anyone else.

He drove his Harley home as if he were a Hell's Angel. He stomped loudly up his front stairs, hoping he was scaring her just a bit. She was going to get the spanking of her life from him once he got inside, and his cock hardened as he thought of her soft flesh beneath the palm of his hand. He could already see her ass turning pink under his assault, and could taste her come on his lips.

He turned the knob and the door opened. "Jolene," he called, but got no answer. She wasn't in his living room or the kitchen, so he walked down the hall and heard the water running in his master bath.

When he walked into the room, his little nun was lying naked beneath the hot water, smiling wickedly.

He was so angry and so aroused he growled, "What the hell are you doing?" but she just sank deeper into the water and said, "I want you to soap me up."

"You what?" he exploded.

She shook her head at him and pinched her lips into a tight line of disapproval. "You heard me," she said crossly. "You are going to soap me up.

"The hell I'm going to," he said, and she rose up angrily out of the tub.

"You big jerk," she cried as water poured off her naked body. "I'm asking you to do one simple thing, and all you do is use blasphemy!" She made a fist and said, "Now get over here and do as I say!"

Zane leaned against the door, crossed his arms, and said, "Make me."

Narrowing her eyes at him, Jolene took a deep breath and stepped out of the tub. Walking towards him, still blessedly naked, she grabbed a towel off of the rack and threw it onto the floor in front of his black boots. Kneeling in front of him she undid the button on his jeans and unzipped the zipper, letting his cock spring free of its overly tight confines.

Jolene had never taken him into her mouth before. Because she was such a novice, he'd never forced her to blow him, happy to sink into her tight, wet pussy every night instead.

He was shocked by her new brazen behavior. His arousal was so acute he was afraid he'd shoot into her mouth the minute she so much as kissed the head of his cock.

Running her fingers up and down his penis, she stuck the tip of her sweet little tongue out and licked him once, twice, and then suddenly sucked in several inches of him, moaning as she did so.

Instinctively she reached between his legs and cupped his balls, massaging them as she throated his cock as well as any professional courtesan might have. Zane knew he was a goner, but he couldn't do anything about it, so he just threaded his hands into her silky blond hair and pulsed deeply into her mouth, gratified as she swallowed every last drop of his come.

He didn't know how long it was before he was done shooting into the back of her throat, but his legs were shaking. He didn't have the strength to fight her, to show her who was boss, so he let her pull him into the tub.

He lay back against the rim and she straddled him and kissed him on his mouth, tasting his lips, playing with his tongue, nipping at his bottom lip.

"Jolene," he said, "I've got to tell you something."

Her face fell and her lips quivered slightly. He couldn't keep from laughing out loud. Did she actually think for one minute that he'd break up with her? Didn't she know he loved her more than life itself?

"Stop laughing at me!" she cried and pounded his chest with her fists.

He grabbed her hands and held them still, saying, "What I wanted to tell you, you little fool, is that I'm in love with you."

Jolene grew completely still, then said, "Say that again?"

He reached for her face and pulled her down for a hard kiss. "I love you," he growled as he took her lips again. Already hard, he plunged his cock deep within her, taking immeasurable pleasure in filling her pussy with his shaft, in shooting his seed deep into her womb, in hearing her cry out his name.

Later, as she lay on his chest, with her head in the crook of his shoulder, she said, "I love you too, Zane," and he smiled and said, "Thank god," vowing to go to church again the next day, to give thanks for the woman in his arms.

Candace saved her file, quickly proofread it, and then printed it off for the contest. Sealing the envelope, she went to the post office and mailed it.

Knowing Charlie was waiting for her to come back to his house, she put the contest out of her mind, stuffed her deception and guilt away from her heart, and got in her car to drive straight to heaven.

* * * * *

The next three weeks were the most amazing weeks of Candace's life. She and Charlie spent nearly all of their time together and had even begun to collaborate on an erotic novel together. Were it not for the black cloud of her dishonesty hanging over her head, she would have felt complete joy in being with Charlie.

The problem was, every time she had an opportunity to tell him about her manuscript, she couldn't bring herself to do it. He was so damn good—so sweet and loving and tender—she hated the thought of ever seeing anything but love in his eyes.

Candace was desperately afraid he'd leave her if he found out how she betrayed the promise they'd made to each other. What had happened in their lessons was supposed to forever stay in their lessons, but by writing Jolene and Zane's tale she had broken that pledge.

As the days dragged by and she didn't hear a word from the contest judges, she began to irrationally hope that her entry had gotten lost in the mail. Or perhaps if she were lucky, the judges had hated it so much they just threw it away.

If Candace had it all to do over, if it meant preserving Charlie's love, she knew she never would have written the manuscript.

Over the past few weeks she had spent every night at Charlie's house. Every day more of her clothes appeared in his closet. He wanted her to move in with him, but she told him it was too soon for such a big commitment.

A voice in her head said, *You would move in with him in a heartbeat if he knew what you had done and said he loved you anyway.*

Candace shook the voice off, and tried to stick to her story about needing more time. He was getting harder and harder to put off with each passing day, as they discovered depths of passion and love in each other's arms that neither had dreamed was even possible.

Her heart sank into her stomach as she saw the thick envelope waiting for her atop her pile of mail by the front door.

Feeling like she was suffocating, she picked up the envelope and sat down on the bottom step of her staircase. Sliding her finger underneath the seal, she slipped the papers out.

Dear Ms. Whitman, the cover letter read, *we are pleased to inform you that you are the Grand Prize Winner of the 15th Annual Erotic Writer's Contest! We hereby request your presence at the awards ceremony July 3rd. We are certain you will be thrilled to receive your medal and $10,000 check from our secret celebrity judge.*

The paper fell through Candace's hands. "Oh my god," she whispered, "I won!"

She jumped up off of the step and screamed, "I won! I won!" and ran into the kitchen to call Charlie. She stopped as everything crashed down around her.

"Shit!" she exclaimed.

Tell him now, her rational inner-voice nagged her.

"He'll leave me if I tell him," she said aloud and her words reverberated off of the shiny counters in her state of the art kitchen.

Unwilling to risk his love, Candace decided not to tell him about winning the award. And now she needed to think of a good excuse for why she was going to be busy on Saturday night.

"Damn it," she muttered as she went back into her foyer to pick up the contest papers that were strewn all over her hardwood floor. "I wish I had never entered this stupid contest in the first place," she declared as she began to compose her newest lie in her head.

Chapter Thirteen

"Baby," Candace said as she lay in the crook of Charlie's arm, "I have a family matter to attend to this Saturday."

"Oh good. I've been dying to meet your family."

Inwardly she cursed herself for saying the wrong thing. "Actually," she said, "it's a private matter. I promise to tell you everything once things are ironed out, but for now, the lawyers have insisted we keep it within the family."

Charlie kissed the top of her head. "Sounds serious. Are you sure you don't want me to come along for moral support?"

"Definitely not!" she exclaimed. Realizing she had been far more fervent with her protests than was necessary, she stroked her hands through the golden hair that dusted his muscular chest. Trying to keep her tone light she said, "Hey, you'll finally get a day without me. I'll bet you've been dying to hang out with the guys to drink beer and eat pizza and watch sports, huh?"

Charlie chuckled. "Honestly? No. I haven't been the least bit interested in hanging out with the guys."

"Really?" she asked in an uncertain voice.

"Are you kidding?" he replied. "Only a madman would choose beer and pizza over you."

She tilted her head up and kissed him softly on the lips. "I love you, Charlie Gibson."

* * * * *

Charlie had planned on asking Candace to the Erotic Writing Contest ceremony, but he kept forgetting. By the time he learned she already had unbreakable plans, he figured there was no point in mentioning it at all.

Backstage, in his dressing room, Charlie clipped on his bowtie and evened up the sleeves of his tux jacket. Looking at himself in the mirror he saw a man in love looking back at him. His eyes were clear and bright, a smile was permanently plastered on his face, and he was thrilled to know that he and Candace were going to share the rest of their lives together.

He was planning on asking her to marry him. In fact, he had dropped by Tiffany's that very afternoon and purchased one of the biggest diamond rings he could find.

He couldn't wait to slip the solitaire on her finger, knowing she'd be in his bed, in his heart, for all eternity.

Steve Holt stuck his head in the door. "Hey Charlie, I thought you might want to check out the winning manuscript before you present the award to the winner." Steve put the thick bundle of pages on the table nearest the door. "It's pretty fuckin' hot. I can't wait to get a look at the woman who wrote it when she walks up on stage tonight."

Charlie cocked his head to the side. "You don't recognize the writer's name?"

"I think it's a pseudonym. Nobody would name their daughter Candy Lane."

Candy? Charlie felt a squeezing sensation in his chest, but brushed his sense of foreboding aside. Of course Candace hadn't turned herself into Candy Lane.

Then again, he had never asked her if she wrote under a pseudonym.

She would have told him if she entered this contest, he knew she would have. They told each other everything — all of their dreams, fears, hopes.

He shook his head to clear the insanity from it and picked up the manuscript. "Thanks Steve. I'll take a quick look at it. See you out there."

"I'll save you some champagne," Steve said and then loped off down the hall.

Charlie shut the door behind Steve, sat down on the leather sofa in the small dressing room and read, "*Jolene was a good girl...*"

* * * * *

Candace walked into the beautifully decorated ballroom of the Fairmont in Union Square and slid her hands over her red silk dress, smoothing out invisible wrinkles. She was incredibly nervous about accepting the award for her story, *Hell's Angel*. Yet again, she wished she had told Charlie about it, so he could lend her the moral support she so desperately needed.

A stunning blond greeted her at the doorway. "And you are?"

"Candace Whitman," Candace replied with a smile.

"Ooo, how exciting!" the woman exclaimed as she spontaneously gave Candace a hug. "Charlie Gibson was your mentor this year, wasn't he?"

Candace nodded. "That's right."

The woman leaned in closer and said, "Jessie was spitting nails for weeks after losing out on the chance to work with him. I hear you nabbed him the minute he walked into the conference hall."

Grinning, Candace said, "Pretty much," liking the woman immensely and feeling a great deal more at ease.

"I'm Sherryl Ann," the woman said with a shake of her perfect blond ringlets. "Charlie was my mentor last year and I learned so much from him. I'll bet you did too."

The smile froze on Candace's face. "You worked with Charlie last year?" she asked, striving for an even tone.

Sherryl Ann winked. "He's quite a hunk, isn't he?"

Candace felt all of the color rush out of her face just as a loud buzzing started in her ears. "He is," she said quickly. "Could you point me to the ladies room?"

"Sure thing, honey. It's just down the hall to the left. You don't look so good all of a sudden," the woman added, clearly concerned.

"Probably just something I ate," Candace lied before spinning around and practically running down the hall.

Once she had locked herself into a stall, she let the tears stream down her face. "I can't believe I'm such an idiot," she whispered. "Of course I wasn't the only female apprentice he's ever had." She sniffled and rolled some toilet paper into her fist, dashing it angrily at her face.

Painful memories crashed down around her. Walking in on her first boyfriend while he screwed the head cheerleader. Bravely letting her next boyfriend have sex with her, only to have him tell her she was a cold fish. Swallowing her pride as she found signs of her latest boyfriend's affair, and realizing it was with the woman she thought was her best friend.

And now Charlie. He had probably slept with every woman in the room on a "mentor/apprentice" basis.

"Damn him!" she exclaimed.

Her tears ran dry and she heaved in a shaky breath. "I'll show him," she declared. "I'm going to accept this award, shove it in his face, and move on with my life. Without him."

She unlatched the bathroom door and made her way to the mirror. Quickly fixing her makeup, she strode into the banquet hall and tried to ignore the voice in her heart that said she could never live without Charlie by her side.

* * * * *

The words played in endless repeat in Charlie's head and swam before his eyes.

"He hooked his fingers into the edges of her cotton panties and slowly slid them off her."

"Suddenly the buzzing started up again between her thighs, but this time, she knew that somehow, some way, Zane was manning the controls to her vagina."

"'You're not wearing panties,' he said. 'I was wondering when you'd notice.'"

"I want you to soap me up."

Charlie ran his hands through his hair and dropped the manuscript back onto the table.

He had read the words, but he still couldn't believe it.

Candace had detailed their lessons act by act, scene by scene, in her book *Hell's Angel*. He couldn't deny that it was powerful writing, and yet the hole in his heart was so deep he could hardly feel anything at all.

"She promised," he said aloud in the small room and closed his eyes, wiping away the moisture that had crept beneath his eyelids.

"Damn it!" he exclaimed as he punched his hand into the wall. Some of the plaster crumbled beneath his fist just as the event organizer knocked once.

"What?" Charlie said in a gruff tone.

"We're ready for you," said the voice from the hall.

"I'll be right out."

He had thought he was special to Candace, but now he wondered if he was just a fool for believing that she truly loved him. For all he knew, she was going to take her new knowledge and find another "mentor", one who knew more than he did, who could give her things he couldn't.

Charlie took a deep breath and tried to compose himself. And then he stepped out of his dressing room and down the hall to greet the person he loved most in the world, wondering what the hell he was going to say to her when they finally came face to face.

* * * * *

The MC said, "Thank you for coming to the 15th Annual Erotic Writer's Contest awards ceremony! We had some incredible entries this year, but for the first time in the history of this contest, our judges voted unanimously for the winner. Here to present the $10,000 check to our winner is none other than best-selling author, Charlie Gibson."

Sitting out in the audience, Candace was hardly aware of the raucous hoots and hollers from the crowd. Charlie was the surprise celebrity guest?

She looked around for the nearest escape, but knew that she couldn't take the coward's way out. Not this time.

Even if she ran tonight, he'd find out that Candy Lane was her pseudonym, that *Hell's Angel* had been inspired by their astonishing lovemaking.

It was finally time to face the punishment.

Charlie took the stage and she could see him scanning the crowd, looking for her. His eyes locked with hers and she forced herself not to look away. She didn't know what she expected to see in his eyes—pain, hatred maybe—but not the awful blankness that radiated down to her in the audience.

Her stomach heaved, but she swallowed the bile back into her throat and clasped her hands tightly in her lap, her spine as straight as rebar.

"Writing is a funny thing," he began, as he looked out over the large, well-dressed crowd with a small smile. "We think that we can separate ourselves from the stories we weave, but no matter how much we lie to ourselves, there is always a piece of us in there. Some where, some way, we can never disguise what's in our heart."

"An hour ago Steve Holt handed me a copy of the winning manuscript. Truth is, folks, I couldn't put it down. It was compelling. It was sensual. And most of all, it was honest."

A tear began to slip down Candace's cheek, and she shook her head, whispering, "Stop, Charlie. Please, stop."

"It is with distinct pleasure that I award this year's Erotic Writer's award to Candace Whitman, for her erotic novel, *Hell's Angel*, writing as Candy Lane."

The applause was deafening as Candace unsteadily rose to her feet. Strangers reached out to shake her hand in congratulations. She smiled and murmured thanks, but she was held prisoner by the intensity of Charlie's gaze.

I love you and I'm sorry, her heart cried out to him, but by the look in his eyes, she knew he was lost to her.

Wiping away the tear that had rolled down her cheek, she carefully climbed the small flight of stairs up to the podium where Charlie was standing.

"I'm sorry," she mouthed to him, but he ignored her, his face devoid of all emotion.

Putting the check into her trembling hands, without touching her, he stepped back into the shadows. Fearing her knees were going to buckle beneath her, Candace clutched at the podium and held on for dear life.

Looking out at the rapt crowd waiting for her acceptance speech, she swallowed nervously.

"Hi," she said softly into the microphone, surprised by the volume of her voice through the speakers.

"I, uh, want to thank the judges for..." She cut herself off, shaking her head, her face crumpling. "The truth is, I can't accept this award. I'm sorry," she cried as a sob escaped her. Holding her hand over her mouth to quiet her weeping, she ran off of the stage and down through the tables and chairs in the banquet room. She continued to run through the lobby and out into the cool evening air, not stopping to breathe until she tripped in her high heels and landed hard against a street lamp.

Clutching the street lamp, she sobbed and gasped for air, hating herself more and more with every passing second.

She felt a warm hand on the small of her back through her thin silk dress.

"It's a wonderful book, Candy," Charlie said as he gently rubbed her back.

She shook her head so hard, her gold clip fell out of her hair and clattered to the sidewalk. "No. It's not. I'm sorry. I'm so sorry." She sniffled and wiped her nose with the back of her hand.

"Sweetheart," he said, his voice tender, "I love you."

She finally turned around to face him, anger mixing with her sorrow. "Is that what you told Sherryl Ann last year?"

"What does Sherryl Ann have to do with this?"

Candace crossed her cold hands across her chest and held onto her shoulders, rocking slightly back and forth as if to comfort herself.

"What kind of *lessons* did you set up for her? Were they hotter than ours?"

"God no! I edited a couple of her manuscripts and then passed her off to my agent."

Candace knew the look of shock and disbelief on Charlie's face was pure and she felt like an even bigger fool than before. "Of course you did," she said quietly, all of the fight back out of her. "I understand if you never want to see me again, Charlie," she said, staring at the dirty sidewalk between them.

He slipped one of his fingers underneath her chin and forced her to look him in the eye.

"Candy, I won't lie to you. This hurts like hell. I thought you knew you could tell me anything. Anything at all."

"I do," she protested, but he quieted her by pressing his thumb over her lips.

"The truth is I'll love you until the day I die, no matter what. So if you think I'm going to let the content of one of your future best-selling novels get in the way of our future, you're very much mistaken. It's gonna take a whole lot more than a few hot love scenes to change the way I feel about you, sweetheart."

New tears had formed in Candace's eyes, but this time they were tears of joy. She launched herself onto him, wrapping her long legs around his waist and kissed him with all of the love in her heart.

"Oh baby," she said when they stopped devouring each other's lips for a moment, "I love you so much."

Charlie just smiled and held her closer to him, heedless of the stares from the strangers as they walked by.

"Thank god," he murmured as he bent his head and captured Candace's lips in a kiss that went straight to her soul.

"Now, let's get home so that I can punish you for your very bad behavior."

* * * * *

And so it was that Charlie finally got to enact the scene he had been choreographing in his imagination since the day he first lay Candace naked upon the bed in his guest bedroom and tasted her sweet pussy.

Charlie sat down on the edge of their bed, still wearing his tuxedo. "Come here," he said.

Candace couldn't hold back the smile on her lips as she walked towards him.

"What could you possibly be smiling about," he said, trying and failing to hold back his own grin, "when you are about to get spanked until your ass is pink and stinging?"

Candace made a show of demurely lowering her eyes. "Forgive me, oh benevolent one." She looked up at him through her long lashes. "I am a very bad girl, and I deserve to be punished."

"Lie across my thighs," he ordered.

"What about my clothes?" she asked him, gesturing to her ankle-length red silk dress.

"Leave your clothes to me. Now get over here."

Hiding another smile, but unable to disguise the twinkle in her eyes, Candace draped her body, face down, across the tops of Charlie's thighs.

Through the smooth, thin silk of her dress, he rubbed her round, firm ass.

"No panties?" he said hoarsely.

In a subservient voice she said, "I wouldn't dare wear panties. Not when you're already about to discipline me."

"Good girl," he said, licking his lips.

Unexpectedly, he ripped the seam of Candace's dress open from her ankle to her waist. She gasped and he said, "See how upset I am with you?"

She nodded and waited expectantly for his onslaught to begin. Already, her pussy was moist and swollen, ready to be touched, sucked, and fucked.

Again, he rubbed the palm of his right hand on her ass, warming up her chilled flesh. "You have such a beautiful ass," he murmured. He lifted up his hand and then brought it down firmly on her round globes.

Candace gasped again as pleasure and pain got all mingled up inside of her. He brought his hand down again and liquid dripped from her cunt to her thighs.

"Am I hurting you?" Charlie asked her, his voice hot with need.

"A little," she said in a small voice, equally wracked with the need to be possessed by the man she loved.

He ran his hand down her ass cheek to the very top of her thighs and then slid an index finger inside her swollen pussy. "What about now?" he asked, his breath coming in quick bursts. "Am I hurting you now?"

Candace nodded again. "Yes," she said, "I need more."

Abruptly, Charlie ripped the dress all the way up to her shoulders. She was completely naked underneath and he lowered her to the soft rug in front of his bed. She looked up at him with love in her eyes.

"Now for the final punishment," he said, as he unzipped his pants and let his huge, throbbing shaft spring free.

"Please, Charlie," she begged him, her hands moving to fondle his cock, to pull it towards her ready cunt.

Settling himself between her legs, he pushed into her wet, hot pussy, inch by inch.

"Charlie," she moaned, her head writhing on the floor.

"Oh god," he roared as she moved her hips slightly, taking him all the way to the hilt. Roughly he grabbed her hips, and plunged in and out of her lips, feeling her muscles contract around him as her pleasure spiraled out of control.

Right before they came, Charlie forced their bodies to go completely still. Holding her hips in his hands, watching the rise and fall of her breasts as she panted beneath him, he said, "I love you Candy. Don't you ever forget it again."

He plunged into her hot folds, and she milked him dry as a soul-shattering orgasm rocked through them both.

The next day, they wrote their latest lovemaking into their new tale of erotic romance and then headed back to the bedroom for another round of "research".

About the author:

Before plunging wholeheartedly into writing erotic romance, Bella got a BA in Economics at Stanford University, worked as a marketing director, and strutted hundreds of stages as a rock star. She currently lives in Northern California with her fabulous husband, who thinks his wife is cooler than his friends' wives, because she writes romantica.

Bella Andre welcomes mail from readers. You can write to her c/o Ellora's Cave Publishing at P.O. Box 787, Hudson, Ohio 44236-0787.

Why an electronic book?

We live in the Information Age—an exciting time in the history of human civilization in which technology rules supreme and continues to progress in leaps and bounds every minute of every hour of every day. For a multitude of reasons, more and more avid literary fans are opting to purchase e-books instead of paperbacks. The question to those not yet initiated to the world of electronic reading is simply: *why?*

1. *Price.* An electronic title at Ellora's Cave Publishing runs anywhere from 40-75% less than the cover price of the <u>exact same title</u> in paperback format. Why? Cold mathematics. It is less expensive to publish an e-book than it is to publish a paperback, so the savings are passed along to the consumer.

2. *Space.* Running out of room to house your paperback books? That is one worry you will never have with electronic novels. For a low one-time cost, you can purchase a handheld computer designed specifically for e-reading purposes. Many e-readers are larger than the average handheld, giving you plenty of screen room. Better yet, hundreds of titles can be stored within your new library—a single microchip. (Please note that Ellora's Cave does not endorse any specific brands. You can check our website at www.ellorascave.com for customer recommendations we make available to new consumers.)

3. *Mobility.* Because your new library now consists of only a microchip, your entire cache of books can be taken with you wherever you go.

4. *Personal preferences are accounted for.* Are the words you are currently reading too small? Too large? Too…ANNOYING? Paperback books cannot be modified according to personal preferences, but e-books can.

5. *Innovation.* The way you read a book is not the only advancement the Information Age has gifted the literary community with. There is also the factor of what you can read. Ellora's Cave Publishing will be introducing a new line of interactive titles that are available in e-book format only.

6. *Instant gratification.* Is it the middle of the night and all the bookstores are closed? Are you tired of waiting days—sometimes weeks—for online and offline bookstores to ship the novels you bought? Ellora's Cave Publishing sells instantaneous downloads 24 hours a day, 7 days a week, 365 days a year. Our e-book delivery system is 100% automated, meaning your order is filled as soon as you pay for it.

Those are a few of the top reasons why electronic novels are displacing paperbacks for many an avid reader. As always, Ellora's Cave Publishing welcomes your questions and comments. We invite you to email us at service@ellorascave.com or write to us directly at: P.O. Box 787, Hudson, Ohio 44236-0787.

Printed in the United States
22516LVS00001B/46-144